I0666689

The Tamar Black Saga - Book Two

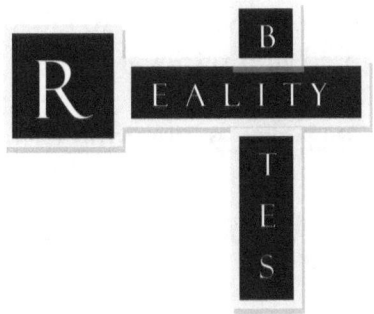

BY NICOLA RHODES

© copyright 2009 Nicola Rhodes

All rights reserved. No part of this publication may be reproduced, stored in a retrieval system, or transmitted, in any form or by means, electronic, mechanical, photocopying, recording, or otherwise, without the written prior permission of the author.

IBSN: 978-0-9561495-1-0

AUTHOR'S FOREWORD

This sequel has been a long time coming. Not because it took a long time to write, just a long time to get published.

For those of you who have been patiently waiting to hear more about Tamar and Denny, I apologise. I hope you feel it was worth the wait.

For Mike – my wonderful husband.
Without you to constantly support, help, encourage, nag and believe in me, this book might have lain in my computer files for evermore and never been unleashed upon the world. Thank you.

~ Prologue ~

TAMAR BLACK, former Djinn, current superhero was lurking. Lurking, of course, is not your standard superhero behaviour, but Tamar was doing something that she knew in her heart she probably should not be doing.

Denny Sanger, her – for want of a better word – sidekick (Denny himself would certainly be none too happy to be described in those terms) would be furious when he found out, and would almost certainly have tried to stop her had he known what she was up to, hence the lurking.

Not that he would have been *able* to stop her, being a mere mortal with no powers such as those Tamar possessed, but he would have tried very hard to talk her out of it, and may very well have succeeded.

Denny was her former master from back when she had been a Djinn and old habits die hard, besides which, she had a lot of respect for him. More than she had ever had for any other mortal. It was because of him that she was no longer a slave of the bottle.

The current slave of what had been for several millennia *her* bottle (and who was, in fact, also the original slave of said bottle, and the one who had tricked her into to it in the first place) the former Djinn – former sorceress (don't ask) current Djinn (again) and Arch Nemesis, AKA Askphrit, was the reason for the lurking.

When Tamar, with Denny's help, had tricked Askphrit back into the bottle, and she had become human again, although retaining her Djinn powers because that had been the wish she had made (and how she had been tricked into taking his place in the bottle) and a wish cannot be undone, they had decided that he should stay in the bottle as punishment for what he had done to her.

And, of course, so that he could not cause any more trouble, by granting any more wishes.

Wishes always come with hidden consequences as Tamar, having been both a victim *and* a Djinn knew very well (which was exactly why she was feeling so guilty about the fact that she had just let Askphrit out of the bottle). Oh Denny was going to be furious.

Askphrit was grinning hugely and lighting up the alleyway like an oversized firefly, thus completely ruining the whole lurking aspect of things.

Tamar ignored him as much as she could. She took a deep breath. 'I wish ... and you can wipe that smile off your face – believe me, I know what I'm doing. And you're *not* going to like it.'

Askphrit stopped grinning.

'That's better. Now then I wish ...'

Part One: The Darkness

~ Chapter one ~

THERE WAS A smoky room, and it was inhabited by two shadowy figures (smoky rooms are always inhabited by shadowy figures, if they were not, the universe would probably collapse, some things are a law of nature – or at least of narrative).

One of them was wearing a long cloak with a large hood concealing the face; the other was a tall, thin man with an untidy beard and a tweedy look about him. (He looked about as menacing as a librarian.)

He too, seemed to be trying to conceal his face by standing in the shadows, well away from the single candle burning on the table. He handed the other a piece of paper.

'That is the man,' he said. 'You are to follow him and do not let him see you.'

'And that's all?' said the other.

'For now, yes.'

'I see.'

'I do not think you see as much as you think you do. The purposes of the dark forces are not clear even to me, not yet. However, he has a weakness that it may be useful for you to know about.'

'Yes?'

'It's all in the information I have given you.'

The other read the paper briefly. 'Oh.'

'Yes, yes, I know, such manoeuvrings are distasteful, but it may be necessary.'

'Yes, I see that.'

'Do you indeed?' The thin man stared hard at the other.

'I should start at once?'

'Yes, do you think you can find him?'

'Not a problem.'

'Good, you must find him at once, then ...'

'*Find* him at once? I'm not allowed to start by *looking* for him, then? – 'cause I can do that, but it draws attention.'

'Risk it. Find him at once, I said. Now remember no contact and he must not suspect you are following him. Is that clear?'

'You know my reputation.'

'Indeed, good luck. I will contact you – soon perhaps.'

'Goodbye.'

'Goodbye.'

The hooded figure slipped silently from the room, and the other poured himself a drink from an elaborate decanter and sat down in an easy chair, smiling. He had every confidence in his new friend.

~ Chapter Two ~

DENNY WAS DREAMING. Actually, he was trapped in a hellish nightmare. Like all nightmares, it had started off well enough with him flying over the city looking down on happy people or busy, preoccupied people. Ordinary people just going about their business. Children playing in parks or in the streets, they all looked like ants from up here (Denny was not very imaginative.) It was a bright sunny, day, and he was enjoying himself. It all felt strangely real as dreams do, even the weirdest ones, and it never occurred to him to wonder how he had suddenly learned to fly. He felt godlike looking down on all those ordinary people, so unaware, so safe and secure in their normal lives. He wondered if this was how Tamar felt all the time.

It started so slowly he hardly noticed it at first. The clouds gathered, and below him, the darkness was not falling, but creeping on the city like a thick oil slick, slowly crawling along the streets and over the houses, slow but unstoppable, it turned the city black. This was utter blackness – not just the absence of light, but like a living thing.

Denny felt a sick horror as he watched helplessly. The

screams of the people, silenced as they were swallowed up by the darkness until there was nothing.

Denny hung in empty space, impenetrable blackness all around him. Then he heard the voice. It came from all around him, from everywhere and nowhere at once.

'**HE IS COMING!**'

Denny woke up shivering and yet sweating. The shadowy figure at his bedside melted away without being seen.

Tamar was out, she usually was. Night was her time. He was acutely aware that she needed remarkably little sleep. In fact, he was not sure that she needed any. She seemed to look upon it as a recreation. As a Djinn she had not been able to dream, and now that she could, she reveled in it. Denny was wishing that he did not have to dream, not like that anyway.

He wondered if he should call her, but decided against it. It would be too bad to interrupt her if she was in the middle of kicking some low-life's πίσω πλευρά. Not that she would leave in the middle of that anyway, she liked it too much. Leaving hapless victims in the lurch with a note reading "save you later" was not her style either. She would be back soon.

He got up and went into the kitchen to make some strong black coffee – for some reason, he did not want to go back to sleep.

He drank the coffee in one gulp and then headed for the living room where he began to beat and kick the hell out of the fight training equipment (pads and a dummy) that Tamar had insisted on providing. And that he trained with for three hours every day. He was getting quite proficient – a surprising development in a man whose most noticeable characteristic had been his laziness. It made him feel better too. And right now he needed the release

'Want to spar?' Tamar had appeared behind him and he leaped three feet in the air. He should have been used to this by now, but he was still feeling jumpy.

'Sorry,' she said laughing. She eyed the coffee pot and glanced at the clock – four a.m. 'Can't sleep? Did you have that dream again?'

'Yes, same one.'

'That's what, four nights in a row?'

'Five, I think it must mean something.'

'Like a premonition?'

'Maybe – he says "He's coming". Every time, what does it mean?'

'It means you're going round the twist – sorry but, *premonitions*? There's no such thing.'

'How would you know? You don't know everything you know. You were wrong about the ...'

'Okay, okay, you're right, so what *does* it mean? *Who's* coming, Father Christmas, The Antichrist?'

'I'm going to go with the second one.'

Tamar narrowed her eyes. 'That bad, huh?'

'You don't know – you can't imagine the feeling, the evil, it feels so *real*. I'm experienced at nightmares; this is nothing like I've ever felt before. Anyway, how can you say there's no such thing? What about that dream you had last year?'

'Yes I know, but I thought that was just a ...'

'Coincidence?'

'Guess not huh.'

'Still, it doesn't help; I still don't know what it *means*.'

'We'll figure it out. Why don't you leave that?' she gestured to the coffee, 'and go back to bed.'

He hesitated.

'You can't go without sleep, and it won't come back tonight, it never does.'

'That's what my father used say. I haven't had bad dreams like this since he died actually. Well, they weren't as bad as *these* dreams I suppose. No, the real nightmares happened when I was awake.'

Tamar looked at him curiously.

'You know, you're always saying stuff like that,' she said. 'What was so bad about your father anyway?'

Denny cleared his throat. 'Micks,' he said obscurely, as far as Tamar was concerned, and in a voice that was not quite his own. 'Don't talk to me about the bleedin' Micks,' he continued.'

'Huh?' said Tamar.

'I mean, you've got your loyalists and separatists and the fundamentalists. Bleedin' 'ell – they're all Micks when you come right down to it, aren't they? They should drop a bloody great bomb on Ireland; that's what they should do, that'd sort out all the troubles wouldn't it?'

Tamar's eyes widened. 'Oh, I see,' she said.

Denny ignored her. 'The only thing worse than the bloody Micks are the bleedin' poofs. Now that lot ought to be put up against a wall and shot – the whole bloody lot of them. Don't you agree boy? Ha, course you don't, you great wet liberalist pansy. I'm not so sure you're not a bloody poof yourself. Why don't you get a haircut, you long haired pretty boy? I despair of you, I really do. Prancing around like a tit. Why can't you be more like your brother?'

'Did he really talk to you like that?'

'That's nothing,' said Denny, relapsing into his usual manner. 'You should have heard my mother.'

'Are you serious?'

Denny sighed. 'I never fitted in with them. My father was a great big bloke, a real man's man. And my brother was the same; *is* the same. I take after my mother. Physically, I mean. So you see, I didn't match up to either of their ideas of what a man should be like. My mother was worse than my dad. She admired big strapping blokes; that's why she married one I suppose. And my dad wanted a son to take after him. Miles, my brother, *was* that son. I was just a disappointment to them both, and they never bothered to hide it.

Tamar was shocked. 'But, didn't they – didn't they … love you?'

'*Love* me?' Denny snorted. 'Ha, some people don't know they're born.'

Tamar could only stare in silent sympathy. This explained so much, so much.

'Miles was okay when we were small, but now, he's an even bigger git than my father was,' Denny told her.

'Where is he now?'

'I don't know, and I don't care.'

'Why, "pretty boy"?' This remark had been puzzling

Tamar. Denny was pale and thin and scruffy. He looked like a drug addict. The last thing you would call him was pretty.

'What?'

'Why would your father call you a pretty boy? I mean, you're not exactly ugly but…'

Denny gave a wan smile. 'He just thought it was an insult, because I had long hair and looked like my mother. I think he just thought it was another way to call someone a "pansy" or a "big girl's blouse", that sort of thing.'

'Hmm.' Tamar was not so sure. She looked at Denny, really looked at him for once, and tried to imagine what he must have looked like ten years ago. Before he stopped shaving, before he even needed to shave, and didn't. And perhaps with a little more colour in his face. He had good cheekbones she noticed, surveying him critically, and his mouth although not full was even and well proportioned, straight nose and teeth and gentle blue eyes. And his hair would be quite a bright, almost white blond, if it were cleaner.

He was not classically handsome, but still… if he were not so … and if he had a decent haircut. Well, she could see it now. He *would* be kind of pretty; in an unconventional way. Funny that she had never observed it before. She decided not to mention it. Obviously, he did not want to be – had been convinced by his upbringing that it was unmanly, and, therefore, went out of his way to look as shabby and unimpressive as he possibly could. He had done this so successfully that she had known him for more than a year and had never detected it.

He looked sulky now; his face was pinched and his expression stony. Evidently, he did not like talking about his experiences in a world that had not wanted him.

'I'm going back to bed,' he mumbled, 'see you later.' And he sloped off without another word.

Tamar watched him, aching with pity and love. If only she could go to him and comfort him, but it was impossible. Tamar's powers were too overwhelming for a mortal to handle close contact with her for long. Even a hug was out of the question; unless she wanted to risk killing him.

She waited a few minutes and then went out again.

~ Chapter Three ~

THE HOODED FIGURE was watching from the rooftop opposite. Hood pulled up, melting into the shadows, invisible as people came out of the building below. *Aha, there, that must be him.* Not quite what the watcher had been expecting; older, perhaps mid-forties, and maybe wiser. He looked like a good man, and he evidently commanded a certain respect. The watcher was impressed.

The man turned up a side street and the watcher hesitated. Was it the right man?

Somebody called out to him. 'Goodnight Mr. Stiles.' *Ah.* The watcher slid silently off the roof and followed the man home.

* * *

Denny and Tamar were out patrolling the streets together. The streets of Perth as it happened. It was late, around 2 a.m. and very quiet; suspiciously so.

'Do you think we should move?' said Denny suddenly, *apropos* of nothing.

'Yeah, there's nothing much going on here tonight is there? What about New York? That's usually busy.'

'Actually, I meant move home. Get a house or something.'

'Why?' said Tamar. 'We can be anywhere in the world in the blink of an eye – what does it matter where we're based?'

They were still living in Denny's grotty flat, stylishly transformed by Tamar into a large warehouse conversion and now boasting a training room (for Denny's inconvenience) with a tasteful collection of bladed weapons, which Denny was becoming, if not adept, then at least competent at using. It looked like the Batcave after a trip to Ikea.

'I just think I'd like to live in a house. I'd like a garden.'

'Why, what for?'

'I'd just like one. I've never had one. I was brought up in a council flat, and then I lived here. I always wanted a garden – and if the world *is* going to end ...'

'It's not.'

'Isn't it? It's got to end some day and my dream ...'

'Oh for God's sake! That's such typical human thinking – the Apocalypse myth! Why do people need to have such dramatic explanations for everything?'

'What are you talking about now?' asked Denny, thinking she was going off at a tangent.

'Just what I say. Take the dinosaurs; it must have been a meteor hit you say? But there's no evidence of it; it's far more likely that they just died out naturally. The fossil record suggests it.'

'What's that got to do with anything? And what would you know about fossils?'

'I'm getting to it. It's human nature to seek the most dramatic explanation everything's got to be a big deal. So you envision a terrible apocalypse "The end of the world" and write a prophecy about it. The fact is, that when and *if* humanity comes to an end it'll happen gradually, and you'll probably bring it on yourselves.'

'World War III you mean?'

'No! You see, there you go again – drama! Here we are in the middle of a fertility crisis brought on most likely by our pollution of the planet, we're destroying the Eco-system, disrupting the food chain that we rely on; disease is rife. I could go on, and yet the first thing that comes to your mind is a bloody big explosion that'll wipe us all out in one go.'

'What was your point again?'

'Just that the Apocalypse – Armageddon whatever you want to call it, isn't going to happen. Things just don't happen like that. Humans just *think* they do.'

'I only said I wanted a garden.'

Tamar sighed. 'You did, didn't you? Okay then.'

There was a thin scream from somewhere up ahead.

'Later,' said Denny. 'Come on Batman.' They ran.

Up ahead three men were dragging a struggling girl along the street. Although they were doing this quite openly, nobody was doing a thing to intervene.

Denny and Tamar stopped short in some confusion. Was it an arrest? Were these actually plain clothes policemen … jeering and shouting obscenities while trying to herd her toward a ratty looking old van? Er – no then.

Now, Tamar had some fairly strong opinions about men who attacked women – that death was too good for them – but it would have to do.

(Her opinions on people who stood by gaping while men attacked women are unprintable.)

It was these very people who were causing her main problem. Her usual approach in these situations would be to – well, she had a variety of approaches, but they all involved using magic, and in front of all these witnesses, a display of that kind of power would be, to put it mildly, inadvisable.

She looked at Denny in a panic. 'What do I do?'

Denny shrugged. 'What does it matter? They'll never believe it afterwards anyway. Isn't that what you always say?'

'There's too many of them.'

A fundamental problem of the theory that people always just believe what they want to believe, and only ever see what they want to see, and then just generally rewrite events in their head afterwards, was that it tended not to work when a large group of people all saw the same thing. They still did it of course, and all in their own way. So that, what you ended up with was a large group of people all arguing about what they actually saw, but at least all agreeing that they saw *something*. And then selling their story to the papers, so that an even larger group of people could argue, sometimes on national television, about what a large group of people saw.

It's much harder to convince yourself that it was just a weather balloon, when half a dozen other people saw the aliens playing the world's largest synthesiser and are arguing about the tune. [*]

This was an exposure risk that was just too large to take. Humans *en masse*, are just not ready to know about "virtual reality".

The men were almost to their van. One of them had split off and was opening the back. Tamar still hesitated.

Denny let out a snarl of impatience and ran forward to confront the men.

* * *

Tamar was wringing her hands in panic. Denny was, not to put too fine a point on it, getting the περιττώματα beaten out of him. And one of the men still had hold of the girl.

Tamar looked up at the sky for inspiration. The moon came out from behind a cloud, a full moon. It gave Tamar an idea.

The fight stopped abruptly as she let out an unearthly blood curdling howl that shattered several nearby shop windows. Every head turned; Tamar concentrated and lengthened her ears and teeth. Her eyes glowed yellow in the street light.

She let out another howl. She was beginning to enjoy herself. She decided to really let herself go. She let out another shattering howl and fell forward onto her hands, shaking her head from side to side, like a maddened bull. Then she snarled. Her shoulders grew and lifted into haunches and her entire body mass trebled. All this time, of course, she was growing hair all over her body and face. She looked totally fearsome.

The entire street was, by now, frozen in a horrified tableau – Denny included. They looked as if they would never move again.

---

[*]The world has, in fact, been invaded by aliens seven times. Government conspiracies, ha! Governments are amateurs. It's much bigger than that.

Tamar gave one last howl and bounded forward toward Denny. The men shrieked and ran. Denny did not even flinch. He turned to the terrified girl. 'Run, I would,' he told her. Then he realised she was going to faint. 'That's enough Tamar,' he said sharply.

Tamar whisked round like a dog and charged a small group of onlookers (they deserved it, she felt). That was enough for most of them; they scattered, *like cockroaches*, she thought, and screaming like banshees.

The girl fainted gracefully into Denny's waiting arms. It had been a long night; she was probably tired.

* * *

'What the bloody *hell* was that?' Denny exploded when they got home after depositing the unconscious girl at the nearest outpatients.

'What?'

'What do you mean *what*? You turned into a bloody *werewolf.*'

'Not *really*, it was just a glamour.'

'I don't give a rat's danglies. If you were going to use magic anyway, couldn't you have been a bit more subtle?'

'The thing is…'

'I mean for God's sake, Tamar, people *saw* you,' he raged. 'You might as well have just flown over their heads.'

'No, I couldn't have done that.'

'What's the difference?'

'Well, for one thing, people can't fly…'

'People don't turn into werewolves either.'

'Oh yes they do.'

'I mean for… *what*?' Denny skidded in mid-fury.

'It's true. Werewolves are real. Okay, so it's not usual, I admit, but I couldn't think of anything else that wouldn't expose me for what I really am. I mean when I saw the full moon, it was like a gift.'

'If you say so.'

'You're still angry aren't you?'

'No.'

'Yes you are. I know what'll cheer you up.'

'What are you doing?'

She clapped her hands and then opened a door that had not been there before. Through the door was a beautiful garden. It had a pond, fir trees surrounded it, there was a maze somewhere in the distance and the lawns were "Bowling Green" perfect, bordered by a riot of beautiful flowers – unusual in November.

Denny pursed his lips and narrowed his eyes, reminding Tamar of a look her mother used to give her.

'I meant a *real* garden, at the back of a *real* house, with weeds and insects.'

'Ingrate! Okay, we'll look for somewhere. In the meantime,' she gestured to the garden, now slightly more untidy and jungly, 'try it out.'

'Um, can I have weeping willows?'

'No sooner said than done. Well I'm going out.'

'Again?'

'I won't be long.'

'Where are you going?'

'Same as usual.'

'Oh, right, need any help?'

'Not this time, anyway aren't you due at work?'

'I hate Monday morning.'

'So give up your job. It's not like you need it anymore.'

They had had this discussion before. Denny refused to give up his mouldy job on the grounds that it would be immoral to live on magic. Tamar, who had lived in a bottle for thousands of years, thought he was insane. He wasn't an ordinary person any more, she said. He was a champion of the weak and oppressed now. Ordinary rules did not apply, besides he had no apparent objections to living in a magically transformed home or travelling by teleportation. That was different, he said. But she couldn't help feeling that hanging on to his job was just an excuse to get away from her sometimes. It probably was. Some men have a shed, Denny had a record store, and like a shed, Denny only went there when he really had to. Bo, the manager, never noticed when Denny did not turn up for weeks at a time. As long as he made sure that he was there for stock takes and pay-day, he had that job for life.

* * *

Tamar went out; Denny decided to stay at home. He went into the garden she had created; he thought it might help him think. The dream he had been having had been preying on his mind. What he needed, he decided, was more information, like *who* was coming, that might be a start.

~ Chapter Four ~

THE TIME HAD COME; the shadowy figures had been gathering about Stiles in ever-greater numbers, as the man in the smoky room had predicted. The hooded figure, who had been watching, followed the man to the pub. He was depressed, surrounded by raucous, happy drunks. He was drinking orange juice, only there at all out of custom, and a reluctance to go home to an empty house.

The watcher knew all this; it was the perfect time. Silently, like a shadow, the watcher waited behind Stiles's chair. When he put his glass, the hooded figure reached inside the long robes and took out a bottle of vodka and poured a large quantity into the nearly empty glass, then slipped the bottle into his coat and glided away unseen.

* * *

Later the hooded figure slipped into Stiles's office. It was nearly midnight, and nobody was about, but the watcher was cautious, silent as always. The desk was unlocked; there was a drawer that Stiles often reached into automatically, it was empty; the watcher placed a bottle of whisky and left silently feeling a pang of distaste for these shady manoeuvrings. Still it had to be. Nobody could be on the watch all the time, not even the best. Perhaps it was time to recruit some help.

* * *

Detective Chief Inspector, Jack Stiles was sat in his office, feeling tired. He ran his fingers through his hair and rubbed his stubble wearily, he then patted his pockets for his cigarettes; he lit one and then leaned back, wearily. He had just dismissed a distraught young female officer who had had a bad reaction to her first brutal case, a serial killer. He had thought she had handled it well; she had brought the man down herself. But when she had been faced with his grinning un-repentance, and even delight, in his evil, she had broken down. 'I didn't know anyone could be so evil,' she had sobbed. 'How can a human being *act* like that? I'm sorry sir, what must you think of me?'

'I think you're human,' Stiles had replied. 'It's okay to be upset, what kind of a person would you be if you didn't cry the first time you see the evil that men are capable of doing to each other? I did.'

She had blinked in disbelief; he knew what was going through her mind. *Jack Stiles? Famously tough and unfeeling at his work, the archetypal hard-bitten cop, had once had feelings just like everyone else?*

'You *did*?' she had said, incredulously.

'It was a long time ago,' he said. 'You toughen up, learn to cope, but you never stop caring.' He had smiled at her. *God was I ever that young?* 'You'll be okay,' he told her.

She had left, almost smiling, comforted. Another good one who might have thrown it in, was saved. *She would make a good cop in the years to come*, he thought.

It was late; he really should go home, but he did not want to. *Yes, I had feelings once, and look where they got me?* The office was dark; outside was a neon sign flickering, turning his face pink, orange, pink. Stiles stubbed out his cigarette, got up to close the blinds and then he sat down at his desk with his head in his hands.

As it had so often before, his hand reached for the empty drawer, it was not empty; he felt his hand brush something cold and smooth, something familiar, in some surprise, he drew out a full litre bottle of Whisky. Now how the hell, had that got there? He sat for some time, just staring at it.

~ Chapter Five ~

TAMAR AND DENNY were at a fabulous party being held at a prestigious private club in New York. (The name of which I do not intend to tell you, for legal reasons.) They had not been invited, naturally, but that was a minor detail.

They were not there on business, just for fun. Magic, had its perks, and, as Tamar said. 'There have to be some compensations for all the περιττώματα we have to wade through every day'.

Denny had had his objections at first, not to the idea in principle, but to the choices of venue that the high-flying Tamar invariably came up with. He would far rather have gone to an ordinary night club, or even just the pub. But he was coming around to the idea, it was even fun sometimes even if he did feel out of place at times – all the time actually. Funnily enough, though, no one ever seemed to notice, even if he turned up in his jeans and half a week's growth of stubble on his chin.

Naturally, Tamar always looked fabulous. Tonight, she was stunning in iridescent pale blue silk. (Her dress was not bad either.)

Denny was drunk; although he had a feeling that his headache owed more to the haw-hawing and cackling around him. He did not like the rich. The women made his teeth ache and the men made his fists itch.

Someone else at the party felt the same way, and was about to do a lot more about it than imagine them covered in tar and feathers.

The lights all went out suddenly; this caused a certain amount of panic naturally, and it seemed that this was the reason for it since they came back on again just a minute later. As the lights came back on, the screaming and running stopped abruptly. The ballroom was full of armed men, wearing the latest thing in armed terrorist black and sporting the latest thing in machine gun chic. Denny warmed to them immediately. At least they were not wearing Gucci.

Tamar sighed. 'Everywhere I go ...' she murmured. She waved a surreptitious hand at the weapons and disarmed them; a move that Denny did not fail to perceive. He nodded. At least the people were safe, for now. Although, there did not seem to be much else she could do for them. It was the old problem; there were too many witnesses.

The silence seemed to have been going on forever before a short, stocky man stepped forward and spoke jovially, in a slight accent, that Tamar could not place, but which reminded her irresistibly of Count Dracula. 'Ladies and Gentlemen, we are the people's liberation front of –. We do not intend you any harm at this stage, so please, do not panic. We shall hold you as hostages until our demands are met by your government, but we would prefer you to think of yourselves as our guests. So please no foolish heroics for your own sakes.'

He paused to let this sink in, then continued. 'You are the wealthy and the famous. I do not think your government will let anything happen to you, heh? It was for this reason that you were chosen. Heh? Our demands *will* be met, heh? And then everybody can go home, all right, hokey dokey? Good.'

This extraordinary statement was met with a stupefied silence. From somewhere at the back of the room came a muffled sob.

'Hokay, everybody now we are going to make a little movie, heh? For the folks back home, yes? Leon, the video camera.' He was smiling with all his teeth. 'Good, good, it is all good, heh? Everybody happy? Everybody wants to be in the movies, yes? All Americans wants to be a movie star. You have chance for big break now.'

Tamar sent a thought into Denny's mind. He jumped; she had done this before, but not often enough for him to get used to it. 'There's something funny going on here' she told him. 'There's more to this than meets the eye. What do you think?'

Denny shot her an agonized glance.

She tutted in his brain. 'I can read your thoughts, silly.'

'Well don't.' he thought petulantly. Then he simmered down 'I think you might be right.' he conceded. 'This guy's not real, he can't be. And what would you call that accent?'

'Transylvanian?'

Denny choked on a laugh.

The man in question was bustling about with his video camera. 'Now,' he announced. 'We make movies. Show the man in charge who we have here, heh? Who wants to go first?' Nobody moved. 'Come on,' he cajoled. 'Everybody want to be famous, heh? After this, you *all* be famous. Some of you *already* famous, yes, that why you here, heh?' He scanned the room. 'Hokay Jules.' He turned to a burly man in a ski mask. 'Line them up.' Suddenly his diction was chillingly clear, and his voice lost all its joviality.

"Jules" waved the gun threateningly; he pointed to a blonde woman in a scarlet dress. 'You.' he said. She tottered forward reluctantly. The leader gripped her around the shoulders in an ostensibly friendly fashion, but you could see that he had her in an iron grip that was anything but friendly.

The woman faced the camera and stuttered out a few words then was dismissed.

Several other people did the same; the leader kept up his cheery banter in between "takes", and the atmosphere became more and more laden with menace as the leader grew more loquacious.

He turned eventually to Tamar. 'Your turn,' he said. 'You're a pretty girl; don't you want to be famous? Of course you do. Come along now.'

Tamar fixed him with an unfriendly eye. She faced the camera in silence.

'Just a few words for the folks back home,' said the leader.

Tamar grinned mischievously. 'Okay,' she rolled her eyes and looked directly at the camera. 'Where's Bruce Willis, when you need him?'

'Don't push it,' Denny warned her silently, but the leader just smiled and nodded mockingly, as if she had just told him something.

That seemed to be it for the video cameos. The whole party was herded into a small room and locked in with a burly guard.

'What now?' Denny asked, without a word.

Tamar shrugged mentally, a difficult feat, but Denny got the message. 'I don't know. We'll just have to see what happens; hope we get a chance to do something.'

* * *

'Nice plan,' thought Denny. 'What do we do now?'

'At least these people won't get hurt as long as we're here.'

'Granted, but still ...'

'I guess we just ride it out.'

'We could try to find out what they want.'

'I don't think they want *anything*.'

'Don't be silly, they're not doing this for *fun*.'

'That's just it, I think they *are*.'

'Christ, we could be stuck here for *weeks* in that case.'

'Until they get bored,' Tamar agreed.

'We *can't*, we have to get out of here.'

'I know, believe me, I'm working on it.'

'Work faster.'

'Why don't *you* think of something?'

There was a long silence eventually Denny spoke.

'We have a real problem,' he said.

Then the power went out.

* * *

The candles flickered and flared in the darkness. The tall,

thin man walked to the head of the table and addressed the figures sitting around it.

There were five of them; a "cabal" would have been an appropriate description, although, any sort of description would have been difficult to achieve in the half light. None of them looked directly at any of the others.

'Gentlemen,' said the thin man. (This was a disputable description; some of them did not even look human). 'We have, as you are aware, hit a problem. Our – agent – is in need of assistance. I know – I know,' he held up a hand. 'But our enemies are moving faster than anticipated. There is one,' here he nodded, and his audience murmured. 'Yes, you know who I mean. So, do any of you have any suggestions?'

There was a long silence, and then one of the cabal spoke. 'Uh, what was the problem again?'

The thin man sighed. This could take some time.

~ Chapter Six ~

TAMAR WAS GETTING frantic; two days and no ideas, it was ridiculous. On reflection, it had probably been a bad idea to restore the power, but the hostages had panicked, whereas their captors had taken it calmly, as if they had been expecting it.

There seemed little chance of the Stockholm syndrome developing. The terrorists said little to their hostages. After the filming, they had tired quickly of bullying and all they did was watch silently in shifts. The leader had taken a few strolls among the hostages. He seemed to have a fascination with Tamar. On one occasion, when she had been pretending to sleep like the others, he had lit a large cigar and then deliberately dropped it on her. Without opening her eyes or moving a muscle more than was necessary, she caught it between her fingers and took a long drag before opening her eyes and smiling at him. After that, he avoided the hostages entirely and insisted that they all be tied up. Denny, who had seen this parlour trick, was annoyed and berated her at length – in silence of course. Until she explained, that she was trying to divert his malice toward herself to spare the others.

'I want him to hate me,' she explained. 'Really hate me.'

Denny had to concede that it appeared to be working.

* * *

They had still made no demands or any threats that the hostages knew of. Their calm demeanour suggested that they were simply following orders, and those orders seemed to be simple enough. Keep the hostages tied up and watch them. All in all, the overriding feeling, even among the hostages, was boredom.

As far as Denny was concerned the whole thing had a surreal quality to it. He was conversant with the behaviour of bullies, and boredom usually resulted in bloodshed – as Denny's hospital record from his schooldays would testify to. In the circumstances, then, their behaviour was abnormally restrained. And then there was their attitude towards Tamar, (and one other very pretty girl, come to that). There had been no leering, no suggestive remarks or fumbling hands. In fact, they seemed almost wary around her as if they somehow sensed or had been warned that one false move and she would break every bone in their face.

* * *

On the third day another man arrived, he carried no weapon and wore no mask. He had bleached white hair and, apparently, a bleached face, which contrasted sharply with his very dark eyes. 'Like pissholes in the snow,' as Tamar observed. He looked over the hostages and disappeared into an adjoining room without saying anything.

About half an hour later one of the others came in and started to untie Tamar. 'Boss wants to see you,' he said.

'*No!*' Denny cried out. Instinct told him that he did not want Tamar, even with all her power, to be alone with that ghoul. Something was dead wrong here. Incredibly he struggled to his feet and interposed himself between Tamar and the man, who immediately clapped the gun to Denny's head and ordered him to sit down.

Denny froze automatically. Then he remembered that the guns were inert. On the other hand, he was tied up, wrists and ankles, and there was nothing to prevent a gun being used as a blunt instrument.

Tamar put out a hand and gently pushed the gun out of the way. She turned to Denny and smiled reassuringly. 'It's all right,' she said. 'I'll go.' She smiled, kissed Denny's cheek, and held out her hand to the man. 'Shall we?'

As she reached the door she turned and snapped her fingers, she winked. Denny felt his ropes loosen suddenly.

What? Then he realised the moment had come. The man had left the door unlocked only two guards remained, and one of those was sleeping. It was probably a trap but what the hell? It was now or never. He did not stop to wonder what Tamar was going to do; he just hoped that his feeling about the white faced man was wrong.

* * *

The watcher was stationed in a dark alley waiting for Stiles who often used this route as a short cut home. The dark figures were clustering more thickly around him lately, and the watcher was worried. Time for some action

From an interesting vantage point, positioned in a handstand above the street on some handy scaffolding, the watcher could see that Stiles had picked up another stalker, a large, muscular man who moved with surprising stealth for someone so large.

Stiles himself was oblivious to all his shadows. He was staggering – drunk as a prom queen – that was *something* at least.

As Stiles turned into the alley, the dark figures attacked. The watcher was ready for this and swung down form the scaffolding pole in a smooth motion knocking two of them aside. The muscular man ran forward and grabbed another by the neck, flinging it easily into a wall. The watcher now recognised him as a friend and colleague of Stiles one of his subordinates. The watcher broke an iron bar off the scaffolding with amazing ease for such a slight person, and began batting heads with incredible speed and dexterity.

Stiles struggled from his stupor and recognised his friend. 'Finchley?' he said. 'Is that you?'

The watcher turned to Finchley. 'Take him home – I'll deal

with this.'

Finchley nodded; he was not, from the watcher's observations, overly bright. But even he could see that the mysterious hooded figure, whose face he could not see, could handle this alone, and he should get his boss, who was his priority anyway, to safety.

In any case, Finchley was programmed to take orders without question – not one of life's leaders.

The watcher called out after them as they lurched away. 'Make sure you stay with him, and for God's sake don't let him sober up.'

'*What*?' Finchley was shocked. But the watcher was busy; Finchley shrugged and took his boss by the shoulders and guided him, swaying, away from the carnage.

* * *

They had treated Denny like a hero – there's a first time for everything. Yet it had all been surprisingly easy, too easy really – or was he just being paranoid?

He had shaken off his ropes, lunged at the guard and hit him with a telephone; the guard had gone down with a grunt and lay still on the floor; Denny had grabbed his knife.

Then the sleeping guard had woken up and fired his gun at Denny with no discernible result. He had shaken it and looked down the barrel in confused fear, backing away as Denny rounded on him pointing the knife threateningly. He collapsed in a corner whimpering. Just to be sure, Denny took the gun from him and brought it down on his head with a sharp crack. The hostages cheered and Denny shushed them, pointing meaningfully at the door. He then cut their hands and feet free, and they stood up painfully cramped and crippled with pins and needles.

'Come on,' he whispered. In the outer room, they found the third guard lying dead over the bar.

'Tamar?' wondered Denny. The way was clear, however, so he sent the others out into the cloakroom and looked around for her. There was another door; it led to a small office. He went in; Tamar was there, white faced and shaking, there was no sign of the man with the blanched face and Denny did not ask.

'Later,' he thought.

Outside the police wrapped them in blankets and gave them cups of tea. A strangely orange complexioned TV journalist interviewed Denny, but, as he knew that Tamar would futz up the film in the camera, he was not overly worried about that.

When the news crews finally left, the police insisted that they all go to the hospital to be checked out, and they were bundled into ambulances. They slipped out at the hospital and Tamar teleported them home. In all the confusion, they were unlikely to be missed and, even if they were, hospital staff are far too busy (sneaking out to the car park for a crafty smoke) to go chasing after patients who don't want to be helped.

* * *

'That's not journalism,' said Denny switching off the TV, 'that's lying with style.'

'I especially liked the part where the big bearded guy took your place as the hero of the hour,' agreed Tamar laughing. She had completely recovered her equanimity, but had so far refused to discuss what had happened in the small room with the white faced man.

'I'll tell you sometime,' she said evasively. 'Just not now, don't worry about it, he didn't hurt me.'

'But *something* happened,' Denny persisted. 'You were in a right state.'

Tamar looked shrewdly at him. 'It wasn't your fault you know. I don't blame you; it was my choice; I knew what I was doing.'

Denny subsided; it would have to do, for now.

'I wonder who those guys were – really,' Denny was saying. 'I don't believe for one minute that they were escaped convicts like the TV said, we'd have heard about it before.'

'I don't think *they* know who they were either, they just have to say something.'

'It makes you wonder.'

'What?'

'How much of what's on TV is just a load of drivel.'

'All of it, I'd say.'

'At least entertainment shows are honest about the fact that it not supposed to be true.'

Tamar glanced outside; it was getting dark.

'I have to go,' she said, she held up a hand as Denny opened his mouth to offer to go with her.

'I'll see you later.'

She was not to know just how much later.

~ Chapter Seven ~

'WHAT DO YOU mean, he's gone?'

Finchley was backing away from the infuriated figure. Just because he could not see a face, did not mean that he could not still tell that the person inside the hood was snarling.

'I – I couldn't help it, he let them in and they took him. It was like he was in a trance.'

'Damn it! You idiot, all you had to do was ... you let him sober up, didn't you?'

'Of *course*. He's an alcoholic – I ... wait a minute. It was *you*, wasn't it? You put him back on the drink again. Who are you? Why would you do such a thing?'

The figure pushed back the hood and Finchley gasped.

'I had good reason; you'll just have to trust me. Now, which way?'

Finchley pointed automatically then he suddenly moved himself into the figure's path.

'Wait,' he said. 'You tell me what's going on. What did you do to him? What are those ...?'

The figure sighed. 'I haven't got time for this. I really am very sorry about this.'

'About wh...?' said Finchley before he sailed off to dreamland on the end of a right hook

* * *

D.C.I. Jack Stiles was flying. He had sobered up some time ago, but his head felt like it was full of pink cotton wool. He was feeling no surprise that he was up in the air. All he felt was a sense of calm contentment; it was like being drunk, only better. The world felt – right somehow. Everything was how it should be.

There were three of them, he thought through the fog in his head, beautiful women – angels perhaps. They were supporting him carrying him; they would not let him fall. They would protect him; it was wonderful; everything was wonderful. It did not matter that he could not even remember his name let alone where he was or how had got here. It was a familiar state of mind for him anyway.

Now he was lying on a cloud, the angels were there too. Was he in heaven? Had he died? Did it matter? Nothing mattered anymore this was bliss. *'What's in this stuff and where can I get some more?'*

He noticed, as the fog in his head cleared a little, what appeared to be a door opening before him. *'Uh oh, chucking out time.'*

Snow blew in through it, and a figure appeared, silhouetted against a starry night.

The figure advanced, and his head cleared a little more. He struggled to focus – aware, now that it was weakening, that a strong influence was being exerted on his mind.

The figure raised both arms; enough focus had returned by now that he could see that he was in a large barn of some kind. Well, he thought philosophically, he'd sobered up in worse places.

He saw that the figure was small and that in each hand it held a large heavy looking crossbow. It fired them both at the same time. Two of the women at either side of him exploded in a shower of ash as the third one took off – literally, into the air, and the figure fell forward onto its knees in exhaustion. Stiles reclaimed his mind and darted forward to catch what he could now quite clearly see was a young woman. She collapsed into his arms and passed out. He stared down at her. What the hell?

She was dainty and beautiful although her face showed signs of a terrible strain; her hair was long and dark, and he found himself wondering, abstractly, what colour her eyes were. It was easier than trying to piece together what the hell was going on, who she was and what had happened he was not ready for that yet. It was like he was stuck in a nightmare, his worst trip ever.

Her eyes were dark blue. He saw this when they suddenly snapped open, and she simultaneously shot out an arm. She was not looking at him, but focussing over his shoulder; in her hand was a sharp stick. There was a shriek behind him and an explosion of ash, which landed all over both of them. The mysterious girl met his eyes briefly as she dropped her arm and then closed her eyes again.

The whole thing had taken about five seconds. 'Those are some reflexes,' he thought.

She seemed to be out for good this time, so Stiles laid her gently on a pile of hay and covered her with his jacket. He felt suddenly tired; he glanced at his watch, a little after one. Then he noticed the date, somehow he had lost three days. He noticed the snow blowing in the door and went to close it. Outside he saw miles and miles of empty snow-covered countryside. He was then, apparently, in the middle of nowhere with a comatose girl who had probably saved him from the proverbial "fate worse than death". Tomorrow was going to be one of those days – the kind he had every day.

He wanted desperately to close his eyes, but a strange feeling was resurfacing from the past; was it – integrity? And he felt it incumbent on him to stay awake and keep watch while the girl recovered her strength. After all, there might be more of those – *things* out there. He reached into his pocket and drew out the whisky bottle and deliberately poured the remains of its contents away into the snow, what a waste. He then closed the door and lit a small fire with a pile of straw separated from the rest with a ring of small rocks, thoughtfully provided by the god of convenient coincidences, and settled down to wait for morning. Tomorrow he was going to want some answers, or, at the very least, a lift home and a lot of therapy.

~ Chapter Eight ~

DENNY WAS WORRIED; Tamar had been gone for three days with no contact, and it was the longest she had ever been away without so much as a message. He knew where she had gone and why but he could think of no reason why she should be silent. He had tried calling for her – nothing. She had telepathic abilities and normally she would have spoken to him by now. (She also carried a mobile phone, so she really had no excuses.)

She always called in one way or another, after the time he had lectured her about being inconsiderate and how he worried etc. She had told him that she didn't need a wife, given him curlers and a rolling pin to brandish and had followed him around for days making irreverent clucking noises until he almost decided to go to work. She still referred to him occasionally as "Mother hen", but she had taken the point which was all that really mattered to him. He even thought that, deep down she was rather gratified to have someone who would worry about her.

He wished that he could get the face of the pale skinned man from the nightclub out of his mind. He had a bad feeling about him. If only she had talked to him about it; it was not like her to be uptight; it only made him even more nervous about the situation. Whatever the situation was.

The dreams had been getting worse too; he would have liked to talk to her about that as well. He wondered if the white faced man was the mysterious 'He' who was apparently coming.

He glanced at the clock; it was now almost four days since she had left. She *had* to be in trouble.

Well, he knew where she had gone; he would just have to go after her and try to trace her. To hell with the premonitions of doom, he was not getting anywhere trying to work it out anyway; he just did not have enough to go on. Action, that's what he needed, to *do* something.

He grabbed a jacket, his wallet and a phone and stalked purposefully out of the flat; he got as far as the outer door when he turned back to get his shoes only to realise that he had forgotten his key.

He had picked up quite a few skills in the last year including opening locked doors with a credit card. The only problem was that Denny did not command the kind of salary that permitted having a credit card. He had a video club card, but, unfortunately, it was cardboard. He tossed it on the floor in disgust and kicked the door in. In a testament to shoddy workmanship, the door fell off its hinges in one smooth movement. Denny hoped that it was not a bad omen that he would be starting his journey with a foot full of splinters.

He had hobbled halfway to the station before he gave in and hailed a cab. The driver was disgusted at the small fare (only two streets) and by the fact that Denny spent the journey with his shoes off picking bits of wood out of his toes and bleeding all over the seat. Denny gave him a tenner to appease him. (Denny was the sort of wimp who never complained in restaurants, even if there was a rat in his salad. And he had not even *ordered* a salad; he was strictly a steak and chips man.)

* * *

The station was closed; well it *was* two O' clock in the morning. 'Damned one horse town!'

He supposed he had not really thought this through; he had been carried away up to this point, and now he was stalled – for the next four hours until the station opened. The sensible thing to do would be to lamely slope off back home and wait, but he could not bring himself to do it; it would be such a letdown, like taking a step backwards. He sat down on a bench to wait.

* * *

By the morning, he had collected quite a bit of change; taking off his shoes had earned him even more. He only wished he had had a violin case or even a scruffy hat. Still he had made more than enough for a return ticket.

As the train pulled away, he did not notice the creeping darkness spreading over the streets he was leaving behind

After about ten minutes, Denny's brain woke up, and he realised that he was travelling in the wrong direction; he must have got on the wrong train. 'Damn! Oh damn and hell and – bugger – bugger – bugger.'

He panicked, what the hell was he going to do? Without thinking, he pulled the cord marked "Emergency Only" and, in much smaller letters, the injunction "Improper use will result in a fine"

As far as Denny was concerned, this *was* an emergency. The train lurched and shuddered to a halt halfway through a tunnel. Still operating on automatic or "stupid mode" as Tamar called it, he tried to open the door it was locked, as train doors are during journeys. Had it been a real emergency such as the train being on fire this could have been a problem but apparently nobody had thought of this.

The automatic locking is presumably to prevent children, stupid people and the suicidal from leaping off a moving train. If you want to kill yourself, you will just have to jump off a bridge like normal people, just as long as you do not disrupt the trains. (Of course if you really want to die by rail travel you could always risk the buffet car.)

He heard someone coming. 'Oh hell!' He fumbled and managed to open the window and scramble through; it was a bloody good job he was so thin, he thought. He landed on the tracks and cut his leg and his hand. 'I am *not* having a good day,' he thought, and he ran, or rather limped quickly, back down the tunnel.

After about twenty minutes, he realised that he was still in the dark. 'This is a bloody long tunnel,' he thought. Perhaps he was going the wrong way. The train had only just entered the tunnel before it had stopped, he was sure. Surely he should have been out by now.

He heard voices behind him; he turned and the voices stopped. He carried on limping, and the voices started again, and underneath them, now that he was listening, he could hear footsteps. He stopped and turned again, silence fell again. One more episode of this and Denny lost his temper; he squared up to the shadows behind him.

'Okay,' he snapped, 'who the hell are you? I've had a bloody awful day so far, and it's still only half past six in the morning. I'm just not in the mood to play "Grandmother's footsteps" in the dark. So what do you want?'

He said all this with hardly a quaver in his voice. (His acting skills were really coming along.) The only response was a gust of silvery laughter and a blast of cold wind.

Ghosts? He wondered and shrugged; Tamar had taught him to be unafraid of the ethereal.

'If you're going to be afraid of something' she had said, 'be afraid of the thing that's solid enough to bash you over the head with a big stick. A spirit can't hurt you and mostly they don't want to.'

He had taken her word for it; she ought to know he reasoned and wasn't the world full of enough dangers to worry about. It was nice to know there were some things he did not *have* to fear.

There was anyway, the – to Denny's mind – far more pressing problem of where the hell he was. Since he had not hit daylight yet and he was certain that he should have by now, clearly something had gone very wrong – par for the course really. But he still had to work out what he had done; he was having that strange feeling of destiny again, as if he was being manipulated. The only thing he could do was carry on following the tracks. He looked down; the tracks were gone – Well, of *course* they were! He would have been far more surprised if they had still been there.

'Oh well,' he thought resignedly, and headed off in what he hoped was the right direction. Since he now had no idea where he was trying to get to this made navigation a bit redundant.

He trudged on; the voices were still behind him murmuring constantly. It was annoying, like listening to someone else's Walkman on a bus. He wondered if this were another nightmare; it had that same feeling and the nightmares had been so real. He closed his eyes and tried to open them again in a futile attempt to wake himself up, which is impossible, when you are not, in fact, asleep. It occurred to him that the only time you *think* you're dreaming is when you're not. Apart from the voices (he wondered what would happen if he just turned round and charged at them) he felt strangely calm now; bored even. The nightmarish feeling was ebbing, as was his frantic anxiety about Tamar. He was almost sleepwalking. A cloud of shimmering moths lit up the darkness, and he watched them dazedly, the effect was almost hypnotic. The voices behind him ceased to bother him, they felt almost soothing. It no longer mattered where he was going or why as long as he kept on walking and he felt like he could walk forever.

* * *

Of course, forever is a long time. Denny came to in a small room that was reminiscent of a cell. His head hurt, as if he had been drinking, as did his leg, foot and his hand, all of which had been thoughtfully bandaged by some unknown person. He was lying on a camp bed; he got up and tried the door it was quite naturally locked. He decided that there was no point in shouting for help. He was locked in a cell, and presumably whoever had put him in there had done so deliberately and was, therefore, unlikely to respond to a cry for help by letting him out. Besides which, his head hurt too much; at least he was not tied up.

He sank down on the camp bed; it collapsed, trapping him inside.

'Christ,' he groaned. 'How much worse can this day get?'

He immediately regretted this since asking this question usually guarantees that any minute now you're going to find out.

'That depends on you,' said a voice above him, 'and how co-operative you're willing to be.' A hand reached down and helped Denny to extricate himself from the mangled bed.

'Okay,' said Denny, 'I'll buy it, although you might want to work on the voice – a little deeper perhaps; more Darth Vader and less Julian Clary; that is, if you expect to be taken seriously when you make statements like that.

The man stared coldly at him.

'I was just saying.'

'Hmm, I think that that *female* has had a bad effect on you. Before you met her, I think you would have been properly frightened.'

'Of *you*?' Denny was scornful.

The man stepped into the light. Denny took an involuntary step backward. 'Oh my God!'

'No.' the man gave an evil, fanged grin. 'Not *your* God. But I do move in mysterious ways.'

Denny scanned the cell for an appropriate weapon. He spotted a wooden chair and dived; he smashed it against the wall and it splintered. If he had thought about it, he might have wondered why his adversary did not try to stop him. When he plunged the broken chair leg into his heart to absolutely no effect, it became pretty obvious.

'Oh, just look at that.' The (presumed) vampire simpered in camp tones, pulling the piece of wood out disdainfully. 'A perfectly good shirt – ruined.' He grinned and took Denny by the throat in an iron grip. 'A lesson,' he said. 'I cannot be killed by any means that you possess, puny mortal.'

'*Puny mortal*?' croaked Denny. He was going for withering scorn, but since he was being choked to death the best he could manage was cracked gasping, which is not nearly the same. 'Who writes your lines?' he added caustically.

The vampire (or whatever he was) released him. 'You will stay here,' he said. 'You cannot be allowed to interfere with our plans.'

'Why don't you just kill me?' rasped Denny, and immediately wished he had not. What fatal flaw was it that made him say things like that?

'Fool,' said the vampire thing. 'You have no idea what you are mixed up in, do you? Well let's just say I have my reasons. If it is any comfort to you, you will die soon enough, but I do not have to explain my reasons to you.'

Denny remembered something. 'Tamar,' he said, more to himself than anything else.

His captor turned and grinned evilly at him. 'Tamar Black cannot save you,' he sneered, 'if she's even still alive – which I doubt.'

'She is,' said Denny defiantly. 'She is,' he whispered to himself. 'I'd know – I'm sure I would – I'd feel it.'

~ Chapter Nine ~

'TAMAR BLACK is dead, or she soon will be. We have to send another.' The thin man addressed his cabal.

There was murmuring around the table. 'She's not dead yet,' spoke up one.

'She may yet prevail,' said another, 'she is quite – remarkable.'

'And who else is there to send anyway?' said yet another.

'There is one,' said the thin man. 'He does not realise it yet, but he is already on his way to us.'

'A *man*?' said the first voice. 'But he cannot, only a woman can ... and a woman of great power at that. It has to be her; this is what we decided.'

'I don't see why,' said another voice, and there was some nodding.

'All right, it's got nothing to do with her being a woman; it just has to be *her* then. Only her.'

'Why?'

'Because – shut up!'

'Because, idiots – she is the only one who has the power to

stop the – "Master",' someone else interrupted.

'Oh! – well why didn't you just say so then?'

The thin man waved his arms for silence. 'Yes, yes, I am aware. You have misunderstood me. She is in trouble, and we must send someone to *help* her. And *he* is the only one who can.'

'How can you know this?'

'Because he is the only one who will try.'

* * *

It was morning – just barely, but it was definitely getting lighter. Stiles' head started to nod – the coming dawn meant that the danger was passing. Stiles knew better than this really, but thirty five thousand years of human instinct[*] was taking over.

A shadow fell across him and he leaped up brandishing a handful of smouldering straw. The girl jumped backwards; he burnt his hand and dropped the straw, cursing.

'Sorry,' she said, 'I didn't mean to startle you.'

'It's fine,' he said, shaking his fingers and blowing on them.

She came nearer. 'Here, let me see.'

He held out his hand cautiously.

'You stayed up all night?' she said. 'That's so – chivalrous.'

Stiles felt suddenly tongue-tied. She was so beautiful, and she was looking at him with … what was it, admiration? The close proximity of beautiful young women was not something that Stiles was used to in any circumstances. And no woman of any kind, except his late wife, had ever looked at him with anything other than disinterest at best.

'Oh – well,' he stammered. 'I um – not really – I just – it

---

[*] This instinct is taken advantage of by burglars and hotel thieves the world over – when even the most nervous and paranoid of people, the kind who stay awake all night with a shotgun in their hands finally feel safe and fall asleep. Of course, what usually happens to these people is that the dawn chorus then keeps them awake. – A phrase that sounds a lot more pleasant and musical than the reality of a single magpie cawing incessantly in the eaves (so that, when you look out of the window to throw a stone at it, you cannot even see it) and sounding remarkably like an old man clearing his throat.

seemed – er ...'

She was rummaging in a backpack, which seemed to be mainly full of weapons. Eventually, to his relief, she brought out a roll of bandage and a small jar. 'Arnica,' she said. 'It'll help with the pain.'

It did too; it was remarkable – like magic. (*Very* like magic, in fact.) She bandaged up his hand.

'Is that better, Detective?' she asked.

He waved his good hand dismissively. 'Please,' he said. 'I think, under the circumstances, you should call me Jack.'

She looked intensely pleased. 'Thank-you – Jack,' she said and gave him a dazzling smile. Stiles actually blushed, something he had not done in at least thirty years.

'Well,' he said, looking at his feet, 'I don't know what's going on, but I get the feeling that you arrived just in time.' He looked sideways at her. 'Where are we anyway?' This was starting in the wrong place, but at least it was a start.

'Scotland – somewhere – I think. I'm not sure exactly.'

'Scotland? How the hell did I get to Scotland – on foot – unless?' He glanced at the empty whisky bottle. She shifted uncomfortably, but Stiles did not notice.

'You weren't exactly on foot,' she said.

And he vaguely remembered the flying. 'Oh,' he said and then he shook his head. 'But you ...?'

'Hmm let's just say it's a good job they stopped when they did. I'd just about had it.'

'Are you saying that you followed me from London – on foot in ...' He checked his watch. 'Three days?'

'Um.'

'No wonder you were knackered.'

There was a silence; she waited for the inevitable next question, and it came.

'So, who the hell *are* you?'

There was a further silence, so he began again. 'Let's start simple. What's your name?' He was in good cop mode now, feeling more like himself again.

The girl hesitated for a moment; she was never supposed to have met him face to face; he was not supposed to know about her at all. 'Kitty,' she said.

Stiles saw her glance at a small cat that had wandered in out of the snow. 'Kitty … Winter.'

He looked at her shrewdly. 'Kitty – the vampire slayer?' He indicated the sharp stakes poking out of her backpack.

She smiled. 'If you like – that's one way of putting it.'

'Surely that's a myth – syndicated.'

Kitty shrugged. 'Put it this way,' she said, 'most people think that *vampires* are a myth. I did myself until recently. But now I know different and so do you.'

Stiles docketed this information. 'And why did they kidnap me?'

'I don't know. I – we – the men who sent me to protect you, they only know that they're trying to kill you. But they don't know why. I'm sorry – I know they're working on it.'

Stiles thought about this. 'So, hang on if they're trying to kill me and you're here to stop them – no wait. Why did they bring me all the way out here, and risk you catching up with them? They must know about you. Don't they? And if they got past you long enough to grab me, then why didn't they just kill me in London when they had the chance? You don't have to be a criminal mastermind to see that it doesn't make sense.'

She looked uncomfortable. 'You certainly know how to ask the awkward questions.'

'I'm a copper.'

'I know. I won't forget it. You're a lot shrewder than ...'

'Than what, than I look?'

'No, I just meant ...'

'Look, do you *know* why? It's okay if you don't.'

'No, I do – I think. It's just – well it's embarrassing. You see those were *female* vampires and vampires tend to be – lascivious.' She went pink. 'And you're a man and you're not *bad* looking you know for ...'

Stiles held up his hands, revolted. 'Okay, okay, I get it, don't say anymore – I feel sick.'

'If it makes you feel any better, I'm sure I was in time. I mean you were still fully dressed when I found you. I was right behind them; I don't think anything happ ...'

'It doesn't really; it's just the idea that they wanted to ...'

'Be glad they did,' she admonished, 'otherwise you'd be dead. I got careless; I was distracted – deliberately I think. And then I left you alone with some muscle-bound idiot – when I think what could have happened.'

'Well it didn't. Good job I'm so handsome eh?'

'Yes.'

'I was joking.'

'Oh.'

Stiles was surprised at how easily he had accepted all this, despite the fact that he had seen it with his own eyes. He suspected that it was because he was treating the whole thing like a bad dream. With its good points too of course, he thought, looking at Kitty. For some reason – and not turpitude either – he kept envisioning her in a short skirt and ankle socks waving pom-poms.

'So, what do we do now?' he asked.

'We have to get moving. We'll go to my place; I know somebody who might know what to do. It's time to find out what's really going on with you.'

'And where do you live?'

'It's about two weeks on foot, but we'll hitch or take a train. Got any money?'

Stiles checked his pockets. 'No.'

'It doesn't matter; there's ways and means. If you don't mind bending the law.' She grinned slyly at him.

He looked out at miles and miles of nowhere. 'Got to get back to civilisation first.'

'Yes it's about three or four days on foot. I'm afraid I can't fly?'

Stiles groaned. 'I could use a drink.'

Kitty looked uncomfortable. She made a decision. 'I have a confession,' she said. 'It was me who put that whisky in your desk drawer and I spiked your orange juice.'

Stiles looked at her impassively.

'I had to,' she carried on hastily. 'I didn't want to; in fact I've rarely been more ashamed of myself; the thing is, vampires use mind control, but they find it much harder to work the mojo on a person who's drunk. For some reason, they can't get a grip on a mind that's all over the place. I was trying to keep you safe; I couldn't be there all the time, and I knew about your problem, I hated myself for doing it. I'm so – so sorry.'

'Okay,' he said. 'I understand. You did the right thing. On balance, I'd rather be a recovering drunk than dead. I'd like a cigarette though.'

'You're not angry?'

'No, it's okay, I'm glad you were honest. – About that at least,' he added quietly.

* * *

'So, who's this guy we're going to see?'

They had been going for about two hours now. Trudging through the snow which stretched on featurelessly in all directions. If Kitty knew where they were going, Stiles did not have a clue; he had decided to just go along with it; there did not seem to be much else he could do.

'Just a friend of mine,' she said. 'He's been looking into it for me. I hope he's found something out by the time we get back. Maybe if we knew why they were after you, we could stop it.'

'That's what I don't get. I mean why me? I mean surely I'm no kind of threat, I didn't even know they existed until today. I'm not sure I believe it even now.'

'I know what you mean. And I've seen some strange stuff.'

'What about you? What's your story? After all, you seem to know a lot about me.'

'No story, I'm just me. I help people.'

'Okay, be like that.' Stiles was not giving up though, but he had time and he was an expert at getting people to spill their guts. Rule one, don't push. He would get it out of her, he was sure.

They had passed a few lonely farms and one solitary inn, but Kitty refused to stop. 'We travel until nightfall. Then we have to be indoors, that's when they come out.'

'What if we don't find anywhere?'

'Don't worry; I know where I'm going.'

Stiles gazed around him. 'How is that possible? It all looks the same, or do you have some special spider-sense that lets you know where to go?'

'Nope.' She reached into her back pocket. 'I brought a map.'

A map? – Of nowhere? 'Christ I need a cigarette, takes my mind off wanting a drink.'

Kitty looked away. 'Sorry.'

'Oh it's not your fault; I took up smoking the first time I gave up drinking. Now I just need to give up smoking.'

'It's not a good idea out here anyway. It alerts the wildlife.'

'So? We're in Scotland not Africa. What could be so dangerous out here?'

'You'd be surprised. Not everything has to make sense. Besides where there are vampires, there are wolves – take it from me.'

'Wolves? I haven't seen any wolves. Anyway wolves don't attack humans.'

'They do if vampires are controlling them.'

'You're doing this on purpose, aren't you?'

'I'm not trying to scare you, you'll be fine with me; I can handle wolves. But it'd slow us down. Do you carry a gun?'

'No.'

'Oh well, never mind.'

'I wouldn't shoot an animal anyway.'

In the distance, getting closer, they heard howling. Kitty smirked. 'Are you sure about that?'

~ Chapter Ten ~

LEFT ALONE in the cell, Denny became frantic; there had to be some way to escape. There was a small, barred window, if only there was some way to saw through the bars. He knew he would not have the strength to pull the bars out; he needed Tamar for that kind of stunt. And he was so hungry he could have eaten his own foot.

Not for the first time, he wished that he had wished for some kind of super powers when he had had the chance. Why had he been so stubborn? How many Djinn had he freed in the last year? How bad could the consequences have been, really? If they had been worse than being locked in a dank cell by a mad man awaiting certain death, he would eat his own underpants. He could not even reach the window to try it; he had broken the only chair. And no chance of dinner either – probably.

Well, he had wondered how this day could get any worse.

So *think!* Where was he? Not in the real world he hoped, things tended to be exactly what they seemed to be in the real world; i.e. a solid wall was indeed a solid wall, ditto a locked door or a barred window. In the real world, things worked. But in other less tangible places matter could be manipulated –

as Denny knew from experience. So he tried it; he "drew" a door on the wall with a piece of chalk that he always carried in his pocket these days – just in case. It did not work, what did Tamar always say? 'It's never that easy'. Think! Unfortunately, he was now out of ideas. That was it – just the one. 'I am so useless,' he berated himself, and sank down on the floor with his head in his hands.

After an indeterminate length of time, he stopped feeling sorry for himself. Well, okay, he didn't but he stopped indulging himself in his self-pity. If this was a real cell, he decided, then the only way out was through the door or the window.

'Let's face it,' he thought, 'I just don't have the time to dig myself out *a la* "The Count of Monte Cristo". And he had learned long ago that there are no easy solutions in the real world. 'Christ, what I wouldn't give right now for a bottle of Djinn. –   Hmm, maybe that's it, get all the guards drunk and steal the keys.'

The only problem with this idea was that where there should have been a couple of bored and stupid guards sitting at a small folding table playing poker and ripe for some bamboozling, there was, in fact, a whole lot of nothing.

He did not have any booze anyway, and the guards in this place were quite likely to be vampires; they probably did not get drunk.

That only left the window. He decided to try and fix up the bed as a ladder and try to climb up to it.

He was not too hopeful about this plan; the bars were still iron set in concrete, just as they had been before. But it was something to do.

He unfolded the bed, which predictably snapped shut on his fingers convincing him once and for all that he was indeed in the real world. He cursed – naturally – and unfolded the bed gingerly, then tugged off the mangled mattress. Something clinked; mattresses do not usually clink[*] so Denny, naturally, investigated. He reached inside the mattress and sliced a finger open. 'What the hell?' He ignored the bleeding; there had been so much of it lately that he did not wonder that the vampires were not interested in him. There was probably hardly enough left in him to make an appetiser; he reached inside again with his other hand far more tentatively this time and pulled out a long knife with an intricately engraved handle. It was made of pure silver and had a twisted blade that was so sharp it could have, quite literally, cut the air around him. He recognised it as an Athame, from the word Anathema meaning a thing dedicated to evil (or possibly from the Greek Athéos – without God). A ceremonial knife usually used by demons, often to kill other demons, in theory. It was undoubtedly a magical weapon, so, not the sort of thing usually found a prisoner's cell. Denny was, therefore, immediately suspicious; somebody had left him this little present then. The only question was, why? So that he could fight his way out? But that was insane! If you want to help somebody escape from prison you give them a key and maybe a disguise. In Denny's experience wielding a weapon, especially when you are likely to be outnumbered, is a good way to get yourself killed. Denny did not believe for a minute that any friend of his had left this here for him, and he did not doubt that it had been left for him, he had never believed in coincidences. He dropped the Athame. As it fell, it sliced neatly through the metal frame of the bed. Denny stared; he picked it up and examined it. Maybe there *was* something he could use it for.

* * *

'What do you mean, he escaped?'

The smaller vampire shook with terror. 'Sir, we left him the Athame, as you instructed, sir. But he did not use it to attack Haleb as we anticipated.'

The large beefy vampire in charge interrupted him. 'Haleb?'

The smaller one pointed at a vampire behind him. 'The food server sir. The boy was supposed to attack him to try to escape

---

* Except of course in drug dens, doss houses and the occasional B&B

– so that Haleb could have an excuse for our lord when Haleb killed him. But, when Haleb arrived, the boy was not there.' The smaller vampire closed his eyes and flinched, but the beefy captain held his peace.

'And where?' he asked.

'Well sir, it seems he used the Athame to, er – cut his way through the bars of the window instead.'

'WHAT?' The captain grabbed the other by the collar. 'Did you know he could do that?'

'Technically, yes sir. But – how did *he* know?'

The captain let the other go and rubbed a weary claw over his eyes. 'You couldn't have just given him an *ordinary* knife? He was supposed to die anyway.'

'Sorry sir.'

'Ah well, he has outmanoeuvred us, it takes a seasoned fighter to know when to retreat. We underestimated him; that's all.'

'Perhaps we should have just killed him sir.'

'And how would we have explained *that* to our lord? Our orders ...'

'How are we going to explain *this* to our lord?'

~ Chapter Eleven ~

'WE'RE NOT IN Scotland at all, are we?' said Stiles as the howling drew nearer. 'Where the hell are we, really?'

'Um, perhaps now's not the time.' She was rummaging for weapons in her backpack.

'I just want a straight answer – you're not going to *use* that?'

She had brought out a fairly large axe in three pieces, which she screwed together.

'No, *you* are.' She threw it to him. 'I'm using this one.' And she drew out an even bigger axe, making Stiles wonder if her backpack was some kind of portable TARDIS. He made a mental note to ask her later (one of many such notes – soon there would not be any room left in his head for worrying). Right now, however, the animal rights question was uppermost in his mind. 'They're just animals,' he said. 'Just doing what they do – I can't kill them.'

'Well you can't outrun them. Look I know it's rough, but look at where you are.' There were four slavering wolves emerging from the trees. 'It's them or us.'

He could see her point. 'I see your point,' he said. 'But I still don't think I can do it.'

'You have to.'

'No, I mean I don't think I can *do* it. I don't know how to use one of these things.'

'Like this.' She swung the axe at the nearest wolf and neatly (apart from all the blood) sliced its head off. 'See?'

The remaining three wolves all leaped as one at her throat. Somehow, this galvanised Stiles into action. He took an inept swing at the furry ball of menace, managing to cut off the tip of a tail. The wolf howled and turned on him. 'Oh hell!' The other two followed suit.

Kitty whacked heads and two more fell dead. Stiles got the third in the chest. He was shaking – sure he was going to be sick, but Kitty was perfectly calm.

'Stupid animals,' she said. 'They'll never learn the art of "divide and conquer".' She patted Stiles on the arm. 'Well done,' she said, as he vomited on her boots.

It was around two in the afternoon, and they were still a mile or so from the Inn, according to Kitty, when it suddenly started to go dark.

'Storm coming?' said Stiles.

'Hmm,' said Kitty, doubtfully. 'It doesn't feel like a storm.'

'But it's only two O' clock. It doesn't go dark at two, even in Scotland – *if* that's where we are.'

'Shhh – listen.'

'What?'

'We're being ambushed.'

The vampires came at them suddenly from three directions. It was already too dark to count them. They had arrived in complete silence – Stiles had not heard a thing; he wondered how Kitty had. She was definitely an unusual girl; to witness, the first thing she did was push Stiles to the ground. 'Stay down,' she hissed, 'I'll deal with this.

There then began an eerie and silent battle. Stiles stayed down watching in wonder. The way she moved! She was little more than a blur, and her eyesight must be incredible. "Kitty" was right – she had the night vision of a cat.

She abruptly tossed him a stake. 'On your six,' she called (who talks like that?)

He stabbed wildly in the dark, how had she known? He couldn't see a thing. He closed his eyes – he was not sure that he could not see better that way, and he suddenly choked on a cloud of ash that exploded around him. Then he was being helped up and thumped on the back.

'You all right? I think that's all of them. Let's get out of here.'

Stiles wiped his streaming eyes. 'Okay, that's it,' he said. 'I have to know, who *are* you?'

'I could ask you the same question.'

'What? What do you mean?'

'Well, they sure are determined to get you. You have to wonder why.'

'I told you; I don't know. I can't think of anything.'

'All I know is – it's weird. Vampires, from what I understand, are not the most co-operative of species – more backstabbing than the House of Commons. And yet look at this lot, all working together just to kill one man – you. There must be some compelling reason.'

'Maybe they don't like my politics.'

'This isn't funny, you know.'

'I know, believe me, I know.'

* * *

They had reached the inn before Stiles realised that she had quite adroitly avoided his questioning again. Perhaps he was losing his touch; she was a real tough nut to crack. It only made him more curious about her. Who she was, was more of a burning question to his mind than why a bunch of vampires – *vampires* for God's sake – wanted to kill him.

He was mentally listing what he already knew about her. She had lied about her name for some reason that he could not fathom. She had apparently been watching him for some weeks, incognito, before he had met her, so she was secretive, why? Was she afraid he would have heard of her? This was unlikely in the extreme. He had never heard of any woman who was extremely fast and extremely strong, like superhero strong and fast. She had claimed to be a vampire slayer, but had slipped up here and admitted that she herself had not believed in vampires until recently. Put it all together and you had – what? Absolutely no progress whatsoever; she was a conundrum, one that he intended to crack. It was probably a severe character flaw he realised; he just could not stop thinking like a copper.

He got another clue (there I go again) when they walked into the Inn. "The Stunted Goat" the Landlord appeared nervous of her and yet strangely pleased to have her under his roof. In any case, it was apparent that he recognised her and Stiles intercepted a warning look that she gave him that plainly meant 'keep your mouth shut'. A few other people looked up from their drinks and stared at her silently as she passed, but since they were all of them men, perhaps there was nothing to infer from this, and yet it did seem as if they too knew her, or knew of her. This was no help either he decided.

The Stunted Goat was a smoky den type of place, very ye olde. Very, very, actually, it even had straw on the floor and a fireplace so large that a child of at least ten could have stood up in it easily, if they did not mind being incinerated. For some reason, you got the impression that the blazing fire was a permanent feature, like the patrons, (or were they inmates?) It seemed that they had been there from time immemorial and were fossilised in their seats.

The landlord barely raised an eyebrow when she asked for a single room. But Stiles was distinctly uncomfortable about it. He opened his mouth to object, but with that curious instinct that she seemed to possess she dug him in the ribs to silence him before he even uttered a word; she had not even looked at him. She pulled him aside.

'Rooms cost money,' she hissed. 'Besides, I don't think I should leave you alone, especially at night.'

Stiles shrugged. 'Okay.'

She handed him the key. 'You go upstairs,' she said. 'I have something to take care of, I won't be long.'

He left feeling puzzled. More mystery, what was she up to now?

The mystery was cleared up pretty quickly when she reappeared in the room five minutes after him and rather sheepishly handed him a grubby packet of cigars. 'I got these for you,' she said, almost shyly. 'They um didn't have cigarettes and anyway cigars are more ... more *you*, I think.' Stiles was touched and surprised. 'You didn't have to.' Was all he could say; it sounded wrong – ungrateful.

'Oh, I think I did, because of – you know. And you said ... well anyway ...' She looked around. 'Nice room.'

It was, in fact, surprisingly un-awful, not at all what the downstairs led you to expect. Of course, it might be riddled with damp by daylight, but by candle and firelight, it looked cosy, with heavy velvet curtains framing a leaded diamond pattern window, and a large easy chair by the fire and a four poster bed with damask curtains. It was embarrassingly like the honeymoon suite in a country retreat.

Stiles settled in the chair and lit a cigar from a handy candle. 'Ah.' He sighed. He ran an impressive line in smoke rings, and she watched for a while, fascinated.

'You take the bed,' he said chivalrously. 'I'll be fine right here.'

'Don't be silly,' she retorted. 'There's plenty of room for both of us, we'll need a proper night's sleep, if we can get it. I think I can trust you.'

Stiles looked acutely self-conscious. 'I don't think it's a question of trust,' he said. 'I mean, from what I've seen, one wrong move and you'd break me in half. Not that I would. It's just, well – it wouldn't seem right. I don't think I ...'

'Don't be silly,' she said, again. 'We'll be fully dressed. Would you be this prissy about us sharing the same pile of straw?'

'No, but ...'

'Then it's settled. If it makes you feel any better, I'll put a bolster down the middle of the bed – okay.'

Stiles gave in. 'Okay'

She lay down on the top of the covers with her head propped up in her hand. 'Mmm. I love the smell of cigars – it's a proper smell for a man. You smell of cigars all the time, you know. Cigars and old leather, better than poncey after-shave or that lieutenant of yours, Finchley? He smelled of soap – not that men shouldn't wash, but *soap*, I mean it's not very manly is it?' she gave him a look that made his knees tremble. But he was also alert. She was trying to distract him.

Like a shark in the water, Stiles sensed a weakness here. She was babbling nervously, and why was she nervous? Stiles guessed that it was because she was now trapped with him, with no distractions, no way to avoid his questions. Time to move in for the kill, but first to put her off guard, approach her from an unexpected angle.

'So,' he began, 'what did you mean downstairs, about not leaving me alone? What I'm getting at is I thought that vampires couldn't get in a place unless they're invited. Or is that just folklore?'

'No, it's true enough,' she answered readily enough, 'but, this is a public building, in fact more than that, it's an Inn, a place where they actively encourage visitors so it's a sort of permanent open invitation to all comers, vampires can come in here just fine.'

'Damn!' he thought. She fielded that one nicely. He had been hoping that she would have been forced to admit that she had made a mistake, which would put her off balance. She was damn good at this; he had to admit that maybe he had met his match. Perhaps he should stop thinking of her as a suspect and more as just a person. The trouble was she was acting so damn suspiciously.

She was smiling at him. 'I can't tell you any more than I have already,' she said. 'Let's just get that out of the way right now, shall we? I'm sorry; I really am. I like you, I think you're a good man and you deserve better than all this. I will tell you this: I intend to help you if I can. I'm going to find out what's going on and stop it.'

'Who sent you?' he demanded.

'I don't know – exactly, just some men who asked for my

help, and that's the truth.'

'And why you?'

She shook her head. 'Sorry.'

'Do you think that *they* know what's going on?'

She shrugged.

'Oh, come on – you've got to give me something.'

'I've told you everything I can.'

'Except who you really are. Why did you lie about your name?'

She was silent.

'Okay, forget it.' He realised he had pushed too hard. For the first time, he realised that there was no earthly reason why she should trust him, any more than he should trust her. Less, in fact; trust had to be earned, and he had been acting like a right suspicious git ever since he had met her. Pushing and probing and questioning, it was no wonder she did not want to talk to him. She must have some strong reason for wanting to preserve her incognito and it really was not any of his business, she had not done anything wrong, quite the contrary, in fact. He wondered if there was a self-help group he could join. "Suspicious Bastards Anonymous".

'I mean it, forget it,' he reiterated. 'It really doesn't matter, maybe you'll tell me when you're ready – or not,' he added hastily. 'It's fine; you've saved my life three times now. That should be enough for anybody.'

She managed a smile.

'And you got me cigars, what more does a man need?'

This time the smile was wider.

'So,' he said, heartily. 'Are we going down to eat? Man doesn't live by cigars alone you know, I'm starving.'

'Mmm, I asked Charlie to bring us something up, is that okay?'

'That's fine, um – what exactly?'

'Oh, I don't know. Shepherd's pie probably. It's always Shepherd's pie in places like this; I think it's a rule or something. Or pasties.'

'Or those huge chips like doorstops with the skin still on them,' agreed Stiles, laughing.

'Yeah.' She smiled at him. 'You know ...' she began and was interrupted by a loud shriek. With instincts natural to them both, they ran for the door without hesitation. Naturally Kitty won; she opened the door to be greeted by a wall of flames. Hurriedly she slammed the door.

'Oh hell!' They were trapped.

~ Chapter Twelve ~

DENNY'S FIRST PROBLEM was what to do with the Athame. It fell straight through the pocket of his jeans spilling loose change on the floor, some of it severed in half. It sliced through his belt, and he was unwilling to carry it between his teeth, since he still needed his tongue for the time being. But he did not want to leave it behind; it would be too useful. There must be something he could sheath it with, but it seemed that it could cut through anything. He settled for carrying it, which was awkward, but Denny was nothing if not dogged.

The second problem was that he had no idea where he was. After he had climbed out of the window, he found himself in a field. It was dark, but he could just make out, behind him, a large country house. That is to say, it was a large house, and it was in the countryside. Funny really, he thought. He would have expected a crypt in a graveyard; he glanced around nervously, no there were no graves. Thank God, the last thing he needed right now was a horde of zombies. Tamar had once told him that there were no such things as zombies, right around the time she had told him that there were no such things as vampires, ha! Although to be fair, she had not said that there were *definitely* no such things, just that she had never seen one, and that the idea was ludicrous, he had just taken it as read that her opinion was more reliable than most people's facts. She was, after all, over 5000 years old.

So, no graves; still this was not much better. Denny was not at home in fields, or woods, or copses or, in fact, anywhere without plenty of concrete and streetlights. Denny liked pavements and shop fronts. He was afraid of cows and terrified of horses, and there was a strange sound, which he eventually identified as complete and utter silence. Something, he realised, he had never actually heard before.

Well, he could not stand around here all night; they would realise he was gone soon. As long as it was still dark, no amount of head start would be enough to escape vampires, who could fly after all.

He headed for a fence that he could just make out in the distance, although there was no moon. It was some time later before he realised that there were no stars either, and yet it did not look cloudy; it was just that the world was covered in inky blackness. He was getting that nightmarish feeling again.

He was so sunk in fear and depression that it took him nearly ten minutes to register a dreary streak of light in the sky ahead. He had crossed the field and half of another by now; he felt a fool when he finally noticed it. Dawn; thank God, of course. He had heard it was darker in the countryside, he should have realised. He kept on walking until he burst out into bright sunlight, as if he had walked through a door. That did not seem right; he looked back, and behind him it was still dark, like a large dark cloud, blotting out a large portion of the countryside. Beyond it, he could see light again, like a corona around the sun. "Vampire City", he thought. Still it was behind him now.

He relaxed and realised that he was hungry, thirsty and tired – not to mention, lost.

As if in response to his unspoken wish, he saw a road not far to his right; and on that road was a café. It looked remarkably familiar, until he realised that this was because it was a "Little

Chef". Nothing particularly remarkable about that, except that it did seem to have appeared out of nowhere, just as he was feeling a yen for a full English Breakfast and maybe a pancake or two, or three … (like many skinny people Denny could eat enough at one sitting to feed a football stadium of sumo wrestlers). He checked his wallet, a difficult manoeuvre with only one free hand; he fumbled and dropped it twice.

Cursing loudly, he scouted around for somewhere to put the Athame. For some reason, he did not really want to put it down. He balanced it on a fence post, being careful not to lay the blade on the wood, and picked up his wallet, keeping an eye on the Athame just in case it vanished or something. He had plenty of money, more, in fact, than he usually had. He picked up the Athame with a strong sense of relief to have it back in his hand, and headed toward the café.

As he reached the door, he was struck with a thought. How was he going to manage to pay for his food, carry it back to the table and eat it without putting the Athame down? Apart from his reluctance to put it down, he had visions of it slicing through the counter top or the table. This was likely to cause comment, and perhaps arrest for criminal damage. Perhaps he could prop it up in a napkin holder, but that would still entail letting go of it, somebody might pinch it. If only he could put it in his pocket, but he would not feel comfortable with even an ordinary knife unsheathed in his pocket. He looked at the Athame, he looked at the door. Torn between mortal hunger and the strange hold the Athame had over his mind. On the one hand, he was starving, and he was not really much of a fighter – more of a runner really. Anyway, he could not go for much longer without food. It was not as if you could wield a knife with any great force when you were faint from hunger. On the other hand, to just abandon it would be wanton ingratitude, it was a gift, it *could* be very useful; how, exactly, he had not quite worked out. But there, hadn't it already been useful? Without it, he would still be in a grotty cell waiting to be sliced and diced or, more likely, exsanguinated.

The Athame won; he turned away from the café with considerable reluctance. 'Damn the thing,' he thought.

'I wish I had a proper sheath for this thing,' he said aloud.

Then the strangest thing happened. Black smoke began to swirl around the blade, thick and oily it formed into a solid shape, but dense and shimmering with intricate patterns that moved constantly like a living thing. He touched it, yes, it was solid enough. He pulled the blade out and slid it back in, out, in, out, in again quite easily.

'Wow!' He glanced around. '*Magic?*' he thought; first the café (he was now pretty sure that it had not been there before) and now this. What was causing it? He was pretty sure he had not opened any bottles or rubbed any lamps. He would have remembered. Anyway, a Djinn was something you could not miss, and the same went for fairy godmothers he was sure. But still – two wishes granted; the mere idea made him nervous. On the other hand, it was too late now; he might as well take advantage of it.

After he had eaten, he decided, he would set off to find Tamar. He was back on track. He jammed the Athame into his belt loop (his belt now abandoned in slices back in the field) and went into the café.

* * *

The camp vampire, who had reminded Denny of Julian Clary, and whom all the others were afraid of for some reason. – Perhaps they suspected him of harbouring a fetish for whips and chains. Although he dressed immaculately at all times in a cream linen suit (an odd choice in itself given his eating habits – surely it must cost him a small fortune in dry cleaning bills) it was not hard to imagine him in a basque and spiky high heels.

Anyway, he was listening courteously to the stammering explanations of the beefy guard and his smaller cohort. He did not lose his temper or interrupt them at all. It was nerve racking, as if he was actually *listening* to them. They both trailed off eventually and stared uncomfortably at the floor.

The "Master" as the others called him, steepled his hands, always a bad sign. 'I see,' he said.

They quavered inwardly; this was going to worse than they had anticipated.

'Hmm.'

Both vampires shook.

'Explain something to me,' he said. Then his voice rose, although he still did not shout. 'Where in the name of Hell did you get an Athame?'

'It belongs – belonged to the cook,' said the smaller one. 'He uses – used it to prepare the vegetables – for the prisoners.'

'And where did *he* get it from? Vampires do not carry ceremonial weapons. *I* should know.'

'Oh, he's not a vampire, he's a demon. I think it belonged to his father.'

'I see, well he will no doubt be anxious to retrieve it. Send for him.'

'Yes my Lord.'

When the master had them, all three in a row – the demon chef was perhaps the most human looking of the three – he waved a hand over them all, and they all combusted into a pillar of flames and disappeared.

He minced over to a mirror to check his fangs; he was smiling. 'They were a predictable lot,' he thought. It was all working out exactly as he had planned. He glanced at the pile of ash where the demon had stood. Well he could not have him going after Denny to get the Athame back, now could he? He had never bothered to find out why a demon would chose to work for a bunch of vampires. It was certainly an unusual choice. Demons were an inordinately prideful race as a rule. Well, he thought ruefully, it was too late to ask him now.

He sent for one of his lackeys. 'Send me a prisoner,' he ordered. 'I'm getting peckish. And when you have done that, send out a patrol for the girl, no excuses this time – find Tamar Black.'

* * *

'The problem is she could be anywhere,' Denny thought. 'The *other* problem is, I could be anywhere.'

Feeling full and satisfied, he had asked the bored looking woman in a pinny at the cash register where he was. She gave him a blank look, which he interpreted as her thinking he was insane. So he explained – the edited version, omitting the vampires and, in fact, most of what had actually happened.

Eventually he realized that the blank expression meant that she did not understand the question. Convincing him, once and for all, that the café was not real and neither was she. Well, thank heaven for small mercies. She reminded him forcibly of Mrs Payne, known as Mrs. Payne in the neck. A school dinner lady who had terrorised several generations of kids at Hall Lane Primary, with an uncanny ability to be in numerous places at once whenever kids tried to sneak back into the classrooms, and who had had a face like a bottle of vinegar.

Denny sloped out of the café feeling dispirited. The only thing to do he supposed, was to follow the road, in the hopes of getting a lift somewhere. Even though part of him had been expecting it, he had to do a double take. The road was gone. He spun round; the café was also gone, having served its purpose.

'So now what?' He glanced at the sun and checked his watch, and then he remembered that he was not a Park Ranger. He had spent two weeks in the Boy Scouts and had hated every minute of it. He hated camping and "joining in", he had not even earned his needlework badge, and as for the life-saving dummy, he had had nightmares about that thing for weeks.

He patted the Athame to check it was still there. He had been doing this at ever diminishing intervals ever since he had sheathed it.

'I have to get out of here,' he thought desperately. 'If only I knew where I was to begin with, even a road would be nice.' He was not really terribly astonished when the road (*sans café*) reappeared as if – to coin a phrase – by magic. Denny sighed; he was pretty much used to all types of weirdness by now God knew, and he ought to be. But he preferred to know, if possible, exactly what kind of weirdness he was dealing with. He usually relied on Tamar for this information.

'Okay, I'll buy it,' he said to the air. 'I just wish I knew how I was doing this.' And suddenly, he did.

It was the Athame of course. (Anyone but Denny would have worked this out sooner.) In some way, its possession conferred demonic powers; this was, he now understood, how demons obtained magic powers. The Athame was designed to steal powers from others. The power it gave him was not the all-encompassing power that Tamar had. Compared to hers, it was quite limited. Limited, in fact, to the powers of the one who had forged it, or rather, whoever he had stolen them from, but still pretty impressive all the same.

'Well,' he thought, 'this wasn't in any of the books.' but then, the fact that an Athame could be used to slice through iron bars (and probably battleships too) had never been mentioned either.

'This is so cool,' he thought. 'I wonder what else I can do?' He was already thinking of the power as his own. He took it out; he could feel its power now; it almost hummed in his hand; he was surprised he had not noticed it before.

'I wonder if I can teleport like Tamar?' He concentrated on his flat – on being there. He was enveloped in a whirlwind which set him down gently seconds later in his own living room.

'Whoa! Whey hey.' He did a little tap dance and mugged a huge grin at himself in the mirror. '*Smokin,*' he whooped.

'This is so much cooler than the way Tamar does it,' he thought.

'Tamar! Oh God, I have to find her.'

'Well, so,' he said aloud, 'I wish I knew where Tamar is.' Nothing, no inspiration, no answers. *Damn.*

Well he knew where she had been headed; he just did not know where she was now. Oh to hell with it; back to the original plan, only this time he would not take the train.

But first – he drew out the Athame and grinned. 'Let's see what this baby can do.'

He felt a small pang of guilt about Tamar, but he banished it. She could take care of herself.

'Poor, useless Denny and all-powerful Tamar,' he thought, with a sudden surge of bitter resentment. 'Stay at home Denny – stay out of danger, I can handle it. Well, just look at me now!' He took a deep breath and unclenched his hands and forced himself to calm down.

Where the hell, he wondered, had *that* come from?

* * *

Denny was enjoying himself. He had discovered that he could "glamour" – that is a fancy, magic way to disguise yourself, far more effective than anything Sherlock Holmes ever managed. This could be useful although it was temporary; he had to concentrate to keep it up, which would take practice, and his imagination limited him to taking on the appearance of people he had seen and could picture clearly. Well, Denny was not vain, but if you're going to disguise yourself, it might as well be as a handsome film star.

Your own good sense will tell you why this was not a particularly bright idea in actual fact, at least not in public.

He had also discovered that he was substantially stronger physically than he had been before and that he could manifest certain objects just by thinking of them, mostly weapons it seemed, but he already knew this. His injuries had not healed, but they were bothering him far less. And when he tried to fix the broken front door he found he could not. This caused him a moment's irritation, but then he realised that he did not really care very much.

He was having so much fun that he had not noticed that, although it was only noon, outside the sky was pitch black.

He still had not noticed an hour later, when he decided it was time to go and find Tamar. He thought he might as well road test his new powers, besides he owed her and she might be in trouble.

'Oh God,' he thought, 'what am I *doing*? I have to go.' He brought out a map and stabbed a finger at it. 'Might as well land in the right place,' concentrated and the man-sized tornado picked him up.

He landed in a (fortunately) deserted street laughing. *My God that was fun.*

'Auntie Em,' he hooted. 'Auntie Em – you know what Toto? I don't think we're in Kansas anymore.'

'Tamar would *love* this.' This thought sobered him up. *Tamar!* It occurred to him that the new powers he had acquired were going to his head; he was getting giddy; this was a problem.

'It's not the powers that are important,' he told himself sternly, 'it's what you can do with them; they are only important as a means to an end – get a grip on yourself.'

He blinked and looked around, where the hell, he wondered, were all the people? He looked at his watch, one forty-five. And why was it so dark?

~ Chapter Thirteen ~

'OKAY, READY? Jump.' They were poised on the windowsill; smoke was curling under the door.

'Pretty much a rock and a hard place,' thought Stiles ruefully. He hesitated.

'It'll be okay,' Kitty said. 'Hold my hand; I'll break your fall. I'm pretty strong.'

Stiles nodded; this was true. 'Okay, on three?'

She caught his hand, scowled, and jumped dragging him with her. They landed in a snowdrift and rolled to a halt against a tree, unhurt.

There were people milling around, coughing and crying. A dishevelled woman came running out of the blazing Inn; flames were shooting out of the windows

She was screaming. 'My baby – my baby! She's inside. Help me.'

Stiles did not miss a beat; he ran back into the building before Kitty could stop him. 'Jack – no!'

He reappeared after a few minutes coughing and covered in soot and ash, carrying a small bundle – which was wailing with immense vigour.

Kitty clasped her hands together proudly. 'Oh Jack!' she said under her breath. She seemed to have developed a proprietary feeling about him ever since she had saved his life.

Stiles handed the baby to the distraught woman, who gave him a look of pure hero worship.

Stiles was in charge now. He organised the bystanders into a bucket chain, using the nearby river, which had almost burst its banks due to all the melting snow. After they had put the fire out, he herded them into a nearby barn.

By the time they were all settled, he had picked up a few more admirers. Several of the women were making "sheep's eyes" at him. Kitty was amused. 'I could have him,' she thought, 'like that!' She snapped her fingers.

She sat on a rock outside; Stiles came out to look for her. 'Aren't you coming in?' he asked.

'No, I'm waiting out here for them.' She looked at him. 'I've had enough of this; I want to find out what the hell is going on.' She waved a hand at the charred building. 'Why would they go so far?' she asked the air.

'You think the *vampires* set the fire?' Stiles was stunned.

'I *know* they did. So much malice, it defies understanding.'

'How do you expect to find anything out?'

'I'm going to take a leaf out of your book,' she told him. 'We keep one of them alive and question him – do you carry handcuffs? It doesn't matter I think I've got some manacles.'

Stiles did not even ask.

* * *

The vampire, who was currently tied to a tree, grinned nervously. ''Ere, what's going on? Just stake me already.'

'Not yet,' said Stiles. He turned to Kitty. 'What are you doing?'

She was rummaging again. 'Aha!' She emerged with a small knife, a bottle and an evil smile. The vampire gaped. ''Ere, I know you.'

'Shut up,' she said.

Stiles was alert.

'You're her!' said the vampire, 'aren't you? You're Tamar Black.'

Stiles shot her a glance; she looked sheepish. 'Okay,' she sighed, 'I suppose it doesn't really matter now.' She turned to the vampire. 'Now,' she said. 'We'd like you to answer a few questions.'

'And then you'll let me go?'

'Maybe.'

'Maybe's not good enough. I want a guarantee.'

'Okay, you tell us what we want to know, and I *guarantee* I won't do this again,' she said, slicing off his little finger in an unconcerned manner.

The vampire howled. Stiles turned away.

Tamar shook her head. 'Just remember, he's not human, he only looks like one.'

She turned back to the vampire. 'Let's start simple,' she said grinning slyly at Stiles. 'Name!' She barked.

'My name?'

Tamar rolled her eyes.

'Pall.'

'Paul?' said Stiles. 'That's a bit ordinary isn't it?'

'I think he spells it P-A-L-L,' said Tamar.

Pall nodded.

'Okay, Pall, who sent you?'

Pall shook his head. Tamar took his hand, almost gently, and held up the knife.

Pall shook his head frantically. 'I don't know, *really*.'

'I don't believe him,' she said to Stiles. 'Do you?'

'No, take it off.'

'Or,' she said opening the bottle, dipping a finger in it, and smearing the contents on Pall's forehead.

He shrieked as the flesh burned away.

'Holy water?' asked Stiles.

'Holy water,' agreed Tamar. 'And it's nothing compared to the pain he'll suffer if I leave him tied up here until the sun rises,' she added threateningly. 'That was just a taster.'

Pall grinned evilly. 'There will be no dawn,' he said in a sinister voice.

Tamar barely faltered. 'Not here perhaps, but somewhere in the world the sun *will* be coming up. I can do it; you *know* I can.'

Pall flinched.

'Who sent you?' reiterated Stiles. 'Just tell us.'

'I don't ... aaagh!' Tamar had poured the contents of the bottle over his hand. It burst briefly into flames and crumbled away.

'He has to die!' shrieked Pall, pointing at Stiles. 'Ran-Kur has decreed it.'

Stiles and Tamar smiled and nodded to each other.

'And who is Ran-Kur?' she asked.

'No.' Said Pall, stubbornly. 'It is forbidden to speak of him to mortals.'

'Well, I'm not exactly mortal,' said Tamar, 'no?' She raised the knife.

Stiles stopped her. 'Let me.' He reached into her backpack and drew out an axe. 'How about the whole arm this time?' he suggested.

Pall squirmed but remained stubborn. 'Do it,' he said. 'I'm not saying anything else.'

Tamar sneered. 'Yes you will. You know you will, in the end.' She smeared some more holy water on his face.

'Okay, okay, I'll tell you if you promise to let me go.'

'No deal,' said Tamar. 'You know I can't. But I'll tell you what, you tell us, and I'll stake you, nice and quick. If you *don't* tell us, I'll let you burn slowly in the Bahamas somewhere.'

Pall hesitated.

'Tick tock,' she said. 'What's it going to be? Staked or parboiled at dawn.'

'Bitch!' muttered Pall. 'All right you mad harpy, Ran-Kur is our god, the creator of our kind; He ordered his death. That's all I know.'

'Vampires have a *god*?' said Stiles, incredulously. 'Now I've heard everything.'

But Tamar had gone white. She walked away silently. Stiles followed her.

''Ere, what about me?' yelled Pall indignantly.

They both ignored him.

'What's wrong?' Stiles asked her. 'What is it?'

She did not answer; she sat with her head in her hands, silently rocking back and forth.

'Oh περιττώματα!' she said eventually. 'Oh God, oh God, Oh God!' She forced herself to calm down. 'Well,' she continued, 'it certainly explains a few things, I've seen the way people act around gods; they're terrified.' She glanced at him sombrely. 'They do whatever they're told to. And they'll just keep coming; they'll never stop. And there's nothing I can do about it. Gods can't be killed. This is a foe that's beyond me.'

Stiles patted her awkwardly on the shoulder. Pall was still yelling.

'Er, what about him?' He indicated the enraged vampire.

'What? Oh yes.' She handed him a stake and went back to her gloom.

* * *

Denny was dreaming. He had given up his search for now and gone home to get some rest. He had been to the CID offices and had eventually found Finchley, who had told him what little he knew. Stiles was gone, and the young woman had gone after him, but he had no idea where. He had been unconscious, he had explained with some embarrassment, when she had gone, and before he could even ask her who she was. He rubbed his jaw reminiscently and Denny could not help but smile. That was Tamar all right. He sympathised; he had a strong urge to punch this idiot out himself. Thanks to him, Tamar and Stiles were God knew where.

So, he decided to get some sleep, he had not slept, he realised, in more than forty-eight hours, unless you counted the sleepwalking.

It was not the usual dream, this time. Tamar was there, and some strange things happened, involving a large animal of some kind and a medal, then the darkness broke. It was all highly allegorical, just an ordinary dream really. And when Denny woke, he forgot all about it. All he remembered was that for the first night in a long time, he had not had the nightmare.

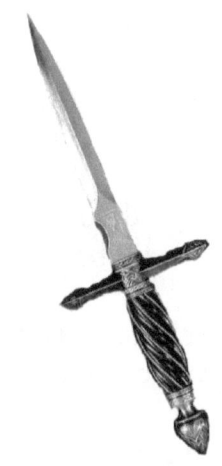

~ Chapter Fourteen ~

'I GUESS YOU want some answers,' said Tamar as they trudged along to where, she had assured him, would be a main road. It was officially eight in the morning, but the sky was still pitch black.

Stiles looked awkward. 'I may *want* answers,' he said, 'but it's really up to you whether or not I get them.' He held up his hands. 'I've learned my lesson. I will tell you this though – I've heard your name before.'

'I know, I've been watching you – remember?'

'Yes, I had an arrest warrant for you. I'm guessing the complainant was one of these guys.'

'I'd say that's a fair assumption.'

'So, I guess that's why you didn't want to tell me your real name when we first met?'

'That's part of it.'

'What's the rest? No never mind. It seems you're pretty well known in ghoul town.'

'Oh yes, a legend in my own lunchtime,' she said dully.

'Why don't you just kill me?' he asked.

'*What?*'

'Or I could kill myself, I suppose; only I don't really want to, but since it's all so hopeless and we're just giving up …'

She gaped at him.

'After all,' he continued. 'I might as well just get it over with; it's all over anyway, isn't it. *You've* given up, so I may as well.'

'Nice pep talk,' she said sourly. 'But I don't need it. I *never* give up; if I did I'd still be trapped in a bottle.'

'Eh?'

'Oh, nothing, another time – just get moving.'

'There is one thing you could explain to me – if you can.'

She sighed. 'Yes?'

'What did he mean, a god?'

'A deity – you know. Like Zeus or Thor.'

'They're *real*?'

'Not anymore, but they were once, until people stopped believing in them.'

'I guess the vampires still believe in *their* god then.'

'I didn't even know they had one. But it makes sense; everybody has to believe in something and supernatural beings tend to cling to the past. Hecaté is still around too; the witches believe in her.'

'There are witches too? Of course there are – why did I ask? I guess vampires can't – you know, believe in the big guy.' He pointed upwards. 'You know God, God.'

'Well no, they *are* from Hell. I suppose if I'd thought about it, I'd have thought they'd follow Satan.'

'I don't believe in Hell, unless you count the one we're all living in.'

'You don't believe in Hell? But you *do* believe in God?'

Stiles changed the subject. 'So, all the old gods are gone?'

'Yes.'

'So, what killed *them*? You said ...'

'They lost all their believers, I just explained all that.'

'And that's the *only* way to kill a god?'

'The only way that I know of; they're not like Kings you know. You can't just chop off their heads.'

Stiles was thoughtful. 'What about Ragnoroc?'

'The Norse Twilight of the Gods, what about it?'

'Well, what you said about Kings. They're human, right? And if one human can kill another, then ...'

'Then perhaps one god can be killed by another. That's brilliant.' She subsided. 'Except I don't know any gods.'

'What about Heck – Heckle ...?'

'Hecaté.'

'If you say so.'

'Hmm, the witches might know how to summon her. Or wait – Denny! He's got books about that stuff, I don't know why.'

'Who's Denny?'

'Oh, he's – I live with him.'

'Is he a superhero too?'

'No, just a regular hero. He's a nice guy; you'd like him.'

'I doubt it,' muttered Stiles.

'What was that?'

'Oh, nothing important.'

'He's a lot like you, you know. He respects me, my unusual abilities I mean. He's not – he doesn't get all intimidated by it, all macho and stupid, you know? He lets me do what I do without getting in my way. You're the same; I appreciate it; it makes it easier for me. I hate it when some macho fool jumps in and puts himself in danger because he can't stand the thought of being saved by a woman.'

'Sounds like he means a lot to you.'

Tamar smiled. 'He saved me.'

'I thought you just said ...'

'There's more than one way to save somebody.'

* * *

Denny was thinking the same thing, only in a different context. 'Maybe,' he thought, 'if I just concentrate on Tamar herself, I can teleport straight to her. That could work. Except I'll probably end up in a bad situation. I should think about this, I mean if she is in trouble, what can I do about it? Even with all this power, I'm not as juiced as *she* is. On the other hand, I *have* got this.' He took out the Athame. The idea of perpetrating some mayhem was extraordinarily tempting. On the other hand, again, the idea of having mayhem perpetrated on him was not so much. He was torn; he could not decide what to do. He actually looked in the mirror to see if there was a little devil Denny on one shoulder and a little angel Denny on the other. (Denny watched far too many cartoons.) That's what it felt like though. The angel was telling him to do the brave and unselfish thing and go and save her. And the devil was not entirely opposed to this plan if there was a chance of breaking some heads, but mostly it was saying, *No, stay here where it's safe. Look out for number one; she didn't* want *your help.* The angel interposed here with. *But now she* needs *your help, you* know *she does*

That's her *problem*, said the devil. *You can always break some heads around here; someone you* know *you can beat. Go – stay – go – stay.* Denny shrugged and went back to his Cheerios.

* * *

'So, what's the plan?' asked Stiles.

'Well, we're nearer to the middle of nowhere than we were half an hour ago. So may I suggest that you save your breath, we may hit it soon.'

'I meant are we going to look for witches? (I just can't get used to talking like this.) Or are we going to fetch this *Denny person*,' he almost spat the last two words.

'Why'd you say it like that?'

'Oh, no reason,' he said hastily. He had no wish to set her off rhapsodising about him again. 'I haven't even met the guy,' he thought, 'and I hate him already.'

'He sounds like a prince,' he said, ill advisedly.

'Then I didn't describe him very well,' she said. 'Most royalty have better dress sense and larger egos, not to mention less brains. Anyway, to answer your question, I think we head for home – my home I mean, and if we happen to find a witch on the way we can change our plans then, okay?'

'Okay, so, we're going for the Hecaté plan?'

'Unless you've got a better idea.'

'Better than brilliant? The Hecaté plan was *my* idea, remember? If there is a better one, it's going to have to come from you; you're the expert, aren't you?'

'Hmm, perhaps I *should* try to come up with a backup plan. After all, even if we do manage to summon Hecaté, she could still say no, and we can't force her. Although in the old days, the gods liked nothing better than a good slaughtering.'

Stiles stopped short and folded his arms. 'Okay. How the hell do you know *that*? You talk as if you'd met them.'

'No, I just get around, hear things.'

'But you *do* talk about them as if you remember them. How old *are* you?' This was a rhetorical question, so Stiles was fairly staggered when she answered. 'Oh, I don't know, I lost count several millennia ago.'

He stared at her; she nodded.

'*Jesus*! You're not kidding, are you?'

'Nope.'

'So, you're *not* human then, you weren't just saying that?'

'Yes I am – now. But I didn't use to be. It's a long story.'

'And we've got *so* much else to do,' he said sarcastically. 'I mean there's still a hundred verses of ninety nine bottles of beer on the wall to get through.'

'Listen you! *I'm* the queen bitch around here. If you're going for the title, you're going to have to do better than that.'

'*Ninety nine bottles of beer on the wall, ninety nine ...*'

'Okay, okay.' She clapped her hands over her ears. 'Christ, do you need special vocal cord surgery to sound that bad?'

She grinned slyly at him. 'Denny can sing like an angel.'

Stiles grunted. He did not want to hear any more about this paragon, but, hear it he did. Tamar told him her story.

By the end, he was amazed, and, if possible, hated Denny even more than he had before. Also he realised something. 'Wait a minute,' he said. 'I *do* know you. I mean in a way; you're "The Demon". You *have* to be, it all fits.'

'The Demon?'

'That's what they call you, it has to be you. I thought it was just an urban legend – well you would, wouldn't you? But you're *real*.'

'*I'm* an urban legend?'

'It has to be you,' he repeated. 'They called you the Demon

Avenger, and then it got shortened to The Demon. A shadowy superhero who saves people and then just vanishes. There couldn't be two of you.'

'It sounds like me,' she agreed. 'You know, the name is strangely appropriate. A Djinn's powers are technically demonic, you know. That's why they cause so much trouble.'

Stiles nodded thoughtfully. 'So, why can't we "teleport" was it, out of here? I mean I see why you didn't before, but now that I know ...'

'Um, you know how you thought we weren't really in Scotland?'

'Yes,' he narrowed his eyes.

'Well, we are, but not exactly. Oh hell, I don't know exactly what they did, but ... look, this *is* Scotland, right?'

'Okay, but …?'

'Oh, Christ, I don't know how to explain it.'

'Try.'

'But I don't know what's going on myself.'

'But you can't teleport?'

'Technically I can, but it wouldn't do any good.'

'Because?'

'Perhaps I should just show you.'

* * *

'What are you playing at?' said the tiny angelic Denny, otherwise known as Denny's conscience. 'How can you think of your stomach at a time like this?'

Denny looked at the bowl (his third) with sudden distaste. 'What am I *doing*?' he thought. 'I have to get moving, what's wrong with me?' His appetite failed as he imagined Tamar in the clutches of the ashen faced man and himself arriving too late.

Before he could change his mind, he concentrated on Tamar and even said out loud. 'Take me to her.'

The whirlwind picked him up and deposited him apparently in a black hole. No, wait, he was outside, it was cold, and there was snow crunching under his feet. He heard a wolf howl in the distance. As his eyes adjusted he found that he could see, just a little bit. He was sure that he was alone.

'TAMAR,' he called. 'TAMAR ARE YOU HERE? *TAMAR*.' Damn it, it had not worked. It looked as if he had just landed at random, and yet, she had been here; he could faintly smell her perfume. That was the thing about Tamar, even after three weeks stuck in a coal mine she would still look and smell good; she made sure of it. It was kind of windy, so she could not have been here too long ago. He looked down; there were no footprints, the snow was like icing on a cake, and it was not snowing. 'That's weird,' he thought. He tried calling again; she was nearby, he thought, she had to be; he could almost hear her. He tried teleporting again and was set down just a few yards away. The perfume smell was stronger here, but there was no sign of anybody. He felt a rush of air, and the scent dissipated. 'What the hell? Was she invisible?' But in that case, why had she not answered him? Well, she was gone now.

* * *

'Okay, take my hand.'

'Where are we?'

'My place – sort of.'

'Then it worked?' Stiles looked around. 'Kind of a dump isn't it? Sorry, that was rude. I think your Denny's out,' he added.

'Hmm, he might be, and he might not be, we wouldn't be able to see him if he were here.'

'What do you mean?'

'I don't know, I just feel it, you felt it too, on some level. You said we weren't in Scotland, but what you meant was – something else,' she finished lamely.

'You mean like a parallel universe?' asked Stiles, getting the idea as he tried to put it together.

'Yes – no, not exactly, that's different. That's still the same world, in a way, but split off because of people's different choices. It's all theoretical anyway. And then there are magical universes, small pockets of virtual reality that co-exist with the real world. This is something else.'

'But this *is* the real world.'

'Yes it is,' she agreed. 'It's more like … *we're* not real

anymore – trust me, I know that feeling.'

'That's ridiculous.'

'Think about it. You said this place is a dump, can you imagine me living here, and leaving it like this?'

'Well, no – but still ...'

'I know, I know.'

'So, okay, all that walking, where exactly did you think you were going?'

'I was trying to retrace my steps. When everything changed, I felt it, I thought if I could find that place again ...'

Stiles shook his head. 'I'm getting a headache.'

'Anyway, we can call it a parallel universe for the sake of argument, and I suppose it is, in a way. The point *is* we're still in it; we travelled within it; we have to go back, so we can find a way out.'

'I'm freaking out here.'

'I don't blame you, and I'm used to this sort of thing.'

* * *

Denny did not know what to do, well would anyone? He went home.

As soon as he got there, he was aware of her presence again, that scent was unmistakable, she manifested it herself. Also, it made sense that she would come here after leaving the snowy field. But if she was here, why could he not *see* her? This was weird, creepy even, not to mention extremely frustrating. *Damn woman!*

What was she up to now? 'Tamar,' he said to the air. 'This isn't funny you know, I know you're there, I'd know that stink anywhere. Come out – come out – wherever you are.' He waited. Okay, this was not working.

She's messing you around, said the devil on his shoulder. *Hasn't she always? She's laughing at you. If she wants to play silly buggers, let her, you don't have to play along, just ignore her.*

Why would she do such a thing? returned his conscience. *You know her better than that. She's in trouble.*

So what if she is? argued the other side of his mind. *There's nothing you can do about it, so why worry?*

'But I *am* worried,' said Denny out loud. 'I just don't know what to do.' He drew out the Athame. 'What do I do?' he cried in frustration. 'How do I find her? What do I have to do? Where is she?'

Those who are quicker off the mark than Denny will not be surprised that as he said these words, the answer came to him. 'Bingo! Why didn't I think of that before? All I had to do was ask. I am so stupid.' For the first time, he wondered what was happening to him. It was as if he did not care. Normally, he thought, he would have asked the question a lot sooner. He shook his head. 'I'm just tired,' he thought. 'So, here I go.' He raised the Athame.

What Denny had realised, of course, was that Tamar was on another plane of existence, not a spiritual plane, but another physical plane. A veil had been dropped between the layers of the universe, separating it into two distinct planes that encompassed the entire world and the people who had been living in the areas where it had started from. This had happened several hundred years ago, in an age when people tended not to travel or have relatives in other parts of the world, so they probably never noticed a thing. How Tamar, and probably Stiles, had ended up there, was still a mystery, but one thing was certain, she would never be able to find her way out.

But if there's a way in ... 'There's a way out,' he said to himself. And now he knew how to find it. He "cut" the air in front of him, in a mystic symbol, the meaning of which he did not know, but he could look it up later – probably. Still, it looked impressive, sort of – it shimmered in the air, like letters of fire. *Cool! – What now?* Then, suddenly the veil came down; he actually saw it drop, although he sensed that the two planes were very much intact. But now Tamar and a man, whom Denny assumed to be Stiles, were back on their own plane. Had he reversed the symbol, he would have ended up on the other plane with them. This knowledge came suddenly and unbidden into his mind, but there was no time to wonder why.

Tamar shivered. 'Did you feel that?' she said.

'No,' said the man. 'What?'

'Oh, it was probably nothing.'

'So,' said the man, who was probably Stiles. 'We're going back to Scotland then?'

'Why would you do that?' asked Denny, from behind them, 'you just got here.'

Tamar spun, and Denny hastily concealed the Athame in his pocket.

'Denny!' She flung her arms around him. Then she drew back, frowning. 'How? What? How did we get back?'

Denny assumed a blank expression. '*I* don't know,' he said. 'I was in the other room and I heard you talking – although,' he dropped his voice to a whisper. 'I didn't hear you come in – did you teleport?'

'No, yes, that's not what I meant,' she glanced at Stiles. 'Oh, it's okay, he knows.'

Denny now tried to look as if he were more confused than ever, it was an expression that settled easily on his face from long practice. 'So, if you teleported, and he knows about it, why are you asking how you got here? What's the game?'

Denny's acting skills had really come on. In the last few days he had gone from Keanu Reeves to Anthony Hopkins.

'No game – I – I ...'

'You know what?' Denny stopped her, why don't you have a drink or something and calm down, you're all shaky. And aren't you going to introduce us?' He indicated Stiles, who was standing behind her, looking awkward.

'Oh, yes, Jack – this is Denny. Denny – this is Jack Stiles.'

'No kidding,' said Stiles, dourly.

'I guessed as much,' said Denny, smiling, he held out a hand. 'Nice to meet you.' They shook hands.

'Is it hot in here?' said Tamar, pulling off layers.

'I'm afraid I haven't been able to find out very much,' said Denny. 'I was too busy looking for you.' He turned to Tamar. 'Where have you been?'

'You were looking for her *here*?' said Stiles sceptically.

'I just got back,' said Denny easily.

If Stiles thought that Denny seemed suspiciously calm for a

man whose girlfriend had been missing for a week, he did not say so.

'It's okay,' said Tamar. 'I – we found something out. I'd better tell you everything.'

Denny listened calmly. 'Well,' he said, at the end. 'I guess that explains why I couldn't contact you. It might also explain why you'd never seen a vampire until recently; I guess that's where they've been living all this time.'

This was a fact, not a guess, but Denny did not explain this. 'I mean, that's probably where they all went around the time the legends faded away. Well, I mean ...'

'I know what you mean,' Tamar said, impatiently. 'The question is why?'

'A more important question,' said Stiles, 'is how *we* got there?'

'No,' said Tamar. 'It's obvious how. The vampires took you there, and I just slipped in on their coat tails, as it were. The really interesting point is – how did we get back?' They both looked at Denny.

'Well, what are you looking at me for?' he said defensively. 'I don't know do I?'

'We *know* you don't,' said Tamar. 'But you might be able to find out.'

'Shouldn't we be concentrating on how to summon Hecaté?' Denny countered, adroitly changing the subject.

Stiles narrowed his eyes. 'Another one,' he thought. Mind you, he had a point.

'Can you do it?' he asked.

Denny shook his head. 'I can't do the summoning, I have no magic power.' (This was a direct lie now, but Denny barely flinched) 'But Tamar does; she's the closest thing we have to an actual witch – no offence,' he nodded to her. 'My job is to find out what to do. I have books on this stuff, but I think I'll start on the 'net.'

'Shouldn't we be trying to find out why this Ran-Kur wants me dead?' asked Stiles, not unreasonably.

'Well, if we can find a way to get rid of him, it won't matter

– will it?' said Denny.

Tamar smiled in agreement. 'Makes sense,' she said.

'Yeah,' said Denny. 'We ice this Ran-Kur, end of problem.'

'But ...'

'There is one other thing,' added Denny. 'Just in case it doesn't work, you two had better hunt us up a witch or three. You know, in case I can't find a summoning ritual, or Tamar does it, and it doesn't work.'

'Okay,' said Tamar, 'good idea, have you got a list?'

Denny sat down at the computer. 'Just give me a sec.'

'List?' asked Stiles.

'Possible covens,' said Tamar

'Yeah, we lost the last one, after Tamar terrified them,' laughed Denny.

'I just hope I don't have to go campaigning for women's rights in dungarees and an unflattering haircut.'

'Well, *I'm* not doing it,' said Denny.

'Why not, you already *have* a bad haircut.'

Denny glowered but held his peace. Why did he put up with her?

'What are you two talking about?' asked Stiles.

'Witches,' said Tamar. 'They hide out, incognito as women's groups. All right, I'll make a start. Hey Denny are you still having that weird dream?'

'No, it's stopped.'

'I wouldn't say that,' she said, pointing at the window, at the inky blackness. 'I'd say, He's here – whoever He is.'

Denny glanced out of the window. 'Well, I'll be damned,' he said.

'It's probably this Ran-Kur.'

'Probably.'

'What dream?' asked Stiles, he was beginning to feel like a quiz show host. *And for the grand prize of a trip to Tahiti...*

'I'll tell you later,' said Tamar. (No one *ever* said that to Chris Tarrant.)

'Stiles sighed; he'd probably never find out, not now that these two were distracting him in tandem. 'It's supposed to be two cops and one suspect,' he thought. 'And I want to know why I'm wanted dead in ghoul town, I hate loose ends.'

* * *

In the end, he decided to go with Tamar. For one thing, Denny made him uncomfortable, he had been prepared to dislike him, nay, even hate him. But this was more than mere jealousy. Denny made him nervous; he did not trust him. He told himself not to be silly, that he was biased, and it was not Denny's fault that he had got the girl, even though he was no Johnny Depp. Because of this, he was trying to give him the benefit of the doubt; after all, he had been suspicious of Tamar at first. Also, it had been Denny's suggestion that he go, citing his own lack of powers. Stiles would be safer with her, he had said. This was indisputable, and it was unfair to suspect him of trying to get rid of them, even though Stiles was sure that he was.

As soon as they had gone, Denny switched off the computer and wandered over to the bookcase. Without even looking, he drew out a large book entitled "Summoning Spells & Incantations". He flipped over the pages. 'Summoning a Deity,' he read. 'Blah, blah, blah, insert name of deity, etc, etc.' He closed the book and grinned. He felt only the slightest pang of guilt as he snapped his fingers and created a small safe in the air, put the book in and snapped his fingers again, the safe disappeared.

~ Chapter Fifteen ~

BY THE MOST remarkable co-incidence, possibly ever, they found a witch almost immediately. Almost! – Five WI meetings had turned up zilch, and Tamar was disgruntled and Stiles was wishing he had not come. The WI-ers had given him some very curious looks, of course he was used to this, and his first instinct, had been to whip out his badge, until Tamar told him not to.

It was getting dark; they were in Staines; the daylight blackout evidently had not reached this area yet. The sun appeared to be setting in the usual manner. They had decided to call it a day and were wandering along dispiritedly.

'Why isn't it ever easy?' complained Tamar, looking for a private place to teleport from. She stopped suddenly and raised her head, almost as if she were sniffing the air.

'What is it?' Stiles asked.

'Magic,' she said, 'there.' She pointed to a house. 'Witch magic.'

'How do you know?'

She shrugged. 'How do you know when it's cold? I just feel it.'

'So, what are we doing, are we going in?'

'Um – no, we know where she is; let's just leave it for now. We may not need her at all, and if we burst in on her now, she may not be here when we come back. Denny was right; witches tend to be afraid of me. Let's just take a note of the address.' She glanced at the sign and laughed. 'Look at this – Mrs. C Pittencherry, Chiropractor. Good cover, there's even a phone number.'

'What's funny about that?'

'Witches don't need phones.'

'They do if they want to blend in, I suppose.'

'Good point. Well, I suppose we should go back and see if Denny's had any luck.'

* * *

When they got back, Denny was not there. Tamar panicked. 'Oh my God, we led them straight here, no wonder they let us out, they took him.'

'Calm down, what would they want with *him*? I thought it was *me* they were after?'

'Who knows? Maybe it was all just misdirection, who knows what's really going on.'

'That's been my point all along.'

'What?'

'I *said* we should try to find out what's behind all this, and you shut me down, or rather he did, and you agreed with him.'

'Oh God, you're right! And now they've taken him, and it's all my fault.'

'Look, you don't *know* that they took him, there's no sign of a struggle, besides how did they get in? He wouldn't invite them, would he? He's not stupid.'

'Mind control – remember? Isn't that how they got you? Anyway, the door's off its hinges, look.'

'It was like that before.'

'It *was*? Are you sure?'

'Positive! Anyway, I thought you knew about vampires, the mind control doesn't kick in until *after* you invite them in.'

'So, where the hell is he? And how did they get into *your* home?'

'Who said they did?'

'Oh, I just assumed.'

'You do that a lot don't you? Anyway, about Denny, can't you find him, contact him, like telepathy? You said ...'

'Oh, oh yes, I can try. But if he's where *we* were, then ...'

'At least you'll have your answer then.'

'Answer to what?' said Denny walking in.

Tamar rounded on him. 'Where the hell were you?'

'I just went out to get a paper, what's the matter with you?'

'A *paper?* At a time like this? What's the matter with *you?*'

'I'm sorry, I was getting nowhere on the computer, and my legs had cramped up. I wasn't expecting you back yet; I just wanted some fresh air.'

'I thought something had happened to you.'

'I think I'll just – go – in – here,' said Stiles, backing into the kitchen.

'I'm sorry,' Denny was saying. 'I didn't mean to scare you, I didn't think. How come you're back already?'

'We found one.'

'Already? That's great. Wait – just *one*? Isn't that unusual?'

'I guess, maybe not though, how do I know? I suppose they don't all live together, like a commune.'

'I suppose not. Have you forgiven me then?'

She did not answer in words; Denny smiled; oh yes *this* was why he put up with her. But she pulled back quickly; it was just too frustrating. So close and yet so far away. Denny considered for a second, telling her the truth about the Athame, maybe now, with his own power, he could be close to her at last. But for some reason he said nothing.

'I have missed you,' she whispered.

Behind the kitchen door, the forgotten Stiles sank to his knees, stuffed kitchen towel in his ears and cringed.

Later, around two a.m. Denny rose and padded through to the living room. He wiped his forehead. Tamar was right; it *was* hot in here. He checked that nobody was around (meaning Stiles) then he clicked his fingers. The safe appeared, and he removed the book and replaced it in the bookshelf. He was not sure what mischievous impulse had made him hide it in the first place, but he felt guilty about it now. The Athame was secreted in his bedside drawer; he had almost forgotten about it.

* * *

The next morning Denny seemed almost himself again, but he did not confess what he had done, nor did he tell Tamar about the Athame. He did "find" the book, however, and they talked about what to do next.

'I think we have to summon this Ran-Kur first,' was Stiles opinion. 'I want to know why he wants me dead.'

'That's far too dangerous,' said Denny. 'You just said it, yourself, he wants to kill you.'

'If he was going to do it, himself, don't you think he would have done it already?' demanded Stiles. 'I don't reckon he can, or else he doesn't want to get his hands dirty.'

'No, Denny's right,' said Tamar (predictably, thought Stiles). 'It's just too risky.'

'Okay, but I still think we should try to find out somehow.'

'Catch another vampire maybe?' said Denny.

'They must know *something.*'

'Maybe we should summon Hecaté first,' said Tamar. 'Ask her if she'll do it.'

'Do you think we should go and collect that witch first?' asked Denny.

'No, I'll give it a try first,' said Tamar.

'Okay, so are we all agreed, we summon Hecaté?' asked Denny.

They nodded.

'Okay then, there's a potion, we'll need a few things.'

'Eye of newt?' said Stiles, 'wing of bat?' He said this with a perfectly straight face, so they were not sure whether he was joking.

They stared at him. 'Anyway,' said Denny eventually. 'You go and get the stuff, I'll make a list.'

'A roc's egg,' said Tamar, startled. 'Oh my God, this'll cause some trouble.'

'Why?' asked Stiles.

They're sacred birds,' explained Denny. 'Especially to the Djinn.'

'But Tamar isn't a Djinn anymore,' objected Stiles.

'Actually, I'm more worried about how damned vicious they are,' said Tamar.

Denny smiled. 'Do you want *me* to go?'

'Very funny.'

'You'll be okay; I have complete faith in you.'

'Easy for you to say,' snorted Tamar and disappeared.

'So, what are *we* doing?' asked Stiles.

Denny held up a finger. 'Wait for it.'

Tamer reappeared. 'Forgot the list.' She vanished again.

'So,' said Stiles again. 'Now what do we do?'

'I'm going on the 'net, to see what I can find out about Ran-Kur, why he might want to kill you.' He gave Stiles a sudden hard look. 'You haven't been sniffing around *his* girlfriend, have you?'

'*What*?'

'Just stay away from her, okay? Do you think I'm blind?'

'I haven't ...'

'Look, let's just get this straight,' said Denny. 'I've seen the way you look at her. I may not look like much but ...' He picked a long knife off the wall rack and bent it into a circle with hardly any effort. 'I'm stronger than I look. If you cross me, I'll kill you, myself – understand?' He straightened out the knife and threw it with pin-point accuracy into the bull's-eye of a target, painted on the opposite wall.

Stiles gulped. 'I wouldn't do that mate,' he said. 'Not even if you were, well ...'

'As pathetic as I look?' said Denny. 'Okay, mate,' he said, suddenly quite amiable again as he pulled out the computer, 'let's see what we can find out.'

'I feel like I should be cackling,' said Tamar, dropping ingredients into a large black pot (not quite a cauldron, but close enough) and stirring it, not over an open fire on stormy hilltop, but over a low heat, gas mark 2, in fact.

'Lavender for purity,' she said, 'phoenix feather, powdered unicorn horn – Hubble bubble, toil and trouble – ha, ha, ha,' she made a good stab at a cackle.

Stiles was in the living room, avoiding her; Denny was still on the computer, but they could both hear her.

'Nutter,' murmured Denny, good-naturedly. He stared suddenly at the screen. 'My God!' he said.

Stiles looked up. 'What?'

'Come here mate,' said Denny. 'Tamar,' he called. 'Can you leave that for a sec?'

'It'll burn.'

'Turn it off then.'

'But ...'

'You have to see this. I'm pretty sure I've found out why the vampires want our boy, Jack here, dead.'

It was a prophecy; there was an image of it on the screen. Denny printed it out.

'What does it say?' asked Stiles. His Phoenician was rusty.

Denny translated. 'One will come in the second millennium after the coming of the messiah. He shall be a bringer of justice and shall bear a shield, and bear the name of a knave that shall be stepped upon. His coming shall be the beginning of the breaking of the darkness, for he shall sire a child whose very life will be the end of those who walk only under darkness and take the life-blood of the righteous.

'Oh my God!' said Tamar.

Stiles looked blank.

'A Knave is the old fashioned term for a Jack in playing cards,' explained Tamar.

'And 'to be stepped upon' added Denny, '– A stile, you know? It's you all right.'

'But I don't *have* any kids,' objected Stiles.

'Yet,' said Denny meaningfully.

'I'm not even married – anymore.'

'Well?'

'Okay, good point, but still ...'

'If you already *had* a kid, it'd be too late for them anyway, that's the point. They want to get you now to stop it happening.'

'It doesn't have to be true anyway,' said Tamar, 'as long as *they* believe it, which they evidently do.'

'This explains it, anyway,' she continued. 'This Ran-Kur certainly wouldn't want *this* to happen. If he's got no followers, he's got nothing.'

'At least I know now,' said Stiles; he did not look very happy about it. There was an awkward silence.

'Right – potion,' said Tamar briskly. 'Let's get on with it.' She headed back to the kitchen.

* * *

The "Master" was sitting in his private quarters of the big house, reading a bundle of reports on Denny, Stiles and Tamar, with evident satisfaction. They were all behaving exactly as predicted, although he had not expected the Hecaté thing. Yes, they had made one or two unpredictable moves, but on the whole, things were going perfectly to plan. Time, he thought, to make his next move.

* * *

'Never heard of him,' said Hecaté bluntly, 'and I do not wish to either. You got me up for this? You are not even witches. I only help witches. When did you,' she pointed at Tamar. 'Give your last offering? – Never that is when. 'Damned cheek.'

It had been quite an impressive manifestation, and Hecaté herself was an impressive figure. Very tall and slender with long dark hair, and dressed elegantly in elegant black rags. She looked rather like Morticia Addams, and was beautiful enough to give Tamar a run for her money. So this harangue was a bit inappropriate, at least to Stiles. Tamar and Denny were used to this sort of thing.

'Would you do it for a witch?' asked Tamar. 'One of your brethren – sisterhood I mean.'

'No,' snapped Hecaté.

'But he's brought darkness on the world,' said Stiles. 'They'll suffer too.' He looked at Tamar for support.

'Tamar nodded. 'They're only human,' she said. 'Pretty

much.'

Hecaté hesitated.

'It's the vampires or the witches,' wheedled Tamar. 'You or him.'

'Prove it.'

'Look outside.'

'I cannot,' said Hecaté. 'I am not really here.' She pondered. 'If one of my sisters asks it of me, I will consider it,' she said. 'But think on, I have never heard of this Ran-Kur, I do not know his power. Even if I agree, I may not prevail. If I were you, I would try to find another way.' She vanished.

Then the vampires crashed through the windows like the SAS.

'Loophole?' queried Stiles.

'Eh?' said Tamar.

'I thought they had to be *invited* in.'

'Later,' she said. 'Get down.'

Denny's thoughts flew to the Athame; it was in the bedroom. Two vampires blocked his way. He beat them savagely and staked them with a broken floor lamp; the first one with one end and then the other with the other end, as they staggered drunkenly against the doorframe. He dashed into the bedroom and retrieved his prize. He did not intend to use it; he just wanted it. He tucked it into his pocket, and felt better immediately; he ran back into the living room.

Tamar was on the floor crying. 'They got him,' she sobbed. 'There were too many of them, I – I couldn't ...'

'Locate him,' said Denny. 'Quick.'

'I can't, they've taken him back through; I can't sense him.'

'Oh!'

You *can find him,* said his conscience. *You have to.*

But you'll have to tell her, said the other little voice.

She'll understand. He'll die – hurry up, you're wasting time.

What do you care? He tried to steal your girlfriend.

Tick tock, tick tock.

In the end, it was Tamar's misery that decided him.

'I've failed,' she sobbed.

'Not yet,' he said, he drew out the Athame.

'What ...? Where did you get that?'

'Later,' said Denny. He started to cut the air.

'What the hell are you ...? Wait – I sense him.' The veil came down and she vanished.

Stiles was lying behind some bins, bruised and battered, but very much alive, the vampires had fled. Tamar was startled, to say the least, when Denny appeared in a whirlwind beside her.

'Thought you might need some help,' he said.

* * *

'And – scene,' said the 'Master'. 'Curtain – perfect.'

~ Chapter Sixteen ~

TAMAR WAS UPSET and totally confused. 'Why didn't you *tell* me? I think it's wonderful, but why didn't you *tell* me?'

'I wasn't sure, it seemed too easy, I kept on expecting it to stop working. I didn't want to rely on it, or ... well I guess I didn't really believe it. I'm really, really sorry.'

By this time, Richard Burton had nothing on Denny. Tamar swallowed it.

'You should have told me,' she said, 'but I guess I understand.'

He put his arms around her – briefly, and the subject was dropped.

'How do you think they got in?' said Tamar. (Meaning the vampire hordes.)

'Isn't it obvious?' said Denny. 'The bloody landlord must have invited them. I am a bit behind with the rent. That may not have helped. He probably thought they were debt collectors. I mean, there's not much difference is there? I'm more interested in *why* they did it,' he continued, 'just to dump him behind some bins? Do you think they thought he was dead?'

'How could *they* not know the difference? Although I have

to say, I can't think of a better explanation,' admitted Tamar ruefully.

'Me neither.' And this at least was the truth.

Stiles was sleeping off his experience in the other bedroom. Denny was hit by a sudden urge to get away from her. He had not told her nearly everything, and he had had a tricky moment explaining why he had not mentioned his kidnap experience, but had brushed it off with. 'It just never seemed like the right time.' He was having trouble looking her in the eye and the guilt was making him edgy. He was filled with a strong desire to do some violence – but not to her. Never to her, he was not that bad, not yet. He excused himself, and, from the bathroom, he teleported himself outside.

By the time he returned, Denny's conscience was hanging by a thread.

* * *

'What are you talking about?' Tamar said, indignantly. 'Denny would never threaten anyone.'

Stiles shrugged. 'Have it your own way. I just thought I should tell you.'

'Well, I don't believe it. You must have misunderstood.'

'If you say so.'

'He's not like that, he's a teddy bear.'

'Really? He struck me as more of a grizzly.'

'*Denny?*'

'Are you sure you know him as well as you think you do? Guys can get funny when they get jealous.'

'But Denny doesn't get jealous, he has no reason to.'

Stiles took the point and sighed. 'Maybe not, but maybe he *thinks* he does, we're guys; we don't always need a reason.'

'I'm telling you, it's a mistake.'

'It's pretty hard to mistake the words "I'll kill you, myself".'

'He *said* that?'

'Look, you know him better than I do, obviously, but don't you think he's acting a little – odd? Maybe something's wrong. I just think you should be careful. I mean where is he now?'

'He's – he went out. I don't own him, you know. He can go out if he wants to.'

'Does he usually go out in the middle of the night without telling you?'

Tamar had no answer for this, so she stalked out of the room. But she was worried, and she resolved to talk to Denny when he got home.

Denny's first words on returning home were an apology. 'I've been acting weird I know.' He even admitted to threatening Stiles, putting it down to stress. He also apologised to Stiles. 'I'm not really like that,' he said. 'I didn't mean it.'

Later, he told Tamar. 'I didn't actually say I'd *kill* him, he's exaggerating. But I think it's best if we just drop it, don't you?'

* * *

It was dark and gloomy and full of smoke in the bar. As Tamar walked in, she saw a large crowd of people, standing around a balcony arrangement, waving betting slips and cheering. Boisterously shoving each other to get a better view of what appeared to be a pit of some kind. 'Cockfighting?' she wondered, 'dogs?' Where was Denny? She had definitely sensed him here. She pushed her way through the crowd of surging bodies, '*ugh, sweaty!*', and looked down through the fog into the pit. It was only a few feet deep, and the floor was sprinkled with fresh sawdust, which did not quite cover the bloodstains, and there he was.

Stripped to the waist and sporting a far more impressive physique than formerly, but still only about half the size of the man he was squaring up to. She cried out instinctively against it, but her voice was swallowed up in the Babel around her. Denny looked perfectly calm, amused even. A bell rang, and she watched in fascinated horror as Denny pulverised the larger man in a matter of minutes, with a kind of furious joy. She even sensed that he was holding back somewhat. The crowd sensed it too.

'KILL HIM, KILL HIM,' they yelled. 'FINISH HIM.'

As the beaten man raised a hand in supplication, Denny

stepped back, the crowd roared, and the bell went again. Tamar walked back outside to wait.

Denny appeared outside shortly afterwards, looking slightly guilty.

'Hi,' he said, 'thought you'd be out here.'

She smiled. 'I needed some air,' she said. 'It's kind of smoky in there.'

'You're not angry?' said Denny, surprised. 'Disgusted? Disappointed?'

'No, why should I be?'

'Well ...'

'You have to get rid of your aggression somehow, all men do. Some women too. And you – well, you've had a lot of unresolved issues lately, I understand. At least you're not out mugging old ladies or beating up innocent bystanders in the streets. Or worse, bringing it home with you. It's better this way; at least these guys signed up for it. On the whole, I approve.'

'You *do?*'

'Yes, real men pick on someone their own size, so to speak. At least you're not a cowardly wife beater.'

'I would *never* hit a woman.'

'That's what I mean, but a lot of men would.'

'I'd like to see the poor bugger who tried to hit *you.*'

'Okay, so I'm an exception, but even if I wasn't, I know that you would never lay a finger on me, otherwise you wouldn't be here. If you were *that* type of man, you'd be out beating up, oh I don't know, people who couldn't defend themselves. And tonight, I saw you show mercy to that man, I never doubted that you would.'

'Christ, I thought you'd be furious.'

'I suppose that's why you came running out here after me without putting your shirt back on?'

'What?' Denny looked down self-consciously. 'Oh, yes, I hadn't even noticed, I'd better um, just go and ...' He stopped and with sudden viciousness, slapped his hand against the wall. 'Moth,' he said. 'Hate the little buggers.'

She slipped her arm through his. 'Let's just go home,' she said, 'unless you're not finished here?'

'No,' he said. 'I am, let's go.'

* * *

Denny was training. He thought it best to keep in shape in case he lost his new source of power. Besides, he needed the release now more than ever, he felt so *angry* all the time.

Stiles and Tamar were discussing whether or not to go to the witch, Mrs Pittencherry, over the top of the pounding music that Denny was playing with a fine disregard for the neighbours. At the very least, she would be another ally. And if she were one of the faithful, and did some top class grovelling, maybe she could get Hecaté to help, although Stiles was dubious about this. 'Do witches grovel?' he asked. It was something he found hard to imagine.

'Not so much,' conceded Tamar. 'But I could probably persuade her. The real question is – would it be worth it?'

She glanced at Denny, who was now staring moodily out of the window. Stiles followed her gaze. 'What is he looking at? Its pitch dark out there.'

'I think that's what he's looking at,' she said. 'I think he's worried about it. I told you about the dreams. That's probably why he's not been himself lately. I mean, how many people get to watch their worst nightmares coming true – literally?'

Stiles was thoughtful. 'You know, you're probably right. I hadn't thought of that, poor guy.'

'Denny?' Tamar called over to him.

'Mmm?'

'You okay?'

'Huh?'

'Are you okay?'

'H' mm, wha?'

'*Denny*!' Tamar was getting exasperated; all conversations with Denny were getting to be like this.

'Ehm, mmm?'

Tamar rolled her eyes. 'It must be wonderful to have a second language,' she jibed. Stiles smiled. 'I speak three languages myself,' he said. 'According to my late wife –

"English", "Irish" and "Rubbish",'

Tamar laughed. 'Denny's fluent in "Bollocks" and "Grunting" – apparently.'

'And what do *you* speak?'

Ah, that would be the highly advanced "Total Bollocks" and a smattering of that language usually known only to men – "Drunken Drivel". I'm not fluent, but I can communicate the basics.

'Which one are we speaking now, do you think?'

'The lesser known "Utter Codswallop".'

'And to think, I never knew I was multilingual.'

'Sounds painful, isn't there a cure?'

'Shutting up.'

There was a knock at the door; Denny turned round and caught Tamar's eye. They smiled at each other. 'Landlord,' they both said.

'I'll deal with it,' she said. 'It's my turn.'

She rose and shimmied to the door; it was amazing, Stiles thought, admiring her. She moved like oiled silk (whereas Denny reminded him more of boiled milk.) She never stumbled or did anything clumsy or inelegant. He glanced round; Denny was watching him, watching her, with a sardonic air.

'Okay, mate,' said Denny. 'No charge for looking.'

Tamar opened the door; outside was the white faced man. He gave a gleaming smile, the most observable feature of which, were the extremely sharp incisors.

'Well now,' he said. 'As it turns out, I think we might be of some use to each other. Can I come in?'

'I don't know,' she replied. 'Can you?'

The vampire smiled. 'Ah ha ha, well – I only want to talk.' He spread his hands. 'I am alone.'

Mount Rushmore could not have been stonier faced than Tamar. Denny and Stiles were rooted to the spot.

'Very well,' said the vampire. 'We have, I believe, a common enemy. Ran-Kur, at least that's what he calls himself, my name is Ecriep.

'That's a funny name,' said Stiles rudely, but Tamar was

laughing.

'Oh dear,' she said eventually wiping the mirth from her eyes. She turned to the others. 'The vampire's most fatal flaw,' she explained, while their visitor looked murderously at her. 'More than stakes and crosses and garlic or any of that gibberish, is the unfounded belief that no one will recognise their name if they only spell it backwards. Isn't that right – *Peirce*?'

'Not that any of us have ever heard of you anyway,' she added maliciously. 'But you vampires are nothing if not arrogant aren't you? Or do you have some other reason for wanting to conceal your identity?'

'Oh all right,' he muttered. 'My name *is* Peirce. And if you were a vampire called *Peirce*, you wouldn't like to admit it either. So, no jokes I beg you, after five hundred years, I assure you, I have heard them all.'

Denny stirred. 'Except the final one,' he said, manifesting a stake.

'A ha ha, yes, indeed. Well?'

'Oh, come in,' said Denny.

Tamar stared.

'What?' said Stiles. 'Just like that?'

'It'll be okay,' Denny assured him. 'Like he said, he's alone. Besides, what have we got to lose? We're running out of options here.'

'What have we got to lose?' exclaimed Stiles. 'Several pints of blood perhaps?'

'He's in a lot more danger than we are,' opined Denny. 'And he knows it, so he must have some strong reason for coming here. I think we should hear what it is.'

Peirce nodded. 'That's right.' He came in. As he passed Denny, he looked at him in some surprise. 'Rough night?' he asked.

Denny turned away; Peirce turned to Tamar. What's happened to *him*?' he asked, in a low voice. 'He looks like one of my boys has been at him.'

Since Peirce had last seen him, Denny had indeed changed. He looked meaner; his features were somewhat handsomer but, also somehow paler and sharper. His pale blond hair was greasy and looked darker, and it no longer fell messily over his eyes, but was slicked back, and his once warm eyes were hard and cold like pieces of flint.

Incredibly, Tamar had not noticed the change in him. 'What do you mean?' she said.

Peirce gave her a curious look. 'I dunno; he just looks different, he's got that sleek 'n' evil look about him, he hasn't suddenly gone off garlic, has he?'

'Don't be so silly,' she said. 'He's just been having a bad time lately.'

Peirce shrugged. 'It's none of my business,' he said. 'But I should keep an eye on him if I were you.'

Tamar narrowed her eyes – gods had quailed before that look. 'What did you want again?'

'Bloody Mary would be nice.' he said imperturbably. 'Hold the Mary – or just knock her out, a ha ha – er ...'

Three pairs of eyes bored into him. 'Okay, okay, maybe not. But we should get settled; this could take some time.'

Denny grinned at Tamar and raised his eyebrows; the complete lack of fangs in his smile reassured her.

Stiles was concerned about the mind control issue, but Tamar explained that she, at least, would be unaffected. They were not sure about Denny, but since Peirce seemed to be afraid of him in some strange way, they decided to risk it. It was too late now anyway.

They plonked Peirce down on a wooden chair and ranged themselves around him, still standing.

'Okay, so spill,' said Denny.

Peirce gulped. 'Well,' he said. 'How much do you know?' He glanced at Stiles. 'Do you know about the prophecy?'

Denny leaned in and brought his face menacingly close to Peirce. 'Try again,' he said. 'We're on to that one.'

'No, no,' said Peirce, nervously. 'That's good; I want to get this straight, I don't believe it, not at all, it's rubbish – okay?'

'So what?' said Tamar.

Peirce shifted uncomfortably and pulled at his collar,

twitchily. 'So, I well – look, a lot of vampires *do* believe it, you see. And this *Ran-Kur*.' Here he spat on the floor. 'He's making use of it; he's got them all running around like a bunch of headless humans. He's got them all convinced that he's their salvation – their god.'

'Isn't he?' asked Stiles.

'Of course not. A god of vampires? It's ridiculous; I never believed in all that hot air. I don't know who this guy really is, but he's not Ran-Kur. Ran-Kur's a myth.'

Denny raised his eyebrows. 'An atheist vampire, who would have believed it?'

'I don't know what he's up to,' continued Peirce. 'But I don't like it. Vampires don't like being ruled, we like to be the rulers, and he's used this prophecy to set himself up in charge, that's all. He's got them all bowing and scraping; it's not natural! So I want to help you to get rid of him, get things back to how they should be.'

'Restore the unnatural order sort of thing?' said Tamar.

Denny grinned.

'And why exactly do we need you?' she continued.

'Got a plan, have you?' asked Peirce. 'Know what you're dealing with, do you?'

'And you do?' said Stiles.

'Well ... we'd have a better chance working together; I have a small group who are with me. Fifteen good lads.'

'Vampires?'

'Of course, what else?'

'And *you're* leading them?' asked Denny, sardonically.

Peirce shrugged. 'Old habits.'

Tamar cut in. 'We need to talk about this.'

Peirce nodded. 'Yes I understand. Can I smoke while I wait?'

Tamar glanced at Stiles, who had been creating a permanent fog since his arrival. 'No,' she said. 'I'm going for death by sun bed.'

They turned away.

'What about *him*?' asked Stiles.

'What about him?' said Denny. 'He came to us didn't he?

He won't go anywhere. This was incontrovertible. 'Besides, who cares if he does?'

Nobody did. They went into the kitchen to talk.

'Why should we trust him?' asked Stiles.

'We shouldn't,' said Denny. 'That's not the point, the point is – he has a point. So far we've got Jack -.'

'What?' asked Stiles, whose attention was wandering to the other room.

Denny paused. 'What?'

'What?' said Stiles, again.

'I don't want him here,' said Tamar. She was twitchy and pale; apparently Peirce still made her nervous for some reason. Denny asked her about it. 'You aren't bothered by *other* vampires, what is it about him?'

'I don't know, just the way he looks at me, as if ... as if he would turn me if he got a chance.'

'But why should *that* bother you? It's not as if he could, you're immortal. You can't be un-dead if you can't die.'

'But I *can* die. A vampire could kill me, he wouldn't find it easy, I'm pretty *hard* to kill, my powers do protect me to a certain extent, but technically, it is possible. Being immortal means I'll never grow any older or get sick or die naturally, but it's entirely possible for me to suffer an unnatural death, I'm human now. I'm not afraid of death, but I couldn't *bear* to be a vampire and lose my soul. That's why *he* makes me edgy, and the others don't.'

Stiles and Denny, both were stunned by this information.

Denny was the first to find his voice. 'I don't believe it,' he said. 'I always thought, I mean I assumed ...' he stopped. 'What makes you think he wants to turn you?'

'Just a feeling, I know it doesn't make much sense.'

'Well that's it, he's out of here!' Denny pronounced. 'I've learned to trust your intuition.'

'No,' said Tamar, 'he's been invited in now. Maybe we should keep him here, where we can keep an eye on him.'

'I'm sorry,' said Denny. 'If I'd known ...'

'Never mind, maybe it's for the best. He might have some

useful information; you never know.'

'Do you think he's right about the prophecy?' Stiles was hopeful about this aspect of it.

'I don't know,' said Tamar. 'It doesn't matter, does it? As long as he means it when he says *he* doesn't believe in it.'

'And if he's lying?'

'I don't think he's lying,' she said. 'But he's not telling us everything.'

'So we question him further?' asked Stiles.

'I think if we decide to take him on, that's going to be a given,' she said.

'But are we?'

'Yes,' said Denny.

'What, just like that?' said Stiles.

'What have we got to lose?'

'You know, you keep saying that.'

'Because I'm right. Look, he wouldn't have come here, if he didn't want the same thing as us. Why would he risk it? And he got us out of that situation with the terrorists – didn't he?' He looked at Tamar.

'No,' she said. 'He just didn't get in our way. He was the one who got us into that mess anyway.'

'We should ask him about that too,' said Denny.

'So, we're agreed then?' said Tamar. 'Back to the interrogation?'

Peirce was waiting for them exactly where they had left him.

'Come and sit down,' said Denny, indicating two leather sofas. 'We have some questions for you, make yourself comfortable.'

Peirce grinned; he was "in". 'Can I smoke now?' he asked.

As it turned out, Peirce had quite a lot to tell them. He started by explaining the terrorist fiasco. 'Oh that,' he said, when Tamar asked him about it.

'Isn't it obvious? I was trying to stall you, and it worked beautifully too – for a while.'

'Why were you trying to stall me? I thought you didn't believe in the prophecy.'

'I don't, and I never did. And so you're wondering why I interfered since that would seem to put me in the Ran-Kur camp?'

'Yes.'

'You good guys can be so stupid; not a devious mind among you, is there? Okay, evil plotting 101 – for beginners: first – misdirection – no? Okay – so, Ran-Kur, or whoever he is, has ordered this man's death, right? So he brought a whole lot of vampires through the veil to grab him, yes? Practically every vampire from here to Lithuania is under his direct control. He has a power over vampire kind that is unprecedented. But if Mr. Stiles here were to die, well – problem solved – no more prophecy, nothing more to fear. This whole thing is about power, not some bogus prophecy. So I tried to stop you from saving him. This served a double purpose when you think about it; on the one hand, I look as if I'm doing my best for the vampire cause – kudos to me. On the *other* hand, the *reality* is that the death of Mr. Stiles would precede the downfall of the impostor, see?'

'And make you a hero to vampires everywhere,' said Denny cynically.

'That doesn't make any sense,' objected Stiles.

'It does once you know the rest,' said Peirce. 'Firstly, I couldn't get near enough to Ran-Kur to kill him; he's better protected than a schoolgirl's diary. And secondly, I let you escape because I had orders to. Top secret orders, which can only mean one thing.' He looked at them to see if they had got the point.

'Ran-Kur *wanted* Tamar there to protect Jack,' said Denny.

'That's how I read it,' agreed Peirce. 'It may even have been he who sent you.' He turned to Tamar. 'At the very least, he knew that *someone* would. That's classic evil plotting, that is. Sending a bunch of assassins after some innocent Joe, while at the same time, sending out a champion to ensure that the assassins fail, keeping the balance of power in your hands – brilliant. You have to give him credit.'

'I'd rather give him a long sword in the guts,' said Denny, viciously.

'You don't still want to kill me, do you?' asked Stiles, edgily.

'No, don't panic, it's too late for that now. Besides *she* wouldn't let me.'

'Why should we trust you?' said Denny. 'You wanted him dead before. You said it yourself; it would solve all your problems.'

'Why are you so certain that this Ran-Kur is an impostor?' asked Tamar.

'I am 500 years dead,' said Peirce. 'I've been around a pretty long time, but I never heard of this Ran-Kur until about 150 years ago, where was he before then? Gods don't just pop up out of nowhere. And the prophecy! – Bit convenient isn't it?'

'The prophecy dates back at least 3000 years,' said Denny.

'Granted, granted, it does, but so do they all. I've seen a lot of prophecies; most of them are bunk – one for every occasion. But this Ran-Kur, he knew his target audience. Vampires in general, are a superstitious lot, worse than humans are. They're real "suckers" (geddit?) for a prophecy.'

'And what if the prophecy turns out to be true?' asked Denny, earning himself a kick from Tamar.

'It's not,' said Peirce. 'And if it is, well, I'll deal with that when it happens – who wants to live forever right?'

'Okay, so say we take your word for it,' said Tamar. 'How can you help us? Do you know where he is? Can you take us to him?'

'Well, no, not exactly,' admitted Peirce.

'What does he look like?' asked Denny.

'I've never actually seen him – sorry.'

'If we *do* find him, how do we kill him? I mean if he's a god, or posing as a god, he must be powerful.' This was Tamar.

'I don't know.'

'Well, what use *are* you?' said Denny. 'You don't know anything useful, do you?'

'I could find out, maybe.'

'Oh no,' said Denny. 'You needn't think we're going to let you out of here now you know all about us.'

'Oh *Please!*' said Peirce, scornfully. 'Who am I going to tell? If you think Ran-Kur doesn't know all about you already, you're kidding yourselves.'

They returned to confer again.

'He's definitely lying,' said Denny. 'I didn't say anything, but I looked up Ran-Kur on the Aethernet, the stories of him go back much further than 150 years. Ask him to explain *that*.'

'So, he *is* a god?' asked Stiles.

'More than likely, yes.'

'It doesn't mean he's lying,' said Tamar. 'Just that he's wrong. The thing is, he's not much use to us either way. I think we have to stick to the original plan. If we assume that Ran Kur *is* a god, then we have to find a way to kill gods and summon him here, like we did with Hecaté.'

'Hecaté wouldn't help us.'

'But she did hint that there might be another way.'

'I'll hit the computer,' said Denny. 'See if I can turn anything up on god-slaying.'

'Are you sure?' said Tamar. 'You haven't slept in three days.'

'I'm fine,' he said. But he did not look it.

~ Chapter Seventeen ~

MRS. PITTENCHERRY – first name Cindy – had in, fact, never been married. She was a well preserved forty, very well preserved actually. She looked no more than twenty-five. She subscribed to the Tamar school of vanity, and believed that there's no point in being a witch if you cannot use it to look good, and that it was cheaper and easier than make-up or plastic surgery.

She was currently doing the magic mirror thing. That is, she was scrying, pausing intermittently to admire her flawless, unlined face and shining blonde hair. She was trying to get a fix on Tamar, although she did not know it exactly, but she had sensed the magic when Tamar had stopped outside her house, and was curious.

She was startled when a face other than her own appeared in the mirror; it had never worked before. Cindy was not terribly interested in magic that was not about herself. She jumped backwards in surprise, knocking over a vase of roses from one of her many admirers.

The face in the mirror was beautiful and noble, with a piercing gaze that emanated power. What was more surprising was that it spoke to her.

'Sister,' it said. 'Do you know me?' The voice was soft, deep and melodious.

'H – H – Hecaté?' stammered Cindy in disbelief. (Not a good beginning for a manifestation – since gods rely on belief to exist)

'Ah, I see you do,' said Hecaté.

Cindy fell on her knees and gibbered.

'Be calm, beloved,' said Hecaté. She stepped out of the mirror and laid her hands on Cindy's shoulders. 'I have come with a message for you.'

'F – For me?'

'Yes beloved, for you. Listen carefully; there is one who will come to you, to seek your aid, a powerful being.'

'I have sensed it, my goddess.'

'Of course you have, my sister. You must not admit her to your home, she brings great danger with her, do you understand?'

'Yes, my goddess.'

'Even more dangerous, is her companion. Beware of them both beloved, and I will give you my protection.'

'Thank you my lady, I will do as you say.'

'My blessing on you, beloved. Now, there is just one more thing I would have you do for me ...'

* * *

Peirce was tied up in the bath. Since he could, theoretically, turn himself into a small rodent or even a cloud of fog at will, Stiles considered this to be an exercise in futility. But Tamar said it showed that they meant business, and anyway, not all vampires could perform such parlour tricks, as she called it.

Denny was out again, having so far come up empty on the god-slaying, he was spending more and more time roaming the streets, and when he was at home, he was moody and withdrawn, and would sometimes pace for hours, like a caged beast. Even Tamar was beginning to notice, but then, Stiles was now getting the same way, and even she was feeling oppressed by the constant darkness and gloomy prognostications of Peirce, who now seemed convinced that they were all going to die horribly.

* * *

Someone else was also convinced of this, and was, in fact, relishing the idea; he was contemplating the reports of their actions, and rubbing his hands together in satisfaction. Peirce had acted exactly as predicted. After the terrorist fiasco, the "Master" had known exactly what his next move would be, and it was exactly what the "Master" had wanted. Still, he *was* technically a traitor, and, as such, should suffer the most horrible penalty that could be meted out to a vampire. Perhaps the tar pit, or a thousand knives, anyway he would have his day in the sun – ha! And as for Tamar Black ... He rubbed his hands together in gleeful anticipation. 'Causing suffering,' he thought, 'is good for the soul.'

~ Chapter Eighteen ~

DENNY WANDERED along the pitch-dark streets. He felt at home in the darkness now, he could see almost as well as in the light. The air was stuffy, and it was sweltering, like a hot summer night, even though it was November. It had been getting hotter and hotter on the streets ever since the darkness had come. Tamar thought it might be a side effect of whatever the vampires were doing to keep it dark, but Denny looked it up and came to the conclusion that it was done deliberately to raise the body temperature of potential victims. Tamar's reaction to this was a predictable 'Yuck!'

He stopped to listen; all around him was the sound of a soft, gentle fluttering, like a thousand moths – large moths. A velvety wing brushed his face. They appeared out of nowhere, and suddenly he was surrounded. Some of them were lit up like fireflies, and some glowed dimly, in the streetlight's glare, with a gentle phosphoresce. They fluttered all around, creating a gentle wind and making the sky flicker. It was quite beautiful in its way, but eerie at the same time. It made the night seem blacker by comparison; he could see nothing beyond the radiant cloud they created.

Denny imagined them lifting him into the air and spinning a huge cocoon around him, pinning him to the side of the building. Slowly he would disappear behind a woven wall of silken threads and be entombed forever. This fancy was so vivid he could almost feel them, their wings brushing his face, buried in his hair, the threads, binding him tightly, until his breath was short. He began to sweat.

But it would almost be a relief if they did, he thought, at least then, he could do no more harm. He wondered where this idea had come from. Denny was not given to flights of imagination.

They were hovering thickly around him, glimmering faintly, but leaving a space all around him, like a black aura, as if he was surrounded by a barrier that they could not, or would not penetrate. He watched them, fascinated, he stretched out a hand and one landed on his finger, flapping lazily. It was huge, like those Jurassic insects you see fossilised in the Natural History Museum, about the size of a bat, perhaps. He turned his hand over slowly, until it sat in the palm of his hand, and then he closed his fingers and crushed it. The others flew away immediately. 'Strange', he thought, 'do moths have a hive mind?' He examined the remains of the one in his hand, it was not quite dead. It examined him back, or so it seemed. Then, although nobody spoke, he heard, clear as a bell in his head, the words. *'You bastard!'*

He dropped the mangled moth, startled. Surely it could not have ...?

He looked around. 'Who said that?' he called; there was a dead silence. 'I must have imagined it,' he thought. 'I'll be talking to myself next.'

The street behind him lit up for a moment, and then dimmed. *Tamar,* he thought. She did not often put on the light show when she teleported, even in the dark, but he guessed that tonight (was it night? Whatever!) even she needed a guiding light. He turned around.

'What are you doing here?' he asked.

'That's what I was going to ask *you,'* she said 'I was worried about you, why do you keep going out on your own like this?'

'You shouldn't be here,' said Denny. 'How could you leave Jack on his own with that pasty faced bloodsucker?'

'He's tied up, besides he'll be all right, he won't do anything; he wouldn't dare.'

'You don't know that, you should go back.'

'Not unless you come with me. Please, whatever it is, we can sort it out.'

'I'm fine, nothing's wrong, I'll come back soon. Please, just go back home.'

'No,' she said, stubbornly. 'I've had enough of this.' She reached out a hand and touched his arm gently. 'Please, come home.'

'You don't understand,' he snapped, shaking her off.

'I would if you'd tell me,' she said angrily.

'Oh, *Saint* Tamar,' he said, scathingly. 'You may be a lot of things, but a psychologist you ain't.' He disappeared.

'Oh no you don't,' she said, and also vanished.

'How do you think I found you in the first place?' was the first thing she said as she reappeared beside him.

'I was hoping you would take the hint,' he said.

There was a rustling behind them. They stopped fighting, and tensed.

'Vampires?' whispered Tamar.

'Probably,' he answered. 'The whole city's lousy with them.'

'Let's get out of here,' she hissed, just as three figures jumped them.

'Too late,' one of them mocked, as he landed on her back; *damn*! She spun and twisted and threw him off.

Denny held out his hand, palm up. There was a blue flame flickering there. 'Choose gas,' he laughed, and made a throwing action. The small flame shot out of his hand in a long steady stream. He hit Tamar's attacker right in the face, he screamed and clutched his head, Denny hit him again, and he became an inferno. Denny spun and hit another one smack in the chest; he went up like a Roman Candle. Denny whooped as the third one took to his heels.

'Denny,' Tamar croaked, over his crowing. '*Denny*!'

'What?'

'They *weren't* vampires; they would have exploded into dust. Those guys were *humans*.'

Denny looked at her; he was bouncing a ball of flame in his palm. 'Whatever,' he said.

'Did you hear me?'

'Yeah. Look they weren't exactly models of virtue, were they? Just because they weren't vampires, doesn't mean they weren't still bad guys, calm down.'

Tamar was backing away from him. 'I don't believe you, who *are* you?' You're not Denny, I'm bloody sure of that.'

'Of course I am, look, I didn't know, okay? It was an accident, I'm sorry.'

'That's just it, you're *not* sorry, and Denny would be. So who are you? Are you some kind of spy? Did you body-snatch him?'

'Tamar, you're being ridiculous, I'm Denny, *look* at me for God's sake. I – I – just – I – never – I – never – *killed* anyone before ... I – oh God, what ...?' He sank down to his knees, his head in his hands, genuinely distraught.

She knelt beside him. 'It's okay, it's okay,' she soothed.

He looked up at her. 'Help me,' he said

~ Chapter Nineteen ~

Dark, dark world. Sick sad world.
All I see are hollow men. And all around are shadows
I died so quietly, just slipped away one day
My soul went up in ashes. And my future blew away
Still it doesn't matter. I'm taking it with me
'Cause no one's getting out of life alive

Now the love has gone. And the pain is gone
All the hope has gone. Still I'm hanging on

Cold cruel world. Dead drained world
There's no redemption on this, earth, and all I know are
  ghosts
Living a lie, it hurts like hell. Sinking into death
Find I'm liking it as well.
As death fills my soul. I carry it with me
And no one's getting out of here alive

It tastes so sweet. It tastes so vile
Send up a prayer. To an empty sky

To wash these sins from off my hands

Now the love has gone. And the pain has gone
All the hope has gone. Still I'm hanging on

Bleak black world. Lost lonely world
I cannot break free, and I'm, not sure I want to anyway

Why should I care? I'm not running away
'Cause no-one's getting out of here alive

Three days later, Denny was still holed up in his room for most of the time, playing this miserable song on his guitar and others like it. Whenever he did emerge, which was not often, he continued his policy of moody silence. Tamar could not get near him. Not that she ever could, the Athame had not changed that after all. Still, at least she knew where he was.

'Just leave him alone. He'll be all right,' she told Stiles, when he complained that it was like living with a moody teenager in a permanent funk.

'Next thing you know, he'll be painting his room black and smoking pot,' he said.

'You should have more compassion,' she retorted. 'You know he's been through a lot.'

'I'm more concerned with what he's put you through.'

'It's not his fault.'

'Well whose fault is it, then, if it's not his? He's the one who ...'

'It's *my* fault.'

Stiles stared. What the hell did *that* mean? He decided not to ask.

'Well,' he said tactfully. 'At least he plays well even if the songs are a bit ...' he bit his tongue. 'He's really good isn't he? I wish I could play an instrument.'

'*What* did you say?'

'I said at least he plays well,' repeated Stiles uncomprehendingly.

It was Tamar's turn to stare.

* * *

Peirce was another problem; he was increasingly morose and demanding. His demands included: - better accommodation, ('how would *you* like to sleep in a bathtub?') A better CD collection, ('haven't you got any Iron Maiden?') He was nonplussed for a moment when Denny in a moment of rare joviality asked him. 'Wouldn't you blunt your teeth on her?' – Typical Denny. No one was sure whether it was a joke or not. A change of clothes, Tamar eventually acceded to this one. The dead apparently smell just as bad as the living if they do not change their socks. And last, but not least, human blood, as opposed to the variety that the local butcher provided – variously, pigs, cows chicken and once an ox, which he almost approved of.

And Stiles was getting restless. 'What are we going to *do*?' he asked repeatedly. 'We have to do something. Or are we just going to sit here while the darkness spreads and the bodies pile up in the streets?' He wanted to let Peirce go and find out what he could about the location of Ran-Kur.

'And we have to get Denny back on board, he's the expert, isn't he? I thought he was going to research ways to kill gods.'

'There aren't any.' Denny had appeared at his bedroom door, looking disturbingly corpse like.

'Christ,' said Stiles. 'You look deader than him.' He meant Peirce of course. Denny scowled.

'And what do you mean,' Stiles continued, 'there aren't any'? How do you know? You haven't even been looking.'

'No, he's right,' interjected Tamar. 'We need another god. There's nothing *we* can do.'

'So, we're stuck? I think it's time we fetched the witch.'

'We could kill every single vampire in the world,' said Denny. 'That'd do it.' The idea of this appealed strongly to him. His taste for violence had certainly increased lately.

'Be realistic,' said Stiles. And Denny laughed somewhat hysterically.

'What?' said Stiles, looking at Tamar, who was also smiling.

'The world is covered in darkness,' she told him. 'The un-dead are roaming the streets, and there's a god of vampires out there somewhere, who wants to kill you. Last week we summoned Hecaté into our living room, and we have a vampire sleeping in our bathtub, and you just told him to be realistic. You have to see the irony.'

Now Stiles also smiled. 'I suppose,' he said, ruefully. 'Still, we have to do *something*, I can't just sit on my rear; it's not in my nature. If it's up to us to save the world, then I say we just get on with it.'

'You're right,' said Tamar, jumping up. 'I should be out there, saving people, it's what I do. You don't save the world by killing gods or destroying all evil, it can't be done, and I *know* that, I always have. You save the world ...'

'One person at a time,' Denny finished for her.

'What are you two talking about?' said Stiles. 'What about Ran-Kur?'

'Irrelevant,' said Tamar. 'At least to us, we can't kill him, we don't have that power. And while we've been sitting around here, worrying about him ...'

'Twiddling our thumbs,' put in Denny.

'Exactly – while we've been doing that, innocent people are dying. Like you said, we can't just sit here while the bodies pile up in the streets.'

'I hate to interrupt,' said Denny, nevertheless doing so. 'But there *are* no bodies piling up in the streets, I should know.'

'What do you mean?' asked Tamar.

'I mean, they're not killing, they're siring new vampires.'

'That's odd.'

'Yes, it is.'

'Why?' asked Stiles.

'Vampires are snobs,' explained Denny. 'They're usually extremely fussy about who they sire. And also they don't want their numbers to grow too large. Imagine a world with all humans and no animals, or no whisky, just lemonade, and you'll understand why.'

'I won't have to imagine it, if the sun doesn't come back soon,' said Stiles.

'And vampires don't even have the "cannibalism" option,'

continued Denny.

'Yuck,' said Tamar.

'You know,' said Denny. 'For someone who has seen as much death and destruction as you have, *caused* as much death and destruction as you have for that matter, you certainly are squeamish.'

'I see your point,' said Stiles. 'So, why are they doing it?'

'Ran-Kur's orders I assume,' said Denny. 'The more vampires he has believing in him, the more powerful he becomes. Gods feed on belief, like all mythical creatures.'

'So he's creating an army?' said Stiles.

'You could put it that way.'

'We have to stop him.'

'No, we have to get out there and start saving lives – killing vampires,' said Tamar.

'She's right,' said Denny. 'That's our job, and I suggest that we start with him.' He pointed at the bathroom door.

Stiles shrugged. 'Suits me,' he said.

'OK,' said Tamar. 'Bring him out.'

Denny and Stiles manhandled Peirce into the living room.

'What's going on?' he asked them. 'Have you decided to let me go?'

'Not exactly,' said Tamar. 'But we have decided to do *something* with you.'

'What?'

'This,' said Denny, plunging a stake into Peirce chest.

Peirce pulled it out easily. 'I thought you might try this sooner or later,' he said. 'You'll have to do better than that. Look at that, you've ruined my shirt.' He laughed at their dumbfounded faces.

'Must have missed,' muttered Denny, preparing to strike again.

'Don't waste your time,' said Peirce, holding up a hand. 'Look.' He pointed to the wound; it was smack in the centre of his chest, exactly where it should be.

'I don't get it,' said Stiles. 'Surely you kill a vampire with a stake through the heart, that's basic folklore, isn't it?'

'It's certainly always worked before,' agreed Tamar.

Denny could have told them of at least one other occasion when it had not worked, but he held his peace, for now.

'Did you really think I'd come here, to the enemy stronghold, without taking some precautions?' sneered Peirce. 'For all I knew, you would have staked me first and asked questions later.'

'What do you mean – precautions?' asked Denny.

'Well, it couldn't hurt to tell you, I suppose, since there's nothing you can do about it,' said Peirce. 'If you must know, I've had my heart removed; it's safe in a vault somewhere.'

'Yuck,' said Tamar, predictably.

'Ingenious,' said Denny. 'It's not as if he's using it,' he explained to the bewildered looking Stiles. 'He's dead; his heart doesn't pump blood like ours, that's why they drink it, to replenish the supply.'

Stiles recovered. 'So, decapitate him,' he suggested.

'Won't work,' said Denny. 'The ritual is, you stake it through the heart and then cut its head off and stuff garlic in the mouth. It's part of the folklore; traditionally the stake through the heart is to hold the corpse in the grave – figuratively speaking. The fact is, with his heart safely stored away, he's invulnerable.'

'What about sunlight?'

'What sunlight?' Denny gestured to the darkness outside.

'Oh, right, well fire then.'

'Nope, when you use fire you have to burn the actual heart, and he's never going to tell us where it is.'

'Actually,' said Peirce. 'I don't know where it is, I never asked.'

'Why don't all vampires have this done?' asked Tamar.

'It's a very expensive operation,' said Peirce. 'Very specialised, to most vampires it's just not worth it.'

'Well we can't just let him go,' said Stiles. 'He might claim to be on our side, but he's still a killer.' Denny blanched, but Stiles did not notice.

'We can't hold him,' said Tamar. 'Tying him up was just symbolic, he could escape easily.'

'Look,' said Peirce. 'Why don't we just put this behind us?

I'm not one to hold a grudge. I mean I expected this, but there's a larger purpose here. I don't even want to know why you suddenly decided to stake me, but why don't you just let me go? You can't stop me anyway, and I'll try to track down Ran-Kur, and report back.'

'And when you've found him, then what?' asked Tamar, following Denny's gaze as he slid his eyes meaningfully towards the mantelpiece.

'No,' she said decisively. 'We're done with all that – lock him up boys.'

Denny nodded to Stiles and winked at Tamar. They shoved him in a broom cupboard, locked the door and quickly blocked up the space under the door, while Tamar grabbed her old bottle off the mantelpiece and held it up to the keyhole. Fog started pouring through the keyhole, straight into the bottle. After a few minutes, Tamar slid a piece of card over the neck of the bottle and hurriedly stoppered it. 'Got him,' she said. 'Or at least probably most of him, good thinking,' she added to Denny.

'Hey, why mess with a winning formula?' grinned Denny, referring to the occasion when they had shanghaied a homicidal Djinn in much the same way.

'Okay,' she said. 'That takes care of him – let's get out there, and do some damage.'

'There are swarms of them,' said Stiles. 'We need an army.'

'Two superheroes and a copper with a grudge,' she answered. 'We *are* an army.'

* * *

The "Master" steepled his fingers in that disturbing way he had when he was displeased, when he heard of this latest development. *'Bloody woman,'* he said.

Damn! Damndamndamndamn.

* * *

They went out in three hour shifts, with Stiles taking every other shift and sleeping in between. He went out with either Tamar or Denny, and they alternately stayed at home with him. They had not forgotten that the vampires were still after him.

Although Stiles possessed no super-powers, he was holding his own with a surprising repertoire of dirty fight moves, picked up when breaking up bar fights in his early years on the force. When, as he told them, the idea was to walk away with all your extremities intact and to hell with ethics. Any fool who tried to fight fair against a drug pusher with a flick knife is destined to have a short career, due to the fact that the police still have not extended their equal opportunities programme to include employing the dead. There seemed to be no trick too low that he would not use it to keep an opponent down, even Denny was impressed.

He was glad, he said, to be doing something again. 'I've been driving a desk for too long.' He said. 'I'd almost forgotten what this feels like, to be out there getting on with it – feels good. This is what it's all about.'

Stiles had been loaded up with stakes axes and various incendiary devices to make up for his lack of a magical armoury, but, as he said. 'You have to catch the buggers first.' And this was where Stiles excelled, small and wiry, he could run very, very fast. But more than that was a sheer love of the chase, a dogged determination. Where others would have given up after they ran out of breath and their legs felt like blancmange, this only seemed to spur him on. 'If I feel like this,' he would gasp. 'Imagine how *he* feels. He'll give up any minute.'

But all this, he was aware, was, for him at least, just a distraction. In his off hours, his brain was working overtime. He was frantic to start the investigation again.

Ran-Kur had sent assassins after him and had caused a whole lot of trouble on the way. Stiles wanted fervently to know why, and he wanted to nail the swine. All this chasing vampires around the streets was just a stop-gap measure as far as he was concerned. A crime had been, and was being, committed. He was not quite sure what it was, well obviously there was attempted murder, and the mass slaughter of innocent people, but those were just the consequences of a far bigger crime, one that he could not quite put his finger on. But he was determined; he would find out what the crime was and, if necessary, give it a name, then bring the perpetrator to justice.

Stiles's thinking had been conditioned by twenty odd years at Scotland Yard, and he also shared with Tamar, a conviction that everybody was guilty of something.

But Tamar and Denny seemed happier now that they had decided on the course of action they were taking, as if they were relieved of a burden, and the chances of changing their minds was remote. Tamar had said that perhaps the answer would come to them, if they stopped looking. But in twenty-five years of police work, that had never happened once to Stiles. You *had* to look; it was just how it worked. Answers or criminals did not ever just drop into your lap. Stiles personally had no case on record of a perp walking into his office and saying. 'It's a fair cop guv; I'm the man you want.' (They often did not even say that, when you found them bending over the corpse with a bloody knife in their hand – or even after ten years in prison.)

Plenty of innocent crack-pots did this, but to date never the actual suspect or guilty party.

Stiles was forgetting of course, that he had left normality behind him quite a while ago. The world he now inhabited did not follow the rules that his mind was imposing on it. In other words, he was wrong, the answer *was* about to drop into their lap.

* * *

Denny was dreaming; he was vaguely aware that he had had this dream before. It seemed important, he tried to concentrate, but it made little sense.

It made even less sense when he awoke and scribbled down a few notes before he forgot it. There had been a talking beast of some kind, with antlers and a *crown*?

Hank? He wondered. Even with all he had seen, he had never come across talking animals, and there had been a medal – this was very familiar; he *knew* that he had dreamt this before. Also, there had been a knife – no, a sword, and it dripped with blood – hearts blood. He knew this because of symbolism in the dream, which he could not quite remember, but he was quite certain of it, just as you are certain, in a nightmare that the monster is behind you, even though you cannot see or hear it.

He looked at his notes in confusion, they read thus: -

1, Animal – antlers – stag? – Deer? (Royal)

2, Sword – hearts blood.

3, Medal – courage?

He scratched his head, *what the hell did it mean?* As premonitions went, and he had no doubt that it was one, it was pretty vague. At least the first one had been absolutely clear. Then he remembered; it had not started that way. The first few times, it had been just as mystifying as this was, it had taken several nights to take shape, but he had hardly slept lately. This was only the second time that this dream had come to him. Maybe he needed to sleep more, but if this was a message, then he needed to try to figure it out. He had a nasty feeling that he should have been having this dream for a week or more, and should have figured it out by now. He felt slightly guilty that he had not. He manifested a cup of coffee and sat at his computer with the notes in front of him.

Tamar appeared behind him. 'Hi, what's up?'

'Can you just – leave me alone for a while? I need to try to work something out. – Actually no, wait.' He handed her the notes. 'Mean anything to you?'

She glanced at the notes. 'No, what does it mean?'

'I don't know. Never mind, I'll figure it out.'

She looked curiously at him and back at the paper. 'More dreams?'

'Yes, how did you know?'

'You made notes like this about the first one.'

'Did I? I'd forgotten. Actually, could you grab me some books? Um, 'Allegorical Animals' and, um – 'Mystical Weapons', there might be something in there.'

'Okay.' She fetched the books. 'What's this?' she brushed his shoulders, and a silvery powder came off on her hands. 'Dream dust,' she said. 'Someone's been *giving* you these dreams.'

'That's very – helpful of them. Although, it might be *more* helpful if they just sent an e mail.'

'That's magic folk for you; they delight in the vague and mysterious. Sure you don't want any help?'

'I'm sure.'

'Okay, then, I'll see you later.' She went back out, leaving Stiles to sleep.

When she arrived back, three hours later, Denny still had not got anywhere, and it was time for his shift on the street. Tamar suggested that perhaps he should carry on his research. But he said that he could do with a break, to clear his head and stretch his legs. Stiles slept on.

Denny found himself going over the dream as he walked, going over each point until it no longer made any kind of sense at all, like when you repeat a word over and over until it loses all meaning. It was frustrating the hell out of him, especially as he knew perfectly well that, as Tamar always said, the answer, when it came, would be obvious. He took out his frustration on a bunch of vampires and decided to go home and get some sleep.

* * *

Denny dreamed. The answer was there, right on the edge of his brain, tantalising him. The earlier research he had done was floating on the surface of his unconscious mind, connecting the dream images together. The answer was there, just out of reach.

He woke with a start and leapt up to the bookshelf.

'Eureka?' asked Tamar.

'Not yet,' he replied. 'I just need to check in "Mystical Animals".'

'What's going on?' asked Stiles, appearing, bleary eyed.

'Shhh,' said Tamar. There was a long silence, except for the swishing of pages.

'Aha,' said Denny, triumphantly.

'What?' they both said, excitedly. 'What is it?'

'I have found a way to kill gods,' said Denny, dramatically. This was greeted with a stunned silence.

'You're kidding!' said Stiles, eventually.

'H – how?' Tamar had found her voice.

'Denny pushed to the book toward them. 'The Purple Hart!' he said, 'a mythical deer whose blood is the only substance that can kill a god.'

'Surely that's the Golden Hind?' said Stiles after a moment's thought.

Tamar laughed. 'That was Homer for you,' she said. 'He used to do that a lot – change the names to protect the innocent. You know what Hercules was *really* called? It was ...'

'I thought Homer was before even your time?' interrupted Denny.

'Oh he was, but I've heard all about him, from people who knew him, you know.'

'Are you saying that this thing, whatever it's called, is *real?*' asked Stiles, feeling that they were getting off the point.

'It must be,' said Tamar, that's why he was having the dream, it was a message.'

'So how come, if you can kill a god this way, you didn't find this before?'

'I didn't know what I was looking for,' said Denny.

Tamar was reading the text. 'This was thousands of years ago,' she said. 'How are we supposed to find one now.'

'Him,' corrected Denny. 'There's only one.'

'Okay, how are we supposed to find *him?*'

Denny shrugged. 'A summoning maybe? What does it say?'

'It says – go to page ninety-seven – typical!'

Page ninety-seven turned out to be an index. Denny found the heading – 'Questing for mythical beasts'.

When Tamar heard this, she groaned. 'Not another quest.'

Stiles looked from one to the other, perplexed at their downcast faces. 'What?' he said. 'What?'

Part Two: The Quest

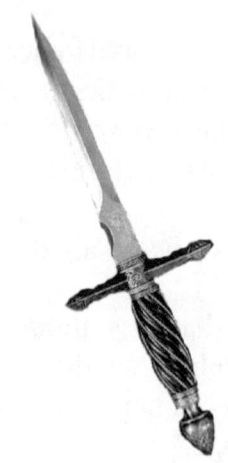

~ Chapter Twenty ~

FIRST, THEY HAD to find a witch.

'No problem,' said Tamar, 'we've already found one.'

'Not just any old witch,' said Denny. 'According to this, we have to find "The old Witch of the Caves", whoever she is.'

'Where do we find her?' asked Stiles.

'It doesn't say,' said Denny. 'It's written as if the reader should know.'

'Well,' said Tamar. 'Most of these old books were written by witches, for witches. So a witch ought to know.'

'Okay, okay, you win,' said Denny. 'You go and ask her. Now, we have to decide who is going on this quest.'

'Aren't we all going?' asked Stiles.

'No,' said Tamar. 'I'm going on my own – someone has to stay here and carry on the fight.'

'I don't think that's a good idea,' argued Denny. 'If the last quest we were on is any guide, you'll get into trouble on your own. Trouble that you might not be able to get out of.'

This was inarguable.

'And, anyway,' continued Denny, 'who says it has to be *you* that goes?'

'I just assumed.'

'Yes – well, I have a few powers now too.'

'Yes, but I'm still more used to this sort of thing than you are.'

'Well, whatever. Whichever one of us goes, I think Jack should go too. He has to stay with one of us and getting him away from vampire central might not be a bad idea right now.'

Tamar looked dubious. 'I don't know. The quest might be dangerous, especially for a mortal.'

'*I* survived. Besides, I think he *wants* to go.'

'I'm standing right here you know?' said Stiles. 'And yes I do want to go.'

'*But not with you,*' he added to himself.

'Okay, so I think we should *all* go,' said Denny, giving Stiles the uneasy feeling that he had read his mind. 'At least as far as the witch, the old witch in the cave I mean, after all we haven't even found out what it's all about yet – what we have to do.'

'What about him?' said Stiles, indicating the bottle in which they had trapped Peirce.

'You think we should take *him?*' said Denny, incredulously.

'I don't mean we should let him out,' said Stiles. 'I just think we should take the bottle with us, to keep an eye on it. We don't want him getting out while we're gone, do we?'

Denny agreed. 'He might even come in handy,' he said.

'Only if we have to throw somebody to some lions,' said Tamar, sourly. 'Once we let him out, we'll never get him back in there. He's not like a Djinn. Okay,' she added, 'let's go find a witch.'

* * *

'You're a *witch?*' gasped Stiles.

'What, you were expecting a hump, warts, skin like sandpaper?' said Cindy acidly.

'No, of course not! But you're just so – so glamorous.'

'Hmm, not as good as "beautiful" or "ravishing" but it'll

have to do.'

Since Cindy was standing in Tamar's company, her considerable attractions had quite a bit of competition. And, anyway, Stiles was not used to, nor any good at giving compliments.

'Can we come in?' he asked.

Cindy hesitated.

'We don't have to,' said Tamar. 'Neutral ground?'

'Um, don't we need to be private?' ventured Stiles.

'It'll be fine,' said Tamar hastily. The witch was clearly nervous enough.

The three of them agreed to go to the "Dangling Prussian" around the corner. Denny would be gutted that he had missed it. They had decided not to all descend on her at once, and, judging from how skittish she was, it had been the right decision, but it had been a long time since Denny had sat in a beer garden in the sun.

Cindy disappeared into the house and emerged with a jacket and a fresh coat of lipstick. She nodded to them. 'Okay.'

'I know what you want,' Cindy said, when Stiles came back with the drinks – two diet cokes and a large Brandy. Stiles looked impressed at this evidence of witchly power; Tamar waited.

'Oh there's no mystery,' said Cindy, 'I had a visit from Hecaté. I can't help you.'

'I don't think you *do* know what we want,' said Tamar. 'Hecaté ...'

'She told me,' said Cindy. 'And she told me not to help you.'

'No, you see, we *did* want Hecaté's help, but now ...'

'You are searching for the Purple Hart,' Cindy told her.

Tamar sat back in her chair. 'Okay, so you *do* know what we want,' she admitted.

'How did she know?' asked Stiles curiously.

'Hecaté?' said Cindy. 'She *is* a goddess you know.'

'Why would she tell you not to help us?' asked Tamar.

'The Hart's blood can kill gods can't it? Isn't that why you want to find it?'

'To destroy Ran-Kur.'

'Hecaté knows this, but you see, technically Hecaté is also a god. Surely you can see why she would not want such a weapon in your hands?'

'But we have no wish to harm Hecaté,' said Stiles.

'No?' said Cindy. 'All right, say I believe you? I'm sure you mean it, but Hecaté told me that the last time a mortal got hold of the Hart's blood six gods died before he could be stopped. Or did he just run out of blood? The point is, he got carried away – the power went to his head; it's too dangerous. Besides, she is my goddess, and she has forbidden me.'

Stiles sighed. 'Please think about it,' he said. 'Ask her again. Ran-Kur will kill me if we don't stop him, and the darkness is spreading. How long do you think *you* can escape?'

'My goddess will protect me,' said Cindy, uncertainly. She looked at Stiles; her resolve was faltering. 'So, you are the one?' she asked.

He nodded.

She gulped down the brandy in one go. 'Can I have another?' she asked, 'while I think about it.'

Stiles rose at a nod from Tamar, and headed for the bar.

She and Tamar sat in silence while they waited. Tamar knew they had won; Cindy was just fortifying herself. Stiles returned with another glass, which she drained in silence.

'All right,' she said. 'I'll take you to the old witch on one condition – that you take me with you – on the quest. I stay with you until you kill this Ran-Kur and then you give me the Hart's Blood, for safekeeping.'

'Deal,' said Tamar immediately. She had expected much worse.

'Oh no,' laughed Cindy. 'I'm not just going to take your word for it. A Djinn and a *man.*'

'Former Djinn,' said Tamar.

'Whatever,' said Cindy. 'Same thing, I want the oath.'

Tamar sighed. 'Do I have to sign my name in blood?'

Cindy looked disgusted. 'Of course not, what is this, the

Middle Ages?'

Tamar spat on her hand, and Cindy did the same. They held their hands up, palms out an inch from each other. A strange shimmering energy sparkled between them.

'Rimminy rimminy rimminy roke – we seal the oath that cannot be broke,' they chanted. Stiles had to stuff his fist in his mouth to stop himself from laughing.

'Come back at ten tonight,' said Cindy. 'I'll be ready then. Will the other one be coming?'

'Hecaté?' asked Stiles.

Cindy laughed. 'No, I just knew. I *am* a witch you know.'

'Yes, he's coming too,' said Tamar. 'See you later.'

When they had gone, Cindy smiled to herself. 'Well, that all went according to plan,' she said to herself.

* * *

'So, how went it with the witch?' asked Denny, when they returned.

Tamar smirked and dug Stiles in the ribs. 'Jack seemed quite taken with her,' she said.

Denny raised his eyebrows. 'Really?' he said. 'Quite the ladies' man, aren't you?'

As this was possibly the worst description of a man, since somebody said. 'He's not such a bad bloke when you get to know him,' of Adolf Hitler, Stiles hung his head and blushed furiously.

Denny laughed. 'Well, you seem to be in a good mood. Do I take it, she's agreed to help?' he addressed himself to Tamar.

'Yes, she's insisting on coming with us though.'

'Well, it could have been worse.'

'That's what I thought,' agreed Tamar.

'Well,' said Denny, 'our hands are in the fire now.'

~ Chapter Twenty One ~

'WE HAVE to walk,' said Cindy. 'There are no shortcuts.'

'Where are we going?' asked Stiles – it would be him, of course. Both Tamar and Denny already knew the answer to this.

'I don't know,' said Cindy, 'we just follow the instructions and we get there. It isn't on any map; that's why we can't jump the astral plane.'

'She means teleport,' said Tamar.

'I was wondering how you did that,' said Stiles. He thought for a moment. 'No, still no idea,' he admitted.

'Well ...' Tamar began.

'*People*,' interrupted Cindy, 'are we going or what?'

'Lead on Mac Duff,' said Tamar.

Cindy took Stiles by the arm. 'I'll explain it to you on the way,' she said sweetly. Denny and Tamar grinned at each other and fell in step behind them.

'You see,' Cindy was saying, 'in order to travel all over the globe in seconds, you have to pass into an ethereal plane, where time doesn't exist, you actually travel within that plane in the normal way – well, actually you fly, well, witches do, and other magical beings I suppose. Non-magical people can't do it at all, so I guess that's not the point. Anyway, you fly along the astral plane; the journey *feels* instantaneous because there's no time there, you see?'

'I – I think so.'

'Obviously you can still see *this* world; otherwise you'd get lost, or land on somebody or something. All that star trek nonsense about de-materialising, well I mean ... what if you re-materialised inside a cliff or a tree or something? Ouch!' She laughed.

Stiles laughed too, just to be polite.

'And that's how invisibility – or rather the illusion of invisibility, is created,' she continued, 'you just pass into the astral plane but stay where you are, see? Better than a hidden microphone – not that I would ever ...'

Denny looked at Tamar. 'Is that true?' he asked.

Tamar shrugged. 'Close enough,' she said.

'It doesn't feel so complicated when I do it.'

'It's instinctive, like blinking – you don't notice what you're doing.'

Cindy was clearly trying to impress Stiles. Her attitude to Tamar was a wary competitiveness. Denny, she had dismissed entirely. Neither handsome nor rich, and anyway quite clearly spoken for, he was invisible to her, but she seemed quite taken with Stiles. And, since Tamar was also spoken for, Stiles had no objection to this.

'How do you know where to go?' he asked.

'Oh, the witch of the caves is an old witch tradition,' said Cindy. 'We all know the story, but no-one's sought her for decades, I don't think.'

'And how ...?'

'Ah, ah, ah,' said Cindy, flirtatiously, tapping her finger on his nose. 'I can't tell you witch's secrets just like that, I only just met you.'

Denny rolled his eyes; Tamar giggled.

'I just hope she knows what she's doing,' Denny whispered.

'Shhh,' hissed Tamar, 'witches have excellent hearing.'

But Cindy was twittering away in a high pitched tone and did not hear him. Denny did not register on her radar anyway. This suited Denny fine; he did not like Cindy much. Besides, he knew he could command her full attention if he chose to.

They were, in case you are interested, wandering along the High Street, apparently aimlessly, stopping occasionally for Cindy to check a piece of paper, which she, rather theatrically concealed from them.

'Aha!' she said, stopping suddenly. 'This'll do.'

'Taxi rank?' said Tamar. 'Are we catching a cab?'

'You might say,' said Cindy.

Tamar snatched the paper from her, before Cindy could stop her. 'Says here, "Coaching Inn".'

'Modern equivalent,' said Cindy. 'Don't forget, this was first written in the middle-ages, you have to interpret.'

'So we *are* catching a cab?'

'Trust me, we just wait. I'll know when it happens. Remember, witches traditionally never used coaches or cabs or any mortal method of transport, so a witch at a taxi rank, well, it's not usual. But I think *something* will come for us.'

'You *think?*'

'Hey, I've never done this before; I'm just following the instructions.'

'Maybe you need to send a signal or something.'

'It doesn't say so here.' She stabbed at the paper. 'Just wait.'

Cindy had turned down three cabs, and it was getting close to eleven when Denny asked. Anyone think we should just take the next one and go clubbing?'

'Mmm, tempting,' said Tamar.

'I'm getting really hungry,' said Stiles.

'There's a burger place across the road,' Denny pointed.

'Now *that's* tempting,' said Stiles.

They were all getting restless, even Stiles. All of their experiences had prepared them for just about anything, except this awful tedium.

By eleven thirty, they were all giving Cindy dirty looks and complaining loudly. By midnight, they had subsided into a mutinous silence and Stiles was asleep on a bench, when suddenly Cindy pointed at some lights in the distance. 'There,' she said.

'It's just another cab,' said Tamar, wearily.

But it was not, the lights were moving in a very odd way, sort of cycling around each other; there were three of them too.

'It's an optical illusion,' said Stiles; Denny had shaken him awake. 'Like headlights in the rain.' But he did not sound either convinced or convincing, perhaps because it was not raining.

'It's not raining,' pointed out Cindy. The lights drew nearer.

'What the hell is it?' said Stiles nervously.

It was a glass coach – motorised, apparently – no horses and no driver.

'You've got to be kidding me,' exploded Tamar. 'I can't believe they're still pulling this stuff.'

'No driver,' observed Denny, dryly. 'Do you think they ran out of mice?'

'Oh hell! Let's just get in,' said Tamar. 'At least it's not broomsticks.'

'Well, it was a distinct possibility,' she said, defensively, when they all looked at her strangely.

They all clambered in. 'Oh yes,' said Denny with caustic sarcasm, 'we won't be *at all* conspicuous in this.'

As soon as they all settled in, they fell asleep.

* * *

When they awoke they were in a field, the coach had vanished. Tamar spotted a pumpkin a few yards away, but held her peace, this was not the time.

'Now what?' she asked Cindy, who was currently more interested in re-applying her lipstick. Tamar had to admire her really; she took vanity to a whole new level.

'Mmm? Oh yes,' Cindy consulted her paper and looked around. 'Where is it?' She muttered.

'Where's what?' asked Tamar. 'The yellow brick road? Three bears cottage?'

'Um.' Cindy looked embarrassed.

'*No?*' said Tamar. 'I was kidding.'

'No, no,' said Cindy, hastily. 'Not that bad. It's – er ...'

'The "Primrose path",' said Denny, pointing at it. 'Leading into a dark and scary forest? Presumably to find Hansel and Gretel.'

'Um, yes, it doesn't say anything about a forest, but – primrose path, yes. I'm sorry; I didn't make it up you know.'

'We know, we know,' said Tamar. 'Oh well, better load up our groins.'

'Er isn't that "gird up our loins"?' queried Stiles.

'I know what I said.'

'Anybody know where we are?' asked Denny.

'Yes,' said Tamar. 'We're being led up the primrose path by a witch, and I'm not sure I like the symbolism of that.' She turned to Cindy. 'If we run into a "Big Bad Wolf" there's going to be trouble.'

'I would say that's a given,' said Denny.

'I meant from me.'

'So did I.'

As it turned out, the journey was uneventful, not so much as a stubbed toe occurred until they arrived at the mouth of a large cave, partially concealed by undergrowth and a trickling waterfall, well more of a drip really. It looked cold, dark and uninviting.

'This is it, all right,' said Tamar, resignedly. She turned to Cindy. 'Any more instructions?' she asked. 'Or do we just go in?'

'Well, we're supposed to ... um, it says ... no, we just go in.'

The cave was all that the exterior had promised it would be and worse.

'It's like being inside a rusty iron lung,' said Denny.

'With extra slime,' said Tamar. 'Yuck.'

'So, where's this witch?' asked Denny.

'Ahem,' said Stiles, from behind them. They turned.

'I think maybe we're too late,' he said.

Beside him, half embedded in the wall of the cave, like a fossil, was a stone figure in the shape of a crouching old woman. There was a constant stream of water flowing over it wearing it away in places, and it was unattractively festooned with weeds and algae.

'That's not her,' said Tamar. 'The water's worn away the rock face, it *does* look a little bit like a ...'

'Face it,' said Denny. 'That's the witch. It's all been for nothing.'

'It can't be.'

'So, what do we do now?' asked Stiles.

Cindy was poking the – for want of a better word – statue. 'Sister? Hello. Sister?'

'Idiots,' said a voice from the back of the cave.

'Now *that's* a witch,' thought Stiles. What faced them as they turned around, was indeed the archetypal witch. A withered, warty crone, with long, straggly grey hair, a hooked nose and a hump you could seat three people on. The only thing missing was the conical hat. She cackled at them revealing three stumps of what could only be her teeth, since they were in her mouth and not a graveyard, and the picture was complete. Stiles had been expecting almost anything but this cliché – a witch who actually looked like a witch – it took him by surprise.

She hobbled towards them. 'Hmm, five of you – there's a thing, so what do you want?'

'Four,' said Tamar.

'So what's that?' cackled the witch, pointing at the bottle containing Peirce, 'Scotch Mist?'

'Actually, I think he's a Londoner,' offered Stiles.

'Ha! So London fog then, what do you want?'

'Don't you know?' asked Stiles in surprise.

'No,' snapped the witch. 'I don't do that clairvoyant stuff.'

Tamar looked shrewdly at her. 'So what did you do?' she asked.

The old witch started. 'What?'

'To end up here,' said Tamar. She turned to the others. 'Look at this place,' she said. 'It's got to be a punishment.'

The crone glared at her. 'It's no never mind of yours what I done – did. So mind your own business.'

'You're quite right,' said Tamar. 'I apologise.'

'What's your name?' asked Stiles.

The old witch peered at him. 'Hmm, a mortal,' she said. 'Well I never. And you!' she poked Tamar in the chest, 'you're no witch you. I dunno what you are, but you ain't no witch. No more are *you*,' she said to Denny. 'What do you want here?'

'We're searching for the Purple Hart,' Tamar told her.

'Ha!' said the witch. 'I should have known.' She gave them a gummy smile.

'Well then, you have to face the labyrinth, which one of you is it going to be?'

'Labyrinth!' groaned Tamar. 'Why is it always so complicated? Why can't they just give you a written test or something?'

'Actually,' said Denny, 'we sort of thought we'd *all* be going.'

'Hmm,' said the witch dubiously. 'I never sent more than one person into the labyrinth before. Mind you, I don't usually get parties. I suppose it'd be all right.'

'Isn't it usually a Minotaur?' piped up Stiles. 'At the centre of a maze I mean, not a deer.'

The witch pupped her lips. 'Another one who reads too much,' she said, derisively. 'Anyway, they calls it a maze, but it ain't what you'd expect – you starts at the centre for one thing and you have to find your way out.'

She spun round suddenly to face Denny. '*You!*' she said. 'You cannot enter the labyrinth; you must stay behind. Go back to where you came from.'

'What? Why?' said Tamar.

'It's okay,' said Denny. 'I should go back anyway. I've been thinking about it – all those people ...'

'That's not the point,' said Tamar. She turned to the witch. 'Why can't he go?' But the witch just shook her head and would not say.

'Just go,' said Denny. 'You have to.' He was taking it very well, considering.

'Okay,' said Tamar, ungraciously. 'What do we have to do?'

The witch nodded and took a large branch and drew on the floor of the cave, a small picture of a maze with a space in the centre, large enough for three people to stand in. 'Stand here.' She pointed. 'I'll do the rest.

Tamar and Stiles stepped into the square; Cindy hesitated. 'I can't,' she said, she was as white as a sheet. She looked at Stiles imploringly. 'You don't really need me do you?'

Tamar and Stiles looked at each other and shrugged.

'I guess not,' said Tamar. 'I don't know.'

The old witch cackled derisively. 'Call yourself a witch? – You ought to be ashamed.'

Cindy went from white to fiery red. She looked up and caught sight of Denny's mocking gaze. It was the first time she had really noticed him.

'You can come back with me and fight,' he said, grinning wolfishly.

'Hobson's choice,' said the old witch.

'All right, I'll go,' said Cindy and stepped into the square. Whatever awaited her in the labyrinth, she felt, could not be worse than being left alone with Denny. How had she not noticed, before, how scary and intimidating he was?

The old witch mumbled a few words and waved an arm. Tamar disappeared.

'Damn!' said the witch. She did it again and Stiles vanished, leaving Cindy alone looking awkward.

'Last chance,' said Denny. Cindy ignored him. The witch repeated the process once more, and Cindy was gone.

The old witch and Denny faced each other.

'Well,' said Denny, drawing out the Athame and unsheathing it. 'You know what I'm going to do I take it?'

The witch nodded.

'And it's what you *want*?'

'It's why I chose you to stay behind. I knew you would do it, soon as I seen you. Them others – they ain't never … they ain't got the stones. But you have, haven't you my lad, it wouldn't be the first time for you?'

'Oh yes,' said Denny, grinning wolfishly. 'I've got the – stones all right. And I can make my own way home, can I?'

'Oh yes.'

'Oh yes.'

'Good,' said Denny, and, striking suddenly like a snake, he plunged the Athame into the old witch's heart.

She fell to the ground, millennia suddenly showing in her face. 'Thank you,' she croaked, before crumbling into dust.

'Don't mention it,' said Denny, with a strange smile on his face. He sheathed the blade, turned and waved a hand. A door appeared in the wall of the cave, through it, he could see the dark streets he had left behind.

'Cool,' he thought, as he felt the witch's stolen powers surge through him. That was how he had killed her; he had taken her immortality. He stepped forward and hesitated. With the witch's power, he realised, he could follow the others into the labyrinth. Should he? He shrugged and tossed the Athame up into the air, where it twirled three times before he caught it, and walked, whistling softly, back into the world. He really did not think he could stand too much more of Cindy's company. Not without a gag on her anyway.

~ Chapter Twenty Two ~

TAMAR LANDED with a bump and was disconcerted to find herself alone on what appeared to be a tropical sandy beach (with the obligatory swaying palms and a sky so blue it made her eyes hurt.)

She waited a full ten minutes, but neither Stiles or Cindy appeared, so she began to walk.

She had felt the difference in herself immediately. She still had her powers, but here, they were a natural thing. It was ironic that Denny should have been held back from here. Magical places were the only places where her powers were not dangerous to mortals.

After a good half hour, she started to worry. Nothing at all was happening and the beach was apparently endless, it led nowhere. How the hell was she supposed to get out of here? And where were the others? Stiles would be okay, she thought, but Cindy would be panicking, unless the two of them were together, of course, but somehow, she doubted it.

Also, although the beach was beautiful it was lonely, she

began to miss Denny, who could be relied upon to make light of the worst of situations.

The sparkling sea was on her right, and on her left was a sheer cliff face, which seemed so high that the top of it was in the clouds. This was definitely *not* a real place, but then she had not expected that it would be. If she had had any doubts, the picture postcard appearance of the beach would have dealt with that. No real beach was without the customary decoration of discarded beer cans and/or dead fish, no matter what it looks like in the brochure.

On the other hand, this place was more desert island than centre of the labyrinth. It gave her a horrible trapped feeling, *where's Robinson Crusoe when you need him?*

Although she knew that her first priority should be to work out how the hell to get out of here, she was far too preoccupied with wondering where the others had got to, to concentrate on this.

There were undoubtedly clues here, but she was too busy searching to notice them if there were any. She wondered if that was not the point.

She slipped off her shoes, and the sand between her toes reminded her of something, *sand?*

It was a lovely beach, Stiles thought. But he would far rather have been where he had expected to be. Not to mention, he had expected Tamar to be waiting for him, surely he had only been a few seconds behind her? He debated whether to try to find her, or to wait, where he was, for Cindy to appear. Like Tamar, he was confused as to why a beach? – As opposed to the centre of an actual maze, with high stone walls and gargoyles, or large, leafy hedges.

When, after a few minutes, Cindy still had not appeared he started to worry. He was definitely alone then? Then he noticed footprints leading away from him; Tamar had been here then. How had she got away so fast, on foot? Stiles was thinking too literally again; he always forgot that he had left normal some time ago. He decided to follow them, maybe Tamar had found something; Cindy would just have to find them on her own, or perhaps she had decided not to come after all.

Cindy was not enjoying the beach. What was the point of a beach with no men around to admire her in a string bikini? She was well aware that she had left normal; she had, in fact, never been to normal as far as she could remember, but this was no help to her in her current situation. She was as lost as the others were, although not as surprised to be on a beach as they were. She knew how witches' minds tended to work. She spotted the exit almost immediately, but it was no use to her by herself, no way was she facing the labyrinth on her own. She was annoyed that they had just gone and left her, as she thought. She was especially disappointed in Stiles, from whom she had had great hopes, although she had not failed to notice his interest in Tamar. But surely no one would be foolish enough to mess with that psycho, Denny?

'Oh well,' she thought, 'might as well get in some sunbathing.' She settled down under a convenient palm tree, and tried not to cry.

'Sand?' Tamar bent down and scooped up a handful. She watched, thoughtfully, as it trickled through her fingers; something stirred in her memory, *the sands of time, trickling away.* Well, that seemed fair enough, time was certainly a factor here. Of course, she could always take an unfair advantage, assuming she had the power in this place.

She thought for a moment. 'Tempus Suspendré,' she said. The sand in her palm froze in mid trickle. The waves were stilled, and the wind through the trees ceased, the world was as still as a photograph. The only thing still moving was Tamar herself, now she had all the time in the world. The only question was – to do what?

She tried to shake the remaining grains of sand from her hand, but, since they were frozen in time, they would not move. 'Oh for God's sake! There's always something!' she thought impatiently.

Out of the corner of her eye she thought she saw a shadow

moving. She glanced round in disbelief and saw – Stiles! He was walking toward her, first at a normal pace and then he seemed to be slowing down like a film winding down until he stopped, as frozen as the rest of the world around her. *What the hell?* There was no time (so to speak) to wonder about this; Tamar was just glad to have found him.

She was glad that her trick had worked at all. Since arriving in the labyrinth, she had felt a definite – not draining of her powers exactly, which was what had happened in the deleted file, but, at the very least, a displacement of them. As if a part of her was elsewhere, but still functioning.

In "other" places, like this, her powers often changed or left her temporarily, but this was different. She wished Denny was here. She would probably have been able to at least give him a hug without killing him. It was ironic that it was he, out of all of them, who had been left behind. She sighed internally, back to work.

She snapped her fingers and time resumed its normal functioning. Stiles continued walking, as if he had not noticed a thing.

'Jack,' she called, 'over here.' She waved her arms. Stiles started, as if she had just appeared out of nowhere, which from his point of view, she had.

'Tamar?' he turned to walk toward her. 'Where the hell have you been?'

'Nice to see you too. And I think the question should probably be – *when* the hell have I been?'

'What?'

'I've just figured it out, I think. What happened in the cave?'

'You vanished first – by yourself.'

'I thought so. We ended up being sent here in different times.'

'Of course we ... hang on – *in* different times. What do you mean?'

'Well, I was sent what, ten seconds ...?'

'Yeah, about that.'

'Ten seconds before you. So you ended up in a time that

was ten seconds behind the time that I'm in.'

'So, how did I catch up to you?'

'I froze time.'

'So – Cindy?'

'Well if she didn't arrive with you, then she's in another time zone, behind us.'

'Look I don't get it, how does it work, just because I arrived at a different time ...'

'Not *at* a different time, *in* a different time. Even if I'd waited here forever, if I hadn't frozen time I'd always have been ten seconds ahead. Ten seconds or ten years, it's all the same thing.'

'So, again I ask – Cindy?'

'Oh yes, Tempus Suspendré.'

Stiles froze, and Tamar had an impish impulse to pull his pants down or tie his shoelaces together. She stifled it and un-froze him, he stared at the world around him in amazement. 'So this is the world in freeze-frame?'

'She's not around here, we'll have to go and look for her.'

Cindy got the point immediately, when Tamar explained what she thought had happened. 'Makes sense,' she said. 'Back when this place was created, there were probably many people at once taking the maze. It wouldn't do to have them running into each other, I suppose. By the way – time freezing – nice power.'

'Thank you. So where do we go from here?'

Cindy pointed to the cliff face. 'Over there I should think, try to find a cave or a passage or something.'

They stared at her.

'Not just a pretty face, am I?' she simpered, looking at Stiles. He missed the point, completely. Disappointed, she turned away toward the cliff. 'Come on then.' She said briskly.

It took some time to find the passageway; they were considerably hampered by the intervention of the shepherd.

The appearance of the sheep milling around in the sand at

the foot of a cliff was a *bit* of a surprise and should have served as a warning that something was wrong. Stiles, who had lived in a city his entire life, postulated that maybe they were mountain sheep, as there were, so he understood, mountain goats. But, as Cindy pointed out, even "mountain sheep" would need grass, surely?

Stiles argued that they probably were not real sheep anyway.

As far as Tamar was concerned the fact that there were sheep at all was a worry; there was something about it that teased her mind. Why sheep? It was frustrating; ever since she had become human she had found that things were harder to recall; she was constantly struggling with thoughts and memories that danced around the edges of her consciousness, but could not be accessed.

The ground shook with a great bellowing, and it came to her.

'Look out for the shepherd!' she called.

'Shepherd?' asked Stiles. 'Where?'

Tamar pointed silently to a huge figure on a ledge above them.

Stiles craned his head back. 'Oh my – opia.'

Cindy gibbered. 'A – a Cyclops.'

'The traditional shepherds of mythology,' said Tamar. 'I should have known.'

Despite its vast size, the Cyclops was making its way down the cliff face with astonishing speed and dexterity; it was brandishing a large club, tastefully adorned with spikes.

Tamar yawned. 'How unoriginal,' she drawled.

Cindy and Stiles stared at her.

'Stand back,' she ordered. 'I'll deal with this.'

'Freeze time again,' suggested Stiles, in a strangled voice. He had seen her fight, but this thing was *huge*.

'Where's the fun in that?' she laughed. It had been too long, and she was itching for a good rumble.

Stiles read her thoughts. 'Tamar, we don't have time for this, we're on a mission. Remember Ran-Kur?'

Tamar sighed. 'Oh all right then. Tempus suspendré.' The

Cyclops kept on coming. 'Tempus suspendré,' she said again, impatiently. 'Tempus ... it's not working,' she stamped her foot. 'Oh well.' She manifested a large spear.

'Come on one eye, let's go,' she dodged as the club crashed down by her head – too close. 'Nice loincloth,' she jeered. 'Did your husband buy it for you?'

Cindy was shivering and clinging to Stiles. 'Why is she antagonising it?' she asked.

Stiles shrugged. 'An angry opponent loses perspective?' he suggested.

'I think she's just crazy,' said Cindy.

'Or that.'

Tamar was dancing about, back and forth, jeering and making stabbing motions, but no actual contact. She glanced at Stiles, 'I *really* wish Denny were here,' she thought.

The Cyclops was advancing on her as she was backing away. 'Jack,' she called, and threw the spear to him, praying he would understand, as Denny would.

Stiles caught the spear and ran forward as she manifested another spear. He ranged himself beside Tamar; she shook her head and nodded towards the Cyclops. He moved back several paces, still in its line of vision. It moved forward and impaled itself on Tamar's spear, and fell dead with a thundering crash on the sand.

'That's the thing about mono-vision,' she said, 'no depth perception.'

'I guess he *did* lose his perspective,' agreed Stiles.

Cindy was still shaking. 'I knew there would probably be guardians,' she said. 'But I expected a hermit or, at the very worst, trolls – you know – in mountains.'

'You *knew* there would be guardians?' exploded Stiles. 'You could have warned us.'

'I'm sorry, I thought you'd know, I didn't think.' She grasped his arm, imploringly.

Stiles shook her off, disgustedly. 'Do you ever?' he said, cruelly.

'That's enough,' said Tamar. 'We're all in this together, so play nice. Or do I have to bang your heads together?'

'Okay,' muttered Stiles. 'I'm sorry; almost dying puts me in a bad mood.'

'Does it?' said Tamar, genuinely surprised. 'I find it kind of exhilarating.'

'You would.'

They faced the passageway through the cliff. 'All right all right,' said Tamar. She turned to Cindy. 'Is this the way?'

Cindy nodded.

'Okay, let's go.'

~ Chapter Twenty Three ~

'WHY DIDN'T THE time freezing work?' Cindy asked; she was addressing all her remarks to Tamar now, understandably.

'I don't know,' answered Tamar. 'But I suppose I shouldn't have been surprised, it's like Denny always says, "it's never that easy".'

'Power displacement,' she thought. 'Like it's being interrupted by something.' She wondered if she should warn the others that her powers were, at best, unreliable in this place.

Cindy gave an involuntary shudder at the mention of Denny's name.

Tamar misinterpreted this gesture. 'It is getting cold, isn't it?'

Cindy shrugged, but Tamar was right. As the end of the tunnel came into sight they saw flurries of snow blowing in.

'Snow?' said Stiles. 'Half a mile back that way is a tropical beach.'

Tamar and Cindy grinned at each other.

'Ah, so literal,' sighed Tamar.

'Oh whence is fled the visionary gleam?' added Cindy, with a smile.

Stiles did not answer this remark, of which he could make neither head nor tail. He suddenly felt outnumbered; those two wicked women had joined forces and were laughing at him. For a moment, life felt normal again.

Until they burst out into the sunlight and were faced with a vast frozen tundra.

'Oh my God!' gasped Stiles.

It stretched on into infinity, an immense featureless wasteland of ice and snow. The biggest ice-skating rink in the world. In the sky was an aurora of shimmering coloured lights, each cloud was rimed in silver and shot through with gold, the whole sky was like a painting done by the hand of God. They stared at it in awe, until the sun suddenly went down, leaving a still beautiful but less awe-inspiring blanket of stars.

The three of them huddled together, united again against the cold and the vastness. Even Tamar was intimidated. 'How the hell are we supposed to get across that?' she said, looking at Cindy.

'Sleds?' said Cindy.

'We haven't got any sleds – oh.' This was Stiles; Tamar manifested a large sled, complete with blankets.

'Can't you see the exit?' she asked Cindy.

'No, but I'm sure we'll know when we've found it, it'll be guarded.' She stole a glance at Stiles, but he held his peace.

'Which way do we go?' was all he said as they piled into the sled.

'Don't know,' said Tamar, when Cindy didn't answer. 'Go,' she said to the sled, which moved off on its own. 'Here we go,' she sang as they rattled away.

'Jingle bells, jingle bells, jingle all the way ...'

Stiles was not amused at the light-hearted way in which "the girls", as he was now thinking of them, were taking this journey. In fact, he was becoming increasingly bad-tempered, and he was beginning to miss Denny almost as much as Tamar was, and he did not even like the feller. But at least he would not have felt so – so out of it with another bloke to talk to. Maybe Denny was not so bad after all. This got him thinking.

'I wonder why that old witch wouldn't let Denny come with us,' he ventured.

Cindy turned away, and Tamar gave him a black look. She had been wondering this herself, and had been unable to come up with a satisfactory answer.

'She probably had her reasons,' said Cindy.

'Like what?' snapped Tamar?

'*I* don't know,' said Cindy. 'I never said they were *good* reasons.' And the subject was dropped. Mainly because of the Yeti.

'Ah,' said Stiles, 'speak of the devil – only kidding.'

It had risen up apparently out of nowhere. Cindy was torn between terror and laughter at Stiles's last remark, and the result was a grimace that would have made a gargoyle look attractive by comparison.

'The second guardian, I assume,' said Tamar, giving Stiles a look that promised trouble later on. She turned to Cindy. 'You look for the exit, I'll deal with him.'

Cindy gulped and nodded; she had already spotted the exit, but did not feel inclined to mention this yet.

Tamar had not moved; she was squinting at the sky. The Yeti did not seem interested in them at all, but they all felt certain that this would change if they tried to get past him.

'Well, what are you waiting for?' asked Stiles. 'Aren't you going to pound him?'

'No,' said Tamar. 'You can't kill a Yeti like that; they're not flesh and blood.'

'So what are you...?'

'Shhh.'

'Fire?' asked Cindy.

'Actually, I had something a little more creative in mind.'

She thought for a while; the Yeti sat on the snow, picking its teeth and ignoring them. Stiles was getting impatient. 'What *about* fire?' he asked eventually.

The sun was now directly overhead. Tamar ignored him.

'Now, do you think?' asked Cindy.

'Mmm.'

'What the hell are you two talking about?' griped Stiles.

'Shhh,' said Cindy. 'She needs to focus.' And she giggled.

'Women!' muttered Stiles, grumpily.

Tamar squinted at the sky one last time and said, 'Okay, *now*.' And sent a large lens flying into the air.

Where the hell it had come from Stiles did not even try to guess. That was Tamar for you. The lens quite naturally focussed a beam of sunlight directly onto the Yeti. Not the brightest of creatures, the Yeti apparently did not notice anything wrong. It did, however, stir uncomfortably.

Tamar moved forward, and it growled at her. 'Calm down,' she said brightly. 'We're not stupid enough to try to get past *you!*' The Yeti subsided. Tamar sat cross-legged on the snow in front of it. She was already sitting in a small puddle. She began to talk airily about nothing in particular. Cindy joined in; she was especially good at this.

Stiles was fuming by this time. 'What are you trying to do?' he hissed. 'Bore it to death?'

It took about twenty-five minutes for the Yeti to completely melt; Stiles had cottoned on to the plan after about ten minutes. 'Well, I'll be damned, it really *is* a snowman,' he exclaimed, his good humour now completely restored.

'Abominable,' agreed Cindy.

'Good job they're so stupid,' said Tamar, rising gracefully from her puddle. 'We won't be so lucky next time. Now where's the exit?'

'I'm afraid it's down there,' Cindy pointed to a fishing hole in the ice.

'Oh Christ, are you sure?'

'Can't see anything else that could be it – sorry.'

'Well, you'd better be right,' growled Stiles. Cindy ignored him.

'Okay' said Tamar. 'I'll go first. Let's get this over with.'

They made ready to lower themselves into the hole in the ice, Cindy gingerly and Tamar planning on a dive, when another yeti appeared this one in full fury, roaring and thumping its chest. Tamar swore. 'Oh to hell with it,' she sighed and threw a fireball at it. 'Sod the compassionate approach,' she said, as it thrashed about melting like the wicked witch of the west. 'We don't have time for this.'

Stiles agreed. 'I don't know why you didn't just do that in the first place,' he said.

'Because I wasn't sure that I *could*,' thought Tamar, but she said nothing.

* * *

Ever slid down the tubes at a water park? This was the experience that followed after they had clambered into the fishing hole in the ice. Only it went on for far longer and took place under the surface of the open ocean. Stiles was fascinated by the undersea world, visible through the transparent walls of the tunnel. He had never seen mermaids before – they were not what he would have expected, and he had never been so close to a shark. Tamar showed the very first sign of fear that he had ever seen in her when this particular incident happened, and he wondered about this, but he supposed that everybody had phobias – she was mysteriously nervous around empty bottles too, now he came to think about it. Cindy was too worried about the possibility of their running out of air to properly enjoy the ride. She was also concerned about the state of her hairdo, but that was just Cindy. Tamar thought she had worked out why Denny had not been able to come. His claustrophobia would definitely have been an issue in this confined space; the fact of their being under water would only have compounded the problem. Stiles, on the other hand, was having the most fun he had ever allowed himself to have. 'Wheee!' he shrieked, like a two year old, (it's always the strong silent ones.) Tamar was amused; she too was enjoying it, she joined in. 'Wheee! – Ouch.' They had landed.

~ Chapter Twenty Four ~

OF ALL THE PLACES they had expected to find under the sea – Atlantis, the Marie Celeste, the last thing they had expected was a library.

It was quite a nice library. Old fashioned, with mahogany shelves and long reading tables, with green reading lamps, and a parquet floor. On one table a chess set was laid out.

That was one end; the other end was more – well, put it this way, there were no books only rows and rows of scrolls, and the floor, not to mention the shelves, were made of stone, and the floor was inlaid with an intricate mosaic. There were signs of fire damage in this older part, and the light was dim; this was because the skylight was covered over with ice.

'It's a library,' said Stiles, somewhat pointlessly. He turned to Cindy. 'Any ideas?' he asked.

She shook her head, apparently as flabbergasted as he was.

'I know you girls think I'm too literal,' he said. 'But I have to ask, I'm sorry, but why is there a library at the bottom of the sea?' He glanced at Tamar, she ignored him. Cindy shrugged.

'Well, there doesn't appear to be anyone here.' He was struggling here, trying to work both ends of the conversation.

'Don't count on it,' said Cindy.

Stiles gave up; he leaned back and knocked over a pile of heavy looking books from the top of a low shelf.

'Ouch!' came a voice from underneath the books, and then some ripe language as the books heaved and out from under them, struggled a small hairy figure, dressed in a tweed suit.

'What the ***** do you think you're doing?' it screamed.

'Oh God, I'm really sorry,' said Stiles, picking the creature up and dusting it off. This only served to make the little "man" even angrier. 'Put me down, you great lummox,' it shrieked. Stiles dropped him. The creature turned its back on them and composed itself.

'Er, excuse me,' said Cindy. 'I don't suppose ...'

The little hairy man – he was about three feet tall, turned. 'Hubba hubba,' he said, leering at her.

Cindy backed away hurriedly. 'Urgh.'

Stiles laughed. 'Well if he's the guardian, we shouldn't have any trouble getting past him,' he said.

'Don't count on it,' said Cindy again.

'I've been here before,' said Tamar suddenly, coming out of a reverie. She rounded on the little furry creature. 'This is the lost library of Alexandria, isn't it?'

'Great Zeus!' said the little creature. 'How old are you? – Ahem, yes, yes it is er young lady. I am its custodian, and I got the job on my own,' he added challengingly.

They all stared at him.

Tamar recovered first. 'So, I am Tamar,' she said, 'and this is Jack and Cindy. What is your name?'

'Oh yes, sorry, I forgot my manners in all the concussion.' He glared at Stiles. 'My name is Alcazar, and I am the custodian of the Great Library of Alexandria, and the guardian of this part of the labyrinth. And I got the job on my own.'

'That's great – Alcazar,' said Tamar.

'Wait a minute,' interrupted Stiles, '*The* library of Alexandria? The *actual*...? Oh never mind.'

'Yes, the *actual* library,' said Alcazar. 'I am its custodian. And I got the job on my own. Tea?'

'Yes, you said,' said Stiles. He shook his head at the tea. 'If this is the Great Library of Alexandria, shouldn't it be ... wasn't it?'

'Burnt down?' said Alcazar. 'Part of it was. This is the new annexe, finest teak, those shelves.' He ran a hand along one of them and coughed. 'Urgh huh huh. Dust! Yes well, I built most of this, updated the books and so on, I got this job on my own, you know? Sure you wouldn't like some tea?'

'You know, you don't look like an Alcazar,' commented Cindy. 'You look more like – like a Eugene. I used to have a dog called Eugene.'

Alcazar or Eugene bristled. And bristled, and bristled some more, until he was the size of a small car and covered in scales.

'What the ...?' began Stiles.

'Mesomorph,' said Tamar. 'Shape shifter. Well you didn't really think it was going to be that easy did you?'

Stiles sighed. 'No, I suppose not.'

Eugene, as they would call him from now on, subsided into his incarnation as a small furry man.

'So, what do we have to do to get past you?' asked Tamar.

'Well now, it's a battle of wits, isn't it?' said Eugene.

'Can, can you look like anything?' asked Cindy.

For answer, Eugene transformed into a tall muscular handsome man. 'Is this what you had in mind?' he winked. 'Cutie.' Cindy giggled.

'Or perhaps something like this.' He changed into a pretty good facsimile of Denny. Cindy winced and took a step back. Tamar frowned. 'How did you know ...?'

'Pretty basic mind reading,' said Eugene. 'I got this one from you,' he added unnecessarily.

'Mind reading?' said Stiles to Cindy. 'How are we supposed to win a battle of wits with a mind reader?'

Tamar heard this. 'I think that's the point,' she said sourly.

'Ha!' said Eugene.

Tamar bristled in much the same way as Eugene had and became a dragon. 'Or,' she said. 'You could just save yourself a lot of pain and show us the exit.'

Eugene became a huge monster with a shark's head. 'Don't think so sister,' he said. Tamar winced and subsided. Eugene grinned; with his sharks head, this had a pretty sinister effect. 'I got this job on my own you know,' he said, predictably. He really did seem inordinately proud of this fact. Like it was such a great job!

Tamar squared her shoulders and did a pretty good impersonation of Beelzebub as illustrated in "Dante's Inferno".

Eugene laughed. 'Met him,' he said. 'If the real thing didn't scare me, you've got no chance. This is fun; I've never had a Djinn in here before.'

'Former Djinn,' said Stiles. Eugene ignored him and turned into an enormous bottle.

Tamar actually screamed, before she could stop herself. It was a surprisingly high pitched girlish scream.

Stiles clapped his hands over his ears. He gripped her arms. 'Get hold of yourself – former Djinn, remember? *Former.*'

'Right, right, thank you,' she calmed down. 'We're going to have to change tactics I think. This isn't working.'

'Oh do you think not?' said Stiles, sarcastically. 'I thought it was going quite well.'

'Huddle,' Tamar ordered.

'Well,' said Stiles. 'I don't think we can scare him anyway.'

'The problem is,' said Cindy. 'We don't really know whether he can actually harm us in these forms he can take on.'

'I think we have to assume that he can,' said Tamar.

'So we have to figure out what he wants. Maybe a bribe?' said Stiles.

'Oooh a corrupt copper, I like it,' said Tamar.

'What do *we* have, that he could possibly want?' said Cindy.

'He seems to like *you*,' said Tamar, grinning slyly.

Cindy was horrified. 'You *wouldn't!*'

'Of course we wouldn't. Don't be silly. On the other hand, I don't think he's really dangerous, and he *can* be anyone you want him to be.'

'No!'

'Okay, so what *do* we do?' asked Stiles.

'I don't know,' Tamar shrugged. 'Ask politely?'

'We could try it, I suppose,' said Stiles.

Eugene interrupted them. 'Come on,' he said. 'I'm bored.'

'So, Eugene,' said Stiles. 'How about we talk?'

Eugene laughed and transformed into a sinister hooded figure holding a large scythe. He indicated the chess set. 'How about we play?' he said.

It was decided that Stiles should play him, since he was the only one of them who had played before. 'Don't forget he can read your mind,' cautioned Tamar.

'Bit of an unfair advantage,' said Stiles, but he did not seem too worried.

They sat at the board. 'Do have some tea,' said Eugene.

'The fact is,' Eugene was explaining while waiting for Stiles to move, 'I was supposed to appear to you in this guise and offer to play you for your freedom, but you caught me off guard with your book shoving. Still I suppose it doesn't really matter. Oh dear.' He made his move. 'Check.'

'Oh damn!' said Stiles, glaring at the board. 'So it's the traditional game with Death is it?' he made his move.'

'Oh yes, I don't know whose idea that was, but the actual reaper, was too busy to do it, so they asked me, I got this job on my own. Your move.'

Stiles moved.

'You should take your time more,' admonished Eugene. He was frowning at the board in a puzzled way. Eventually he moved. 'More tea?'

'Oh I don't think so,' said Stiles. 'I think we're done, check mate.'

'What? Well, that's never happened before.'

Tamar and Cindy whooped jubilantly.

Stiles grinned. 'My game's poker really, and since I had the advantage of *knowing* that you could read my mind – well, you can see ... You know, you're not really a very good player.'

'I never needed to be, before this. I got this job on my own you know? Oh well, a deal's a deal. This way.'

'That was brilliant,' said Cindy.

'Masterful,' agreed Tamar.

Eugene, now restored to his former total lack of glory,

pushed a large bookcase aside to reveal, unsurprisingly, a passageway. It was almost properly labyrinth like, in that the walls were made of large blocks of sandstone and there were the mandatory gargoyles and torches in brackets creating eerie shadows.

Tamar looked both ways down the passage. 'Which way do we go?' she asked without much hope.

'Eugene shook his head. 'No idea,' he admitted. 'Sorry, I've never been out of the library, I got this job ...'

'On your own?'

'Yes, did I mention that before?'

'Once or twice.'

'Why don't you come with us?' said Cindy (of all people.)

'What, why?'

'Well, aren't you – lonely? You said you'd never been out of here.'

Eugene thought about this. 'Well, I suppose, but who's going to ...'

'Who cares?' said Cindy. 'Come with us – it'll be fine.' She smiled at him.

'Er,' Eugene blushed under his fur and tugged self-consciously at his collar. He stared at his feet. 'Y – You really want me to come?'

'I never say anything I don't mean.' She leaned in toward Tamar. 'He might come in handy,' she hissed. 'After all like you said, he can be anything.'

Tamar nodded. 'Good idea.'

Eugene was watching his furry feet as he twisted them around each other.

Cindy brought her face close to his and batted her eyelashes in a well-practised manner. 'Well?' she said.

Eugene gulped. 'Okay, yes!' he said decisively. 'I'll come, I hate this job anyway; my brother got it for me.'

* * *

'One more try,' thought Denny, 'and then I'm giving up.'

He swung down from the cliff face for the third time. The roc was waiting for him; she flapped her massive wings in fury and squawked at him; she was creating quite a dust storm.

Denny sighed. 'Okay, Big-Bird, bring it on.' He lifted into the air, as the roc rose up after him; he dived, grabbed the egg and leapt out of the nest. He did not get very far; she had his ankle in her beak, and it was so hard to concentrate through the pain.

'Why didn't I just wait and let Tamar do this?' he thought.

He had decided to gather the ingredients for the summoning of Ran-Kur to save time when they got back. *If* they got back, but he was not letting himself think about that.

Back to the current problem, the roc had a pretty firm grip on his ankle, and he did not really blame her, he *did* have her egg, and he was in danger of dropping it.

He thought for a second, then he dropped it. The roc let go of him immediately and soared after it, but Denny was quicker, he grabbed the egg, and the roc went spinning off into space on the back of a small whirlwind.

Phew, the phoenix feather had been easy compared to that.

He checked his list and ticked off – lavender, phoenix feather, bay leaf, fairy dust? And now the roc's egg. Almost done, good.

He was, of course, just trying to keep busy, in between patrolling the streets and writing lugubrious songs. The flat was a disaster area, but it never occurred to him to tidy up or to mend the broken windows and front door. When the landlord had come round after complaints from Mr. Whinger and other residents about the noise – and the smell, he had turned him into a statue, which was now festooned with dirty socks. Denny found this highly amusing. In fact this trick was handy on the streets, the city was now dotted with new "statues" all sporting fangs and surprised expressions.

He was even going into work occasionally (Bo had apparently not noticed the funny weather and had continued to open; the lack of customers was no change). Anything to fill the empty hours. He was avoiding going to sleep; his dreams lately had been disturbing, mostly involving the men he had killed. He even saw their faces when he was awake sometimes, which was weird, since he had not seen their faces at the time, at least he did not think he had. He was not too sure of anything anymore .

~ Chapter Twenty Five ~

THEY WENT LEFT and trusted to providence. Eugene had changed, at Cindy's suggestion. She thought that he might need longer legs to keep up. He took the point and was now the handsome, muscular man that she had admired, which, of course, was exactly what she had had in mind.

To Stiles, he now looked disturbingly like Finchley, and he suspected that Eugene was well aware of this. Tamar was just glad that he did not look like Denny; she was missing him enough as it was.

Eventually they came to a fork in the road, so to speak. This time they decided to go right, so as to avoid potentially going in a circle. Although, as Tamar pointed out, they would probably end up where they were supposed to anyway sooner or later, no matter which way they went; there was a kind of inevitability about this quest that was growing on them. At the end of this passageway was a door. The gargoyle above the door was extremely unhelpful. 'Dunno.' Was his uniform answer to every inquiry, even when Tamar threatened to smash him. Still, he probably did not count as a guardian, and was obviously mentally challenged. They went through the door.

The blast of heat that met them almost convinced them to turn back. Below them was a river of molten lava and above them were sheer slopes running to a point; they were standing on a narrow ledge looking up at a small circle of sky. They were in a volcano.

'Okay, bad idea,' said Stiles, let's go back.'

They turned back, but the door was gone.

'Of course it is,' sighed Tamar.

Cindy was tugging her arm. 'What are those?' She pointed upwards.'

Tamar squinted. 'Birds?'

'Damn big birds,' said Stiles, doubtfully.

Whatever they were, there were a lot of them, circling above them, apparently enjoying the heat. Some were evidently flying upside down – basking.

'Salamander dragons,' said Eugene, dully. 'Babies.'

'*Babies?*' said Tamar. 'So, where's mummy?'

'What the hell are Salamander Dragons?' said Stiles.

'Rare,' said Eugene, laconically.

'Some sort of cross-breed?' suggested Cindy.

'Who cares?' said Tamar. 'How do we get out of here? Can you see an exit?'

'Up there,' said Cindy, unhelpfully.

'Eugene?'

'On the other side.' He pointed; there was indeed an opening on the other side of the cone. The question was how to get there.

The ledge did not run all the way around, and there was a total lack of a helpful bridge. Tamar tried to manifest one, but it crumbled immediately.

'Sorry,' she said. 'Geology's not my speciality. I don't know what to make it of.'

'Can't you teleport us across?' asked Stiles.

'Oh I never thought of that,' snapped Tamar, acidly.

'There's no astral plane in magical places, 'said Cindy.

'Fly us then?' persisted Stiles, 'we can't stay here forever.'

This was tried, but they got caught in the up-draught, and nearly choked on the ash and fumes. 'Sorry,' gasped Stiles, wiping his streaming eyes.

'What are we going to *do?*' panicked Cindy.

'How vicious *are* those things?' Tamar asked Eugene.

'Adults are extremely dangerous, according to research,' he said. 'But not the babies, don't worry about them, see they're ignoring us.'

Tamar did a remarkable imitation of the cry of the baby salamander dragons. They turned startled and swooped en mass down toward them.

As they came closer, they could see that the scales on the dragons were smooth, like snakeskin and a bright yellow colour with red zigzag stripes along the back. And their eyes were like shiny rubies. They were slender for dragons, but had the traditional bat-like wings, except that they were bright yellow and translucent. They hovered curiously around the strangers in their midst. One of them let out a tiny jet of flame, which rolled along its flickering tongue.

'What the hell did you do that for?' exploded Stiles. 'This is no time for ...' He stopped in amazement as she reached out a hand to stroke the muzzle of the nearest one. 'Hi – hi there,' she was saying softly. 'Good boy, what a *good* boy.'

'My God!' he thought, 'she's not afraid of *anything*. What a woman.'

He was further stupefied when she clambered onto the back of the tamed dragon.

She turned and grinned wickedly. 'Last call for the dragon train, leaving now.'

The other dragons were hovering in imitation as if waiting for the others to mount them. Stiles was the first to risk it. 'Surprisingly comfortable,' he managed in a strangled voice. 'Come on guys,' he added. 'It's this or nothing.'

Cindy hesitated. 'How do we direct them?'

Eugene turned into a small version of the dragon. 'They'll follow me,' he said.

'Can't I ride on you?' asked Cindy. 'I mean – I didn't mean.' She blushed as the others laughed.

'Um, no offence, but this is just an outward form; I don't have their strength; otherwise I could have carried you all as an adult dragon.'

'Okay.' Cindy took courage from the fact that Tamar and Stiles were still alive, and clambered awkwardly on to the back of the smallest one. They swooped away after Eugene.

Tamar and Stiles were exhilarated, but Cindy looked distinctly green as the dragons landed on the ledge on the other side.

'Are you all right?' asked Eugene, looking concerned.

'I'll be fine,' she replied. 'Just get me down before I ruin the upholstery.'

'Be careful,' Eugene warned. 'Mummy's probably in there.' He indicated the passage.

Cindy groaned. 'I shouldn't have come,' she said. 'How bad could it have been to stay behind with Denny?'

Tamar snapped her head round. 'What's *that* supposed to mean?' she barked.

'Nothing,' said Cindy, hastily. 'I just meant with the darkness and the vampires and everything.'

Tamar narrowed her eyes, but let it drop.

The cave walls glowed red, with flickering shadows from the fires below.

"Mummy" was red, with yellow stripes and much, much, *much* bigger than the babies. Curled up in her nest, she looked like a pile of double-decker buses. She was snoring gently.

'I thought dragons slept on a pile of treasure?' hissed Stiles.

'Why on earth would they do that?' Eugene whispered back. 'How uncomfortable. And why would dragons have treasure, anyway?'

'I suppose,' admitted Stiles.

Tamar and Cindy were trying not to giggle.

'If they *did* have treasure,' continued Eugene, not a man to let things drop. 'They'd probably keep it in a vault, like anybody else.'

Tamar suppressed a snort. 'Shhh you two, is this relevant?'

'Mummy' opened an eye; it was yellow and gleamed in the semi-darkness like a flame. Then with a snort, she closed her eye again.

'How do we get past her?' asked Tamar.

'Who says we do?' said Eugene. (What a little ray of sunshine.)

'I do,' said Stiles, grimly. 'We didn't come all this way, to spend eternity in this blast furnace. I at least want to die before I go to hell.'

'That can be arranged,' said "Mummy" from the depths of the cavern. She rose and unfurled her wings casting a humungous shadow on the back of the cavern wall. Even Tamar quailed. 'Now look what you did,' she said.

'Be polite,' warned Eugene. 'And don't lie.'

'Well, aren't you going to introduce yourselves?' asked the dragon. 'I do so prefer to be on first a name basis with people before I eat them.'

'How about we don't tell you our names, and you don't eat us,' suggested Tamar.

'Be polite, remember,' said Eugene.

'What for? It's going to eat us anyway,' said Tamar.

'Any of you a virgin?' asked the dragon wistfully. 'It's been so long.'

Eugene shifted uncomfortably.

'I'll let the rest of you go,' continued the dragon, 'if one of you is a virgin, one virgin is worth ten – um not virgins.'

'No deal,' said Tamar, to Eugene's relief.

'What do you eat when you can't get people?' asked Stiles, curiously.

'What do you mean? There are always people, in the village below the volcano, but no virgins anymore, a dying breed it would seem.'

'I'm not surprised, if the reward for virtue in these parts is to be your preferred lunch,' said Stiles.

'Hmm,' said the dragon. 'I never thought of that.'

'I always thought that dragons made a deal for virgins, you know one a month, and you won't terrorise the village.'

'Now there's an idea,' said the dragon. 'They could breed them up special, make my life easier too.'

'What are you doing?' hissed Tamar angrily. 'Don't give it ideas like that.'

'Sorry I was just thinking out loud.'

'Well don't! You're just promoting an outdated myth. Just shut up.'

'Well. Doesn't the myth also include a gallant knight who kills the dragon to save the princess or whatever?'

'What part of "shut up" do you not understand?'

'Sorry.'

'Knights?' snorted the dragon, who had missed nothing of this exchange. 'They've tried that. Baked in their own armour, they taste quite good.'

'See?' said Tamar.

'Nobody can defeat the great Smog,' said the dragon.

'Smog?' said Stiles blankly.

'That's me,' said Smog the dragon. 'And now, it's only manners to tell me *your* names. Don't worry I've decided to let you all go, I like that idea that the skinny one came up with, I'd much prefer a virgin anyway.'

'I don't think we can trust you,' said Tamar. 'No offence, but you *are* a dragon.'

'None taken,' said Smog. 'I understand. But it's a kosher offer.'

'Sound good to me,' said Stiles.

'No,' said Tamar.

'Why the hell not?'

'Because, thanks to you, big mouth, it's going to use your idea to get virgins, we can't let it; it'd be our fault.'

'Well, surely that's better than what it's doing now?'

'Oh you think so? No, we have to stop it. It's bad enough that it's killing people, but to expect those people to participate, to just hand people over, that's sick. And they would, they'd do it because they'd be afraid; they're just ordinary people, but I'm *not* ordinary people, and I'm not going to make a deal with a monster.'

Stiles was ashamed of himself. 'So, we're back to square one. Our options are either to die, or to kill it,' he said.

'That's how it should be.'

'Kill *me*?' laughed Smog. 'I'd like to see that.'

'Tamar?'

She sighed. 'Stand back,' she said. 'I'll deal with this.' The next second she was a pillar of flame. Cindy screamed; Stiles gasped. 'Oh no.'

She emerged from the flames, a little ashy, but substantially intact.

Smog was taken aback. She drew in a breath to try again. Tamar leapt onto her neck and pulled her head back by the ears, the jet of flame hit the roof of the cavern.

Smog shook her head from side to side, trying to shake Tamar off. She threw Tamar up into the air and opened her mouth to catch her as she fell. Cindy hid her face. Eugene had Stiles by the arms to prevent him from running forward and being sautéed for his trouble. 'We have to help,' Stiles shrieked, as Tamar was swallowed.

There was a silence.

Smog looked smug.

'I can't believe it,' said Stiles. 'She's gone. I thought nothing could kill her. How the hell am I going to explain this to Denny?'

'I don't think that's going to be a problem,' said Eugene, as Smog drew in a large breath.

But she just flamed the roof of the cavern again, in a sort of triumphant salute. 'My offer still stands for you three,' she said. 'Just walk away.'

'No,' said Stiles. 'Tamar was right, and I won't let her death be for nothing.'

'But it won't make a difference,' said Cindy. 'If she couldn't stop it, what can *we* do?'

'Good point,' said Eugene.

'And the quest, someone has to go on,' added Cindy.

But Stiles was adamant, 'No I'd rather die trying.'

'That can be arranged,' said Smog, and drew in a breath again.

Stiles steeled himself. 'Oh please,' he said. 'How far were you going to let us get, before you flamed us anyway? It's a *dragon!*' he added, to the others. 'You can't have really trusted it.'

'Oh just far enough that you'd think you might make it,'

admitted Smog, narrowing her eyes. 'You first,' she snorted, drawing in an enormous breath. She stopped short; her stomach gave an enormous rumble.

It was a spectacular explosion; the walls of the volcano shuddered as bits of dragon splattered all over the walls. The baby salamander dragons shrieked. Stiles, Cindy and Eugene fell off their feet. They were lucky – only superficial burns.

From amidst the debris a voice was heard. 'Little help here?'

They pulled Tamar out from under a pile of dragon guts, still smouldering. From below them the volcano gave an ominous rumble.

'We have to move,' Tamar said, somewhat redundantly. 'It's going to erupt, I was afraid of that.'

Cindy pulled her scattered wits back together. 'Over there.' She pointed to a small pool, mysteriously undisturbed by the tumult. They ran avoiding the rocks bouncing all around them and jumped.

Once under the water, they found that they were rushing upward until they broke the surface. 'That was refreshing,' quipped Tamar as they clambered onto the bank.

'Stiles opened his mouth, then shut it again, too many questions. He settled for throwing his arms around her, Cindy did the same. Eugene shrugged and joined in, and they toppled over in a heaving pile.

'I guess I didn't agree with her,' said Tamar.

'That was one hell of a case of indigestion,' agreed Stiles.

'How did you do it?' asked Cindy.

'I just held on tight to the flame ducts until they backed up. Bit unfortunate about the volcano erupting, we got rid of a dragon but caused a natural disaster.'

'Can't make omelette without breaking some eggs,' said Stiles philosophically. 'On the whole I think that's a big tick in the plus column.'

'So, where the hell are we now?' said Tamar.

It was a swamp by the looks of things, here and there were gnarled trees, and everywhere you looked there was a variety of khaki coloured weed. The water was the colour of, well, what you might find in a portable loo, and occasionally it went "blup" in a disconcerting manner. And a nasty yellow fog hung in the air, swirling oilily, like a living thing. All in all it was pretty unpleasant, but paradise compared to the volcano. But oh, the *smell*.

'Hmmn,' said Cindy. 'No exit, no guardian, could this be it?'

'Surely not,' said Stiles. 'What self-respecting mythical beast would live here? It's a mud puddle.'

'Mud puddle?' came an indignant voice from behind them. 'My home this is? And who be you?'

They turned and saw the weirdest creature yet, the easiest way to describe it was as a half man – half frog. As if in line at the legs counter it had mistaken where it was and ordered the frog's legs, and also the frog's cheeks, which bulged intermittently. They tried not to laugh, as it hopped toward them. 'Who be you?' it repeated.

'What is it?' hissed Cindy.

'Amphibi-man,' said Eugene. 'They're not dangerous.'

'Ohh, not dangerous, am I not?' said the amphibi-man. 'Guardian of the swamp am I. And who be you?'

Stiles folded his arms. 'Cut it out "Yoda",' he said. 'How do we get out of here?'

'Not Yoda,' said the amphibi-man. 'Who be "Yoda"? My name it is Blarrt. And I am not showing you the way out, rude man.'

As he said this, his eyes flickered toward the bole of a felled tree, large enough to fit a person in. Tamar nodded to Stiles, who had also noticed.

Blarrt swelled up to twice the size he had been. 'Defeat me you must.' he said.

Tamar pushed him casually into the water. 'Come on guys,' she said. 'This way.'

~ Chapter Twenty Six ~

INSIDE THE TREE bole was a staircase which they followed down to a door.

'Cute,' said Stiles. 'I feel like I'm in an Enid Blyton book what's behind the door, do you think – elves, gnomes, goblins?'

'None of those things are cute,' said Tamar.

'Who is Enid Blyton?' asked Eugene interestedly. 'I have never heard of this Author; I thought I knew all the mythological volumes.'

Cindy suppressed a laugh.

'Come on people,' said Tamar. 'Are we going or what?'

Not surprisingly they were all reluctant to step through the door. They all felt certain that whatever was behind it would be unpleasant and dangerous. They wanted a break. On the other hand, what choice did they have? 'Maybe it'll be a nice hotel,' said Eugene, hopefully.

'With a pool,' said Cindy.

'And a bar,' added Stiles. 'What?' He said, as Tamar frowned. 'I just meant for fruit juice, besides what are the chances?'

Tamar pushed open the door, and they walked into a raging sandstorm.

'Figures,' said Eugene, gloomily.

Looming through the swirling sand was a large animal, they could just make out that it was sucking the sand into its mouth creating a swirling whirlwind. As the sandstorm cleared, there emerged a large sphinx, which settled calmly on the sand and waited.

'Wow,' breathed Cindy, 'it's beautiful.'

'They're certainly mixing their mythologies aren't they?' said Tamar.

'Is it dangerous?' asked Stiles, practically.

'Extremely,' said Tamar. 'I think I preferred the dragon.'

'That bad?'

The sphinx turned its noble and handsome face toward them slowly and with consummate dignity. 'Well?' it said, petulantly, in a whining tone. 'What do you want? Are you just going to stand there forever?'

Stiles rolled his eyes. 'I suppose after Hecaté I shouldn't be surprised,' he said.

'Ah,' said the sphinx. 'Do you know Hecaté? I have not seen her for an aeon, how is she?'

'She's fine, doing very well, as far as we could tell,' said Stiles.

'Still as beautiful as ever, is she?'

'Oh yes, very.'

'Oh, this is nice, do you know, I have not had anyone to talk to for, oh I don't know how long. You must tell me all the news from the world. The last I heard, Osiris had just married his sister Isis, how's that going?'

'I think they're both dead now.'

'Well, I'm not surprised. Killed each other, did they? I never thought that would work out, a beautiful girl, but what a bitch.'

'Um, it was a long time ago.'

'Oh, tell me about it, I expect a lot of things have changed.'

'Oh, yes, you could say that.'

'Well, you must tell me all about it.'

Tamar interrupted. 'Well, we'd love to, but you see, we're on this quest ...'

'Not unless you can get past me, you're not.'

'And how do we do that?' asked Stiles.

'Shan't tell.'

'He's supposed to ask a riddle,' said Tamar, 'and if we guess right, he has to let us pass.'

'And what happens if we get it wrong?'

'Guess.'

'Oh right.'

'Of course, we can choose not to answer the riddle at all, and go back in safety. He can't touch us. But the catch is you only get one guess, you have to get it right first time.'

'Okay, but there's no harm in hearing the riddle, is there?'

'Oh no.'

The sphinx yawned. 'All right, clever clogs, so you know the drill, but I've decided, I'm not going to ask the riddle.'

'*What*?' said Tamar, aghast. 'But you *have* to.'

'No I don't. Make me. No, I'm bored; I want someone to talk to.'

Tamar glared at him. 'You're kidding.'

'No, besides do you really want to go across that?' He indicated the vast desert behind him. 'You probably won't survive anyway. Wouldn't it be much nicer to stay here with me and have a nice chat?

'But – but.' Tamar was lost for words.

'Look,' said the sphinx. 'I can make it nice and hospitable for you.' An hotel appeared out of nowhere.

'Oooh,' said Cindy.

'It's just a mirage,' scoffed Tamar.

'It's as real as you want it to be,' said the sphinx. 'Go on, check out the facilities.'

'You know, maybe ...' Cindy began, 'or no, maybe not.' She finished lamely, as Tamar glared at her. 'Except, well – we don't *all* have to go on, do we?' she added hurriedly, then looked at the ground.

Tamar thought for a moment. 'You really want to stay?'

'Well, he's not going to ask the riddle unless at least one of us does,' Cindy pointed out.

'But what about your promise to Hecaté?'

'Oh, um well I ...'

'I could stay,' piped up Eugene.

'You?' said the sphinx. 'You don't have any news; you've been here almost as long as I have.'

'What about me?' said Cindy. 'Would you at least ask the riddle, if I agree to stay?'

The sphinx considered. 'We-ell, I suppose so.'

'What about ...?' Tamar hissed.

'I've decided, that this quest is too important,' said Cindy. 'Besides, after your noble behaviour over that dragon business, I think I can trust you.'

'I'll stay too,' offered Eugene. 'I may not have been out in the world, but I managed to keep the library pretty much up to date, I have a lot to talk about.'

'What about you?' Tamar asked Stiles. 'Do you want to stay too; I bet the bar is pretty well stocked.'

'Very funny, I'll come with you, if the sphinx agrees.'

They looked at him; he hesitated.

'It that or we all just walk away,' said Tamar.

'Done!' said the sphinx.

'And we have been,' muttered Stiles.

'You two can go, if you must. But I warn you, they call it the desert of dread. There are no shortcuts, it's ten days across, and no water, are you sure you wouldn't rather ...? No? All right then, off you go.'

'Um,' began Tamar.

'What?' the sphinx said, testily.

'The riddle?' said Stiles.

'Oh yes, forget my head next.'

'Do we really need to?' asked Tamar. 'You've already agreed to let us go.'

She walked past the sphinx and was stopped by an invisible barrier.

The sphinx laughed. 'You can't buck tradition,' he said.

He cleared his throat. 'What's black and white and red all

over?'

'What?' said Tamar. 'That's it?'

'A stabbed nun,' said Stiles.

Tamar groaned.

The sphinx nodded. 'That'll do,' he said. 'I would also have accepted "newspaper".'

They looked at each other.

'Well, off you go then,' suggested the sphinx.

Tamar and Stiles turned to Cindy and Eugene.

'Well, goodbye then.'

'Goodbye, and good luck,' said Cindy.

'Yes, good luck, it's been very nice to know you,' said Eugene.

They turned to go, Stiles turned back to the sphinx. 'Doesn't everybody solve that riddle?' he asked.

'It's usually much harder,' said the sphinx. 'But I thought, what's the point?'

'Oh I see.'

As they walked away, the sphinx could hear them arguing.

'A stabbed nun? What's the matter with you? *Everybody* knows it's a newspaper.'

'That was the one I learned when I was a kid, besides it worked didn't it?'

'You must have had a very strange childhood, that's all I can say.'

'You can talk.'

The sphinx smiled and turned to Cindy. 'Now,' he said, 'tell me all about the world. Who's ruling Egypt these days?'

* * *

Denny was sinking. The loneliness, in his current state of mind, was driving him mad. He would even have welcomed Peirce as someone to talk to, or even Miles, his horrible bullying brother (a man built like a brick outhouse and with the same approximate intelligence) and his squawking wife, what was it Cynthia? Selina? Something like that. Breaking vampires in half just was not as much fun anymore. Once or twice he had seriously considered using the power of the witch to join them on the quest, but how the hell would he explain it?

He had started drinking heavily, but it did not help, the dreams were not getting any better, and lately, he was seeing another face, the mincing vampire from his captivity, mocking him. He had tried to find out who he was, but without success, he wondered if he might not be Ran-Kur himself. What had he said? 'No, not *your* god.' What did *that* mean?

He sighed and went out. He ended up at a notorious nightclub that the vampires had been frequenting lately. *Keep working,* that was the answer, hope that it would distract him, until they came back and they could finish this thing. *She'll be back soon, she's okay; you couldn't kill her with a sledgehammer.*

He leaned against the bar, staring moodily at the throng, he found it easy to spot the vampires these days, they were so badly dressed, besides he could see the void where their souls should be. They made up about two thirds of the crowd. Wouldn't it just be easier to lock the doors and set the place on fire? But he did not want it to be easy; he wanted to keep busy.

A pretty girl sidled up to him; this was becoming a more common occurrence; he really had that mean and moody thing working for him lately. He glanced at her; she was human – no question, he turned away. She moved to the other side of him. 'Hi,' she said, brightly. 'I'm Laura.'

Denny took a closer look at her; she really was very pretty, nothing compared to Tamar, of course, but then, Tamar was not here. For a moment he was tempted. He had been so lonely lately; it would be a distraction. He shoved the thought away.

'You should go home,' he told her. 'This isn't a nice place, and I'm not a nice person.'

She pouted. 'I like it here,' she said.

'Don't you think it's dangerous for you to pick up strange men in bars?' he asked her.

She looked at him as if he was speaking in an alien language. 'Suit yourself,' she said and stalked away.

'She's going to get herself killed,' he thought. He glanced around; the place was full of young women, dancing and drinking. 'They're making it too easy,' he thought. But he understood the loneliness that drove them, the hope that they might meet just one nice guy, men felt the same, at least he had. 'But you don't meet nice guys in a dive like this.'

He kept an eye on Laura; she was dancing now with some bloke; she seemed okay – for now.

He drained his beer; the club would be closing soon, time to go to work. He stationed himself by the door outside. He caught two a male and female, each with a supine prospective victim, then he heard a scream, as he rounded the corner, he saw Laura, in the grip of a vampire. She was putting up a vigorous fight, but there was already blood on her neck. Denny grabbed the vampire, flung it against the wall and staked it; it exploded in a shower of ash.

Laura was shaking; Denny took her by the shoulders, gently. 'Are you okay?' he asked.

She looked at him. 'It's you,' she said in surprise. 'You saved me. I thought you were a jerk. Thank you.'

'No problem. I warned you; this is not a nice place.'

'What was that *thing*?'

Denny hesitated, then he thought 'no point in pretending.' perhaps it would be better if people knew.

'That was a vampire,' he told her and waited for the scorn and disbelief.

'That's what I thought,' she said, surprising him. 'And you? You're like a vampire hunter?'

'That's one way of putting it. The city's lousy with them, you'd be better off at home.'

'Oh, don't worry, I've learned my lesson.'

He smiled. 'Good, now how about I walk you home?'

At Laura's front door, she stared awkwardly at his shoes for a moment, then ... 'How can I ever thank you?' she said, lifting her face up to his, and looking him dreamily in the eyes.

Denny patted her on the shoulder. 'Stay alive,' he said and walked away.

* * *

The Desert of Dread. Ten days across, no shortcuts and no water. Tamar decided it was time to "fess up".

'My powers aren't exactly on top form here,' she said.

'They keep cutting out on me, as if there's something interfering with them, and it's got worse since we entered the desert for some reason. I just thought you ought to know before it's too late to turn back.' she waited.

'Oh I noticed that,' said Stiles airily. 'What *aren't* you telling me?'

Tamar was genuinely impressed. 'Oh you *are* good,' she said. 'Don't you ever miss *anything*?'

Stiles shrugged. 'I might do,' he said, 'but not this time, what's up?'

'It isn't anything important,' she said. 'At least not as far as the quest is concerned. It's just that ... I'm not dangerous here. You know to – Denny – for example.'

Stiles nodded. 'You mean you could touch him without burning away his insides or whatever?'

'Yes,'

'I see,' said Stiles thoughtfully. 'I see.'

They had decided to travel at night, when it was colder, and slept during the day when they would dig a hole and hide from the blistering sun.

Tamar was morose; she was not sleeping, she did not really need to, but she wished she could, the long hours while Stiles slept gave her too much time to think.

It was the third night, and they sat on a convenient rock to rest for a while and eat and drink. Food and water, as it turned out, was not a problem, with Tamar on hand (even if she *could* only manifest egg sandwiches). But she sat silently and ate nothing.

'You miss him, don't you?' said Stiles.

Tamar sighed.

'I know how you feel, I still miss Mary, my wife, you know? At least you know you'll see him again.'

'If we ever get out of here.'

Stiles nodded. 'That's the question, isn't it?'

He glanced at her; she looked so miserable, and unusually vulnerable. He reached out and put his arm around her, she leaned in. 'Tamar,' he murmured. He brushed her hair off her face and then suddenly he was kissing her.

She pushed him away. 'I can't,' she said. 'Don't get me wrong, if things were different – I *do* like you, but ...'

'It *is* safe isn't it?' said Stiles. 'You said ...'

'It isn't that,' she said.

'You love *him*.' It was not a question.

'Yes.'

'I'm sorry, I just thought ... well, what you said. We might never get out of here, and you're lonely and I'm lonely. He need never know. Would it really be so bad to take some comfort in each other?'

'No, it wouldn't. It really wouldn't. But how can *I* take comfort, when *he* has none?'

Stiles' face burned. 'You're right, I hadn't thought of it like that.'

'I could never betray him, he'd know, and it would kill him.'

'I know. He loves you.'

'And you don't, you know,' she told him.

'No,' Stiles admitted, in some surprise. 'I don't. I thought maybe I did, but I just realized, when you said it, you're right. You're very special, but you're not "the one".'

Tamar smiled wistfully.

'You know,' he said, after some thought. 'I reckon we'll get out of here, if anyone can do it, it's you.'

'Liar,' she said. But she smiled. 'Come on, miles to go, and all that.'

They went on their way, both feeling considerably lighter.

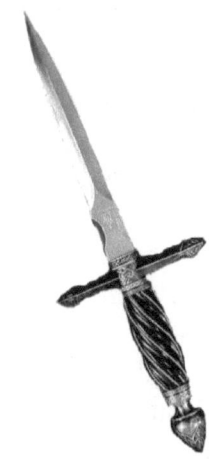

~ Chapter Twenty Seven ~

THE DESERT ENDED abruptly in a hazy shimmer, beyond which appeared to be a forest. It had taken them a week to get there.

'You see,' said Stiles, 'we're ahead of schedule.'

'Do we just walk through, do you think?'

'You're asking *me*? I thought you were the expert.'

Tamar shrugged. 'Not really, Cindy's better at this stuff.'

'Well, Cindy's not here, so make a decision.'

'I'll go first.' She walked through and shivered. 'Oooh it's cold.' But she seemed fine. Stiles followed.

It was a relief after the desert to see so much that was green and verdant; the forest was lush and colourful and so cool and shady compared to the white hot scorching desert.

Through the mist, they saw a large figure with antlers coming toward them. They held their breath, until it came into view.

'*Hank*?' gasped Tamar, in disbelief.

Stiles gaped. 'You *know* this guy?'

Tamar nodded. 'We go way back.'

'Well, well, well, Tamar the Black as I live and breathe,' said Hank, enveloping her in a breathtaking bear hug. 'What the devil are you doing coming in this way?'

'Feeling like an idiot, if you must know, we're looking for the Purple Hart.'

'Yes? Well you came to the right place.'

'You mean he's *here*?'

'Yes, yes, he's here.'

'You mean I went through all that, when I could have just ...'

'No, no, you have to do the labyrinth; it's a test, well, a series of tests really. You can't just waltz into the forest and ask for an introduction.'

'But you never told me.'

'Well, no, I'm not supposed to, I *am* the guardian of the forest. It's my duty to protect it and him.'

Tamar slapped her head. 'Of course, I should have realised. You're the last guardian.'

'And who is this?' asked Hank, indicating Stiles. 'What happened to the other one, the skinny one? Not that this one has much meat on him either.'

'This is Jack Stiles, and frankly Hank, Arnold Schwarzenegger would look skinny compared to you.'

'Arnold who?'

'Ajax then.'

'Oh him, I remember him.'

'So, what do we have to do to get past you?' she asked, giving him a winning smile.

'Oh no you don't,' said Hank. 'I can't bend the rules, even for you.'

'Worth a try,' she said, ruefully.

'Actually the final test is this way, come on.' He led them into the forest.

'So, how is Danny?' he asked conversationally, as they walked.

'Denny.'

'Whatever. How come he's not with you?'

'The old witch wouldn't let him come,' said Tamar

grumpily.

'Ah, I see, that makes more sense, I didn't figure Derry for a coward. Still I can't see why she would do that. Funny things, witches.'

'Yes.'

'Denny knows this guy too?' Stiles was having trouble taking all this in.

'We met last year; it was last year, wasn't it.' Hank scratched his head.

'I think so, it seems longer.'

Hank led them into a sunlit glade. 'Here we are,' he said.

Out of the trees stalked a huge deer. It was indeed purple, with golden antlers. They bowed automatically. It inclined its head and gazed steadily at them.

'What's the final test?' said Tamar out of the corner of her mouth.

'Oh there isn't one,' said Hank. 'That was the desert. I'm just here to guide you, if I deem you worthy. And frankly I wouldn't dare otherwise.'

'I – I see. Um, what now?'

Hank handed her a dagger. 'Kill the Hart. You came for its blood didn't you?'

Tamar took the dagger from him slowly and approached the Hart. She raised the dagger, her hand shaking. The Hart did not move a muscle; it continued to stare steadily at her. She dropped the dagger and fell on her knees. 'I – I can't,' she said.

Stiles let out his breath.

'He won't stop you. I never had *you* down as a coward either,' said Hank.

'It's not that, it's wrong. I can't be a murderer.'

'What about all the lives you will save, if you stop Ran-Kur?'

'It doesn't balance out. Nothing justifies murder.'

'So, why did you come here? You knew what you were coming for didn't you?'

'I – I didn't think, I didn't realise. I'm sorry I can't do it.' She stabbed the dagger into the ground defiantly.

The Hart suddenly changed into a man and stood up. 'You

have passed the final test,' he said, in a booming voice.

Tamar gasped. 'W – What?'

The man smiled. 'One, who would take my blood by force, would only bring death upon himself – *herself,* I should say in the present case. Only one pure of heart can wield the power to kill a god. You have proved yourself, that your intentions are pure. Now you may ask of me what you have suffered so much to find.'

'I – I need your blood to kill Ran-Kur, but I can't ask it of you.'

The man nodded. 'I know of this scourge. Many innocent lives have been lost, and there will be many more. You *must* ask.'

'You won't have to die, will you?'

'Only a few drops will be needed, but how can I know for certain?'

'I – I ...'

'How many more must die, before you find your courage? Ask.'

Tamar bit her lip. 'Forgive me,' she said. 'But may I please have a few drops of your blood to save my world?'

'You may.' And so saying, he took the dagger and sliced it across his palm; he let the blood drip onto the blade. 'Take this dagger,' he said. 'And plunge it into the heart of the evil one. It will kill him instantly. If you miss the heart, death will come, but it will take longer, and he will assuredly try to take you with him if you give him time.'

'At least he'll be gone.'

'And so will you, a needless death. Heed my words; your work in the world is not done yet. You will be needed.'

Tamar bowed her head.

The Hart took her chin in his hands and raised her face to his. 'Be careful,' he told her.

'I will,' she answered a little impatiently.

He released her and stood back – he seemed slightly fidgety, he crossed and uncrossed his arms a few times and cleared his throat, rubbed his nose and seemed about to speak several times, but always stopped himself.

Tamar frowned, but Stiles knew what these symptoms meant. 'Oh, no,' he thought, 'he's going to ask her ...'

'I don't suppose you might consider coming back someday,' asked the Hart, nervously, 'for a – um – social visit maybe?' and he smoothed his hair self-consciously.

Tamar gaped.

'Well, we need to be getting back,' interrupted Stiles meaningfully. '*Denny* will be worrying about you!' he tugged on Tamar's arm.

Behind them, they heard Hank sniggering.

Tamar recovered herself and, standing on her considerable dignity, she said. 'If I were not already spoken for ...'

The Hart interrupted. 'I see,' he said, 'Well, I wish you luck, and remember my warning.'

And the forest vanished. They were home.

'He did go wanking on, didn't he?' asked Stiles.

* * *

Denny was startled when for a moment, a forest appeared in the living room, and he thought he saw Hank waving at him. Then he saw Tamar.

'Denny,' she squealed. 'How are you, what have you been doing?'

Denny grinned. 'Oh this and that, you know, cleaning up the streets, Wombling free.'

'Nutter,' she said affectionately and threw her arms around him.

Stiles sloped off into the other room smiling.

* * *

'Do you get the feeling, there's something we're supposed to be doing?' asked Denny lazily.

Tamar sat up abruptly. 'Oh my god, Ran-Kur.'

'Oh, I completely forgot,' said Denny. 'I finished the potion; I thought it would save time, when you got back, well, it was a good idea at the time.'

'You finished it? But the ingredients ...'

'Yes I went for them. Well I had nothing better to do, in between chasing down vampires. I thought I should make myself useful.'

'You're quite handy really, aren't you?'

'I try,' he said, modestly.

'Might I suggest, that we don't summon him here,' he added thoughtfully.

'Why?'

'Well, I did some research, and he's quite – *big*. I think an open space might be more appropriate.'

'What would I do without you?'

* * *

'We thought we might do some tidying up,' said Stiles, when Tamar and Denny emerged.

'Cindy?' said Tamar in amazement, 'and Eugene?'

'They arrived just after us,' said Stiles.

'The desert and the sphinx and everything just vanished suddenly,' said Cindy. And we were at my house, so we thought we should come here, in case you needed any help or anything.'

'Also, we're dying to know how it all turns out,' admitted Eugene.

Tamar shook her head. 'Oh, Denny, this is Eugene, I told you about him. Eugene this is Denny.'

They shook hands, perfunctorily.

Then Tamar spotted the new statue. 'What's that?' she asked.

'Oh nothing.'

'The question, surely, is *who* is that?' said Cindy.

Denny glared at her; she quailed but continued staunchly. 'I'm a witch; we can tell the difference, you know, between a statue and a person who has been turned to stone; the look of surprise on the face is a dead give-away for one thing.'

Tamar peered at the statue. 'My god,' she exclaimed. 'It's the landlord. Denny, what did you do?'

Denny shrugged carelessly. 'I didn't hurt him. He turned up, and I sort of – panicked, and then … well, how do I undo it without him wondering what the hell happened?'

Tamar laughed. 'I'll sort it out,' she said. 'I'll modify his memory; he won't remember a thing, a dose of the flu that's what happened to him, nothing more.'

'Oh good,' said Denny. 'I can't think of anyone who deserves it more. '

He's a bit of a swine,' said Tamar to Stiles, Cindy and Eugene, who were looking dumbfounded.

'I'm glad you could come up with something,' said Denny. 'I was hoping you would. I had no idea what to do with him.'

~ Chapter Twenty Eight ~

THEY FOUND TAMAR in the empty street, looking grim. She had already thrown the potion. The dagger was tucked into the back of her belt.

'What the hell is she doing?' said Denny.

Stiles laid a restraining arm on his shoulder. 'I think she feels she has to do this alone,' he said. 'She'll be okay; she knows what she's doing. She's ready.'

Denny subsided; he nodded. Much as he hated to admit it, Stiles was right. There was nothing he could do, except watch.

They all watched.

'RAN-KUR THE INVADER – RAN-KUR THE DESTRUCTOR – I SUMMON THEE. COME FORTH AT MY COMMAND. REVEAL THYSELF. BE SEEN AND PERISH.'

'I think she added that last part herself,' said Denny. Only to realise that he was addressing a woman that he had never seen before. Tamar's thundering tones had attracted a small audience of surviving locals.

'What is it,' said the woman, 'some sort of street theatre?'

Denny did not know what to say. Fortunately he was spared the necessity of answering as at that moment Ran-Kur chose to make his appearance in an impressive thunderclap and firework display. There was some scattered clapping. Ran-Kur bowed slightly. Gods are like this.

'Oooh its good isn't it?' said the woman, nudging her neighbour.

Ran-Kur was a pretty impressive figure. Around twenty feet tall, he was cloaked and hooded in black from head to toe (or at least from head to the ground.) All that was visible of his features were two glowing red orbs, in the approximate place where you might normally expect to find his eyes.

'PERISH?' he thundered. 'DO YOU KNOW WHO I AM? YOU INSECT! HOW IS IT POSSIBLE THAT YOU, SMALL CREATURE, HAVE SUCH ARROGANCE? I WILL CRUSH YOU, AS I HAVE SO MANY OTHERS BEFORE YOU. AND IT SHALL BE SLOW, SO THAT YOU MAY SEE HOW MANY OTHERS I SHALL KILL BEFORE YOU DIE.'

'He likes the sound of his own voice, doesn't he?' said Stiles.

Denny was silent; he was worried. If it went wrong all these nosy people would die. They would probably all die, even Tamar.

Ran-Kur was growing, thirty feet, forty, fifty. Tamar stood her ground and did nothing, except watch silently. Ran-Kur reached down and plucked her off the ground.

The spectators were watching in terrified horror. This was more than they had bargained for.

Tamar was lifted high into the air; Ran-Kur continued to grow.

Denny was panicked. 'She's stuck,' he said. 'Her arms are pinned; she can't reach the dagger.'

'If she can survive being swallowed by a dragon, she can get out of this,' said Stiles. He sounded calm, but Denny noticed that his knuckles were white.

'Swallowed by a ...?'

'Oh, er, she didn't tell you?'

Ran-Kur was now seventy feet tall at least. He held Tamar out in front of him on his palm, as he brought her closer to look at her, 'I am the mighty Ran-Kur,' he said in relatively quiet, but still rather pompous tones, 'that you, puny mortal have dared to summon, now you shall pay the price. My name, it means "ill feeling" and "spite".'

'Yes, I know.'

Ran-Kur lapsed into normal speech for a second. 'Oh, you speak Demon then?' he asked interestedly.

'No, it means the same thing in human.'

'Does it now? Well there's a thing.'

Tamar saw her chance. She crossed her fingers the dagger seemed pitifully small now, and leapt sliding down the robes and plunged the dagger into the chest as far as it would go. As she did so, she felt all her strength ebb out of her, she let go of the robes as Ran-Kur gave a shudder and fell.

As she hurtled through the air, powerlessly, she thought, 'at least it worked.'

'She's falling,' cried Denny. 'Something's wrong.' And ignoring the death throes of Ran-Kur, he shot into the air to catch her. Before he could reach her, she hit her head on a jutting parapet, by the time he had caught her, she was unconscious and bleeding freely from her head.

'I'll carry her,' he said fiercely to Stiles, as the latter moved forward to help.

The crowd of people watching stepped aside for him to pass, watching in silent sympathy, at his stricken face. As they walked away, neither Denny nor Stiles noticed the sinister figures of the vampires emerging from the shadows.

* * *

'Can you help her?' Denny asked the doctor on call at casualty. 'I think I should warn you that a "no" at this point, would not be beneficial to your career,' he added threateningly.

Tamar was lying on a stretcher, white and still, her breathing was shallow. Denny had never seen her like this. It was terrifying; the more so because in his worst nightmares, he had never imagined that something like this could happen to her. Not to *Tamar*.

'It's a bad head wound,' the doctor said phlegmatically. 'We'll do what we can.'

As she was wheeled away, Tamar opened her eyes. 'Denny,' she whispered.

'I'm here.'

'I'm sorry.'

'Sorry? What for? You got him.'

'I meant for – for dragging you into this … f – farce I call my life, I shouldn't have.' She was gasping, her breathing ragged.

'Don't talk rubbish; you're going to be fine.'

'Liar.' She managed a grim smile.

He realised that he had never told her. Of course, she knew, but he had never said the words to her. 'I love you,' he said. And for a moment, he looked like his old self again, even his hair was back to flopping in his eyes, although this might have been due to his recent exertions.

She reached up and brushed it back gently. 'I know that,' she said, 'fool.'

'Christ,' she added, 'it *must* be bad.'

He shook his head mutely, as she passed out again.

* * *

Tamar opened her eyes and was surprised to find that she was apparently floating. She felt fine; wonderful in fact sort of light-headed and dreamy – *good drugs these.* Then she saw him, a sinister robed figure sitting cross legged and apparently at his ease but floating in front of her about three feet in the air. Lying negligently across his knees was a large farm instrument of some type and he was reading – a novel apparently entitled 'The Passion of Lucille'. The cover was of the lurid "Bodice ripper" type, featuring a nubile yet over-developed woman in a nightie in the arms of a well-muscled werewolf – well he was extremely hirsute anyway, too much so for Tamar's taste. The figure never looked up; he was apparently thoroughly absorbed in its contents.

Tamar was fascinated. Whatever her expectations of the afterlife had been – and she had not really dwelt on it much –

the last thing she had envisioned was to meet the grim reaper (she knew him from his pictures) passing the time before she passed on by reading a romantic novel. The fact that she had obviously died was, to her mind, the least of her problems.

She was also a little put-out by his obvious indifference to her predicament.

'It's all very well to him I suppose,' she thought, 'all in a day's work.' Tamar was not inclined to take the matter so lightly. 'Ahem,' she ventured.

The spectre looked up, embarrassed, and secreted the book hurriedly in his robes somewhere. 'So sorry,' he said. 'I didn't realise it was that time already.'

'Don't mind me,' she said, caustically. 'Take your time, *I'm* in no hurry, I'm just dead, no big deal.'

The reaper checked his watch. 'Thought so,' he said. 'You're early, so there's no need to get snippy.'

'I'm dead,' she retorted. 'I'll be as "snippy" as I like. How would you feel?'

The reaper grinned. 'Ah well,' he said. 'As to that, you're not, not yet anyway – it's not your time yet …'

'All right, so I'm early, in a few minutes I'll be dead, it's all the same thing to me.'

'No, no, you misunderstand. You're early for our little meeting is all. This is what they call a near-death experience, the latest thing in popular theology apparently. And this is about, as near to Death – that's me – as you're likely to get without actually crossing over ha ha, little joke there – no? Oh well, it's playing merry hell with my schedule if you want to know the truth, they never had any of this nonsense in the old days, you either lived or died end of story, but you have to keep up with the times, so they tell me.'

'It's a fad,' said Tamar. 'You know what humans are like.' Now that she knew that she was not dead, she had recovered her equanimity with astonishing speed.

'A fad, yes, I suppose so, well I'll just have to …'

'So, is there any point to this meet and greet, or am I just going to go back in there,' she pointed to herself lying on the hospital stretcher looking wan and battered. 'God, I look terrible.'

'The point? Ah well yes... caught me off guard a bit, sorry about that, rather spoils the drama doesn't it? You were supposed to feel the awe and solemnity of the occasion, but I don't suppose you would have anyway, not *you!* I daresay you've seen stranger things than me in your time, eh? Anyway, I'm here to offer you a choice – you can continue your life from this point on or you can have a new life – in the same body of course – but without the powers and responsibilities not to mention enemies that you have now.'

'Do you always offer people this choice?'

'No you're a special case.'

'No powers?'

'That's right.'

'Is this a test?'

The reaper looked awkward. 'Well now, you can hardly expect me to answer that, can you?'

'I'll take that as a yes. Okay, it doesn't matter anyway; I don't see that I have much of a choice really, no matter what you say. I have to go back to who I was otherwise people are going to die, aren't they?'

'Are you sure? This is a chance to change your destiny. To start again, a clean slate, no consequences I promise.'

'Not for me maybe, besides, destiny's a load of bull anyway. I've made my decision – if this isn't an hallucination brought on by the drugs.'

The reaper smiled. 'You know better than that,' he said. 'So be it,' he added, in a voice that made her shudder. He handed her a packet bearing the legend "Not to be opened until …"

'Until when?' she said. But he had gone. His voice floated across the aether to her, 'See you in hell.' His head re-appeared in mid-air like the Cheshire cat, but not as scary. 'Oops, I shouldn't have said that,' he grinned then he vanished again, this time for good.

* * *

'What the hell went wrong?' said Stiles, as they waited.

Denny shook his head.

'I thought she could fly,' said Cindy. 'I've *seen* her fly.'

'*I* thought she was invulnerable,' said Denny. 'Just goes to show, doesn't it. Now shut up.'

Cindy backed away nervously. Denny had gone from intimidating to terrifying.

The doctor reappeared. Denny leaped to his feet.

'She's stable,' the doctor informed him.

'Don't give me that bollocks,' said Denny menacingly. 'Tell me how she is.'

The doctor backed away involuntarily. 'She's still unconscious but ...'

'Doctor, doctor,' a breathless nurse appeared. 'You have to see this, the patient with the head trauma, if I didn't know better, I'd swear someone had switched patients on us, I've never seen anything like it.'

'What are you babbling about?' said the doctor, irritably. But Denny knew, he barged past the doctor and the nurse and a flustered orderly and into the post op. Tamar was sitting up, looking fine.

'Thank God!' he said, putting his arms around her while he still could. 'I told you, you weren't going to die.'

Tamar's fingers closed on the packet in her hand; she smiled to herself – she thought she could guess what it was. 'Thank God you were wrong,' she said.

'What?'

'Nothing, never mind.'

'We have to get out of here,' she said unromantically, 'before I get written up as a miracle.'

Cue the comic interlude with much dressing up as orderlies and running around with stretchers. Oh no, wait, they could teleport. Denny drew the curtains around the bed. Put it down as another mysterious disappearance.

* * *

Tamar had no good explanation as to why her powers had failed her, but she did tell them that it had happened just as the dagger went in. 'As if he was sucking the life out of me,' she said.

'The Hart did say he would try to take you with him,' said

Stiles. 'He must have realised what was happening.'

'Well he's gone now,' said Tamar with satisfaction,

'So why's it still all dark?' asked Cindy. She had not wanted to bring this up; it did rather spoil the party atmosphere.

'It's as if nothing's changed,' said Stiles.

'It's true,' said Denny. 'The vampires are still out in full force.'

'So, what can we do?' said Tamar.

There was a silence. Denny was frowning. He had been thinking about this and he thought he understood. He had been hoping that the darkness would suddenly clear, that he was wrong, but it was time to face facts.

'I think we have to face the fact, that it's not over,' he said reluctantly. 'There's another. Someone else is behind this. Ran-Kur was just a front, a patsy.'

'Where do you get that from?' said Stiles. 'How do you know the vampires haven't just decided to stay here because they like it?'

'What about the darkness?' said Cindy.

'Exactly,' said Denny. 'Vampires *can* control the weather, but not on this scale, not without help. And anyway, this darkness is something else.'

'But what makes you think there's someone else behind all this?' persisted Stiles.

'It came to me in a dream,' said Denny. 'And I think I might even know who it is. Time to wake up Peirce.'

Part Three : The Reckoning

~ Chapter Twenty Nine ~

THE 'MASTER' was delighted. All was going according to plan; these heroic types were so predictable. It was a shame that Tamar had survived. On the other hand, it would be more fun to kill her, himself. He had suspected all along that he would have to, he quite relished the idea. Then again, an eternity of torture – even better. And she would suffer the worst kind of torture, the mental kind, knowing that she had brought it all on herself, and her friends and her lover. It would kill her – she was so arrogant – to know that she had made the biggest mistake of them all. He rubbed his hands together. If only they would hurry up. Still he had waited this long, he could be patient, if he attempted to interfere now, it could ruin everything. She was not stupid; she just was not as clever as she thought she was.

* * *

'You can't think that *Peirce* is behind this,' said Tamar.

'I don't,' said Denny. 'But he's in deep. He knows what's really going on, I'm sure of it.'

'And if he doesn't?'

'At least he knows where we can find the one who is. He'll tell us if I have to beat it out of him.'

Denny explained, about the dreams he had been having about the "vampire" he had met in the old house. 'It's him, I'm sure of it; I keep seeing him, mocking me.'

'Do we really need Peirce?' asked Tamar. 'If you're so sure it's the house you went to, can't we just go there and see?'

'Don't you think I've tried that? It must be shielded or something; I can't find it; I was asleep when they took me there.'

'What about focussing on the vampire himself?'

'If he *is* a vampire. And no, I can't, he must be shielded too. Like Peirce said, "better protected than a school girls diary". It just makes me more certain that he's the one we're after'

'But how can it be?' objected Stiles. 'Ran-Kur definitely *was* a god, wasn't he, and that definitely *was* Ran-Kur wasn't it?

'Yes it was,' said Tamar. 'The summoning was absolutely specific.'

'So, what could make a patsy out of a god?'

'There *are* things more powerful than gods,' said Tamar. 'Besides, all he would have to do is use Ran-Kur's name, it's been done before.'

Stiles had to concede this. 'So, we're sure, then?' he said.

Tamar nodded. 'I think Denny's right.' She looked at Denny. 'But Peirce?' she said. 'I don't like it, I don't trust him.'

'How else are we going to find that house again?' challenged Denny.

'Well, - I – no, I got nothing.'

'Excuse me,' said Eugene, 'but who *is* Peirce?'

'In the bottle,' said Cindy. 'I told you. I never saw him, myself. But I heard all about it. He's a vampire, remember? I told you.'

'Oh yes, Peirce, ha, ha, good name for a vampire.'

'Why?' said Cindy, blankly.

'Because, pierce, vampires pierce ... and you kill them by ... never mind.'

'It's a good job she's pretty,' he said in an aside to Stiles.

'Can we get back to the point?' said Denny, impatiently. 'Peirce?'

'Oh let him out,' said Tamar. 'I want this finished.'

Peirce, naturally enough was not inclined to be helpful.

'Why should I?' he said. 'You put me in a *bottle.*'

Denny smacked him. 'Keep talking,' he said. 'I could do this all day.'

Peirce began to change back into fog. Denny clapped a jar over him.

'Try that again,' he said when he released him, 'and we'll leave you in bits all over the world.'

'He's scary,' said Eugene to Cindy.

Cindy nodded. 'Attractive, though – if you like bad boys. Which I don't,' she added hurriedly.

Peirce subsided. 'Okay, I'll behave,' he said, mutinously. Bastard!'

Denny grinned, wolfishly. 'You'd better believe it. I'm just getting started.'

Tamar produced the sketch she had done from Denny's description. 'Who is he?' she asked.

'I don't know.'

'Try again,' said Denny, suddenly producing the Athame.

Peirce baulked. 'Where the hell did you get *that*?'

'I'm sorry; I thought *we* were asking the questions.'

'All right, all right! I've never seen him, but I think he's the one they call the "Master".'

'And the big country house, where is it?'

'What, you want me to draw you a map? I can't.'

'But you can take us there.' It was not a question.

Peirce shrugged then squealed as the Athame dug into his neck. 'Yes, Yes I could.'

Tamar made like the good cop. 'Look, think about it, this is the one who's been using the prophecy to control all the vampires. He's the one who's been masquerading as Ran-Kur. You want to take him down as much as we do.'

'Cut it out,' said Peirce. 'I don't have much choice, do I?' He indicated Denny. 'Just keep *him* away from me.'

'Even vampires are afraid of him,' said Eugene, with a hint of wistful admiration in his voice.

Peirce looked around him. 'So, who are these two?' he asked. 'Are they coming too?'

Cindy and Eugene looked at each other. 'Yes,' they said, decisively.

Denny suppressed a groan.

~ Chapter Thirty ~

IT WAS BECOMING increasingly clear that Cindy and Eugene were becoming something of an item, and Stiles felt that he had gone from being a third wheel to a fifth wheel, despite the fact that Peirce was back in the mix, he did not count, he was dead.

Not that he minded. He was glad that Cindy had someone; many someone's really. Eugene could be any man who took her fancy; he was perfect for Cindy. And he no longer wanted Tamar, but – all this coupledom was making him feel out of place or in the way or something.

* * *

Peirce had led them a merry dance so far, in and out the mulberry bush, so to speak. At least that was how it seemed. He said he was looking for something, but declined to explain what. When pressed (round the windpipe) by Denny, all he would say was 'It's complicated, but I'll know it when I find it.'

Denny suggested that they go back to the train tunnel, where he had been taken from, but Peirce said that it didn't work like that. So far he had taken them to a park, a field and a football stadium. There was a pattern beginning to emerge here. Either they had to be in an open space, or Peirce had a yen for the smell of freshly mown grass.

On the third day (cricket pitch), Peirce finally announced. 'I think this is it.'

'What?' said Denny, now thoroughly sick and tired of Peirce and his magical mystery tour.

'The place, the portal the vampires use to get to the house.'

'Portal?' said Tamar. 'You never mentioned a portal.'

'Does this mean it's in the other dimension?' asked Stiles.

'Oh no,' said Peirce. 'It's just a transportation device, technically we could walk or drive there or even teleport, if I knew where it was, but I don't, none of us do. It's a secret; I don't reckon the "Master" trusts anyone.'

'I wonder why?' said Tamar, sarcastically.

'Okay, so this portal, how come you didn't know where it was.' asked Stiles, suspiciously.

'They move it,' Peirce explained, 'and I'm out of the loop, due to the fact that I spent the last few months in a *bottle!*

'It wasn't that long,' muttered Denny.

'What are you complaining about?' Peirce continued. 'I found it, didn't I?'

'So, how does it work?' asked Tamar.

'Well, we just walk through it of course,' said Peirce as if explaining to a small child, how to use a door.

'I *meant* where the hell is it?' she retorted. 'How do we access it?'

'It's right there,' said Peirce, slowly, pointing at a patch of empty air. He frowned. 'Can't you see it?'

Tamar peered. 'Nope, can't see a thing.'

The others concurred.

'Oh,' said Peirce, clearly nonplussed. 'That's – unexpected. Um, well I guess it doesn't matter, just follow me.'

They made to step forward after him, when their path was blocked by a phalanx of vampires, looking like a gang of rejects from the cast of "Grease" (rejected presumably for being *too* greasy) grinning evilly and swinging baseball bats.

They leered at Peirce. 'We thought you might try this sooner or later – traitor.' The front man, in a studded leather jacket, and with longish oily hair, said.

'You can't kill me,' said Peirce with quavering bravado.

'No, but it's amazing what you can live through.'

Denny was counting under his breath. 'Nineteen, twenty, twenty one, twenty two, three, four, twenty five.' He turned to Tamar. 'I think we can take them,' he said. 'There's only twenty five of them.'

The vampires advanced. 'First we deal with you,' said the front man. 'Then we'll have dinner.' He leered at Tamar. 'I call that one.'

Denny exploded (not literally of course) and a pitched battle began.

'Denny!' called Tamar, 'stop pounding that vampire's head and just stake the damn thing. Cindy needs help, and I'm kind of busy.' She had two of them at arm's length, while they tried futilely to hit her.

A vicious vampire with one eye had Cindy on the ground. Denny dusted his vampire and ran forward; he staked the vampire through the back and landed on top of Cindy. It was possibly the first time she was glad to see him, although this was a view of him she had never expected to experience. Before they had time to feel embarrassed, he was yanked to his feet.

Peirce was having troubles of his own; he was tied to a tree, his head was on fire and six vampires were dancing around him jeering. They stopped suddenly, as Denny fireballed them; he resented doing it, but without Peirce, they could not go through the portal. Peirce burst his bonds (Denny did not intend to waste time untying him) and ran for it.

Stiles stopped him. 'Oh no you don't Sonny Jim,' he said. 'This is your fault.

Stiles's fighting technique of low blows and biting back was effectively decimating the foe; he grabbed Peirce by the collar. 'Who would you rather face, them or him?' He indicated Denny, who was doing unspeakable things to a short vampire, who had only one arm, although he had had two before Denny got his hands on him.

Peirce nodded. 'I take your point,' he gulped.

Eugene's preferred fighting technique was to morph into a dragon, between him and Denny's predilection for throwing fire, the cricket pitch was lit up like the town drunk.

When Denny changed tactics and started turning them to stone, the remaining vampires, who still had their legs attached, gave up and ran for it.

'I quite enjoyed that,' said Denny.

Tamar rolled her eyes. She turned to Peirce. 'I guess someone blew your cover.' She said.

'Well, if you defeat the Master, it won't matter,' he said.

'Doesn't it bother you that one of your "boys" turned you in?'

Peirce shrugged. 'Not really, vampires are not known for their loyalty.'

'That's what's worrying me,' said Tamar. '*You're* a vampire.'

'And you don't trust me, so that's all right.'

'Everyone all right?' said Denny.

There were murmurs of assent; although "all right" is a relative term. They were muddy, bruised and spattered with blood. On the other hand, they had all their respective limbs, and nobody was feeling faint.

'Okay, let's go, Peirce – after you.'

Peirce stepped forward. 'You *really* can't see it?' he asked. 'All right, stay close to me, it's not very big.'

'If it's just here, how is it people don't walk through it by accident?' asked Cindy.

Peirce slapped his head. 'Of course, *that's* why you can't see it, that's obviously the point.'

'What is?'

'That people *do* walk through it by accident.'

'Oh, eeeew.'

They all followed Peirce as closely as they could without actually getting close to him. The portal was a disappointment. They stepped forward and then they were in a wood. Peirce said he could see the wood from the other side.

'I don't remember a wood,' said Denny. 'Are you sure this is the right place?'

'The house is over that way,' Peirce assured him, pointing.

Suddenly the air was split by a resounding horn blast, and the sky was lit up by what appeared to be searchlights.

'What the hell was that?' said Tamar.

'I think we tripped an alarm or something,' said Denny.

'Oh no,' said Peirce. 'That's nothing to do with us; that's just the hunt starting.' He sounded wistful.

'The hunt?' asked Cindy. 'You mean like a foxhunt?'

'I suppose, sort of, that's the general idea, but it's not foxes they're hunting.'

'So, what *do* vampires hunt?'

Peirce gave her a sardonic look. 'Humans,' he said eventually, when she failed to figure it out. 'You see,' he continued, to fill the stony silence that had descended, 'vampires are predators; we hunt in the streets or the villages or whatever. But out here, well it's isolated, so they keep people in cages, cells, sort of like fast food.'

'That's disgusting,' said Cindy.

'Is it?' said Peirce in surprise. 'Any more than battery hens?'

'Yes, these are people, with feelings and loved ones and lives.'

'So, what's the hunt about?' asked Tamar.

'They let some people out and hunt them down, you know for the sport, like humans do with animals. Hunting is our natural instinct. Of course, sometimes they get away, but that's the sport you see?'

'I think I'm going to be sick,' said Tamar.

Cindy looked grimmer than they had ever seen her. 'That's it,' she announced. She drew out some candles from her backpack and set them in a circle around her and sat cross-legged in the centre of them, with her elbows resting on her knees, her hands in the air. The candles levitated around her. She pointed to each one and they lit as she did so. She resumed her position and closed her eyes. 'I'm going to give this one last try,' she said.

What?' asked Tamar.

Cindy was not listening. '*Dea Hecaté audite meus vox*,' (Goddess Hecaté hear my cry) she said. Her eyes snapped open; they were blank, with no iris. '*Cursus dedecor trans divum*,' (Course unseen across the sky) she rasped, in a strange guttural tone, the voice was not her own. '*Retraho id veil of infinitas infinitio nox noctis,*' (Draw back this veil of endless night) *Quod permissum sol solis fulsi videlicet quod perspicuous,*' (And let the sun shine clear and bright).

Silence greeted this strange pronouncement. Cindy closed her eyes, and then opened them again; they were now back to normal.

They waited; Cindy sighed. 'Well. I tried.' And then she was lit by a shaft of sunlight that pierced the trees. Peirce ran for cover beneath a shady oak, as the sky brightened. The sun was out, and it was a beautiful day.

'It worked.' Cindy was delighted. 'I tried it so many times and it didn't.'

'How come *you* never tried that?' Stiles asked Tamar.

'I don't have that kind of power,' Tamar admitted. 'How did you do it?' she asked Cindy.

'I didn't,' said Cindy. 'You are witnessing the power of Hecaté. But it's still only a Band-Aid, a short-term fix, it won't last, and it's only local. But at least that poor sod who's being hunted will get away now. The vampires out there won't last long in this sunlight.'

'And now we have a clear run to the house,' said Denny. 'Nicely done.'

Cindy smiled modestly. 'Thank Hecaté.' she said. 'She answered my call.'

'What are we going to do about *him*?' said Stiles, indicating the shivering Peirce.

'Oh hell,' said Tamar. 'Can't we just leave him?'

Denny was in favour of this plan. But Stiles said that he might come in handy, so Tamar manifested a reflective blanket for him and they set off in the direction of the house.

'How do we get in?' asked Tamar.

'Round the back,' said Denny, anticipating Peirce. 'The cells.'

Peirce nodded. 'It's not guarded.'

The darkness was creeping back as they rounded the house. 'Probably just as well,' said Denny. 'We'll be better hidden.'

'Are you all right, sweetie?' Cindy asked Eugene. 'You've hardly said a word.'

Eugene was as white as a sheet and sweating; he wondered why he had come. It was not as if he was any use. 'I don't seem to have much to contribute,' he said.

'Well, *I'm* glad you're here,' she said.

Eugene gave a weak smile, but he did not really feel much better.

'In here,' said Denny. 'They've kept my room for me.' He indicated a barred window with several of the bars severed. 'How thoughtful.'

They had clambered in awkwardly, before they remembered that there was an easier way – for them at least. The cell door was open; they filed out; the passage was deserted. Most of the cells were occupied, but Denny said they should let them out later, after they had dealt with the "Master".

'Let them out now,' he said, 'and it's a party. Vampires like to hunt, remember? And this place is bound to be full of them.'

'Where are they all then?' said Stiles.

'Maybe they were all out hunting,' said Eugene, hopefully.

'We can't count on that,' said Denny.

'They won't have been,' agreed Peirce. 'Only the privileged few get to hunt.'

'So, where are all the commoners?' said Tamar.

They wandered through one deserted passage after another. 'I don't like it,' said Tamar. 'It's too easy.'

Then they heard the singing. It was beautiful. Stiles, in particular, seemed mesmerised. It was coming from a cell further down the corridor.

'Why the hell would anyone be singing in this awful place?' thought Stiles, as he was drawn to the sound. He broke in the door, and there inside was – '*Hecaté?*' Stiles recognised the beautiful witch's goddess from her manifestation in Denny's living room, but there was something different about her, the voice for one thing.

'Have we met?' she asked, in golden tones that made Stiles weak at the knees.

'Don't you remember?' he managed.

Hecaté smiled. 'I'm sure I would have remembered *you*,' she said flatteringly

Tamar appeared. 'It wasn't you, was it,' she said, 'who manifested to us.'

'No I do not think so.' Hecaté frowned in thought.

Tamar met Denny's eyes in a brief moment of communion. They both nodded in unison.

'How long have you been here?' asked Denny glancing again at Tamar.

'Oh a long time, I do not remember.' She held up her wrists. 'These chains are the only things that can hold a god,' she said. 'I remember when they were forged by Hephaestus. Nothing can break them. I am his prisoner forever.'

'I wouldn't be too sure about that,' said Stiles. 'Denny?'

Denny unsheathed the Athame and struck the chains; sparks flew, but the chain remained intact.

'You see,' said Hecaté, sadly. 'Only the one who imprisoned me can release me.'

'How the hell did he get hold of those chains?' said Tamar.

'If *she* didn't manifest that day, then who *did*?' said Stiles.

'The "Master" obviously,' said Denny. 'If we kill him, will it free her?'

'Oh,' said Cindy. 'It must have been he who came to me that day too, in the mirror.'

'I really am going to gag her in a minute,' thought Denny viciously. 'Or cut her throat maybe.'

'We have to free her,' said Stiles, fiercely.

Tamar and Denny were looking at each other, thoughts flashing rapidly between them. Denny nodded. 'We've been set up,' he said out loud.

He turned to the others. 'Eugene, get Cindy out of here. Jack you stay with Hecaté, keep an eye on her, we're going to find this "Master".'

Stiles, Cindy and Eugene all opened their mouths to argue, but Denny's face was set. 'Do it,' he said. 'And don't argue.'

* * *

Left alone with Hecaté, Stiles was tongue-tied; he had never seen anyone like her. Even in chains she exuded a dignity that was extraordinary.

'You should follow your friends,' she said. 'What can you do here?'

'You heard him,' said Stiles. 'You don't argue with Denny.'

'You have the advantage of me,' she said. 'You know my name, but I do not know who you are.'

'Oh, I'm sorry; my name is Jack, Jack Stiles.'

'Then you were very brave to come here, I have heard your name mentioned here. I know who you are.'

Stiles reddened. 'That's precisely why I *did* come here,' he said. 'I prefer to have things out.'

There was a silence in which Stiles fidgeted uncomfortably.

'You wish to go,' observed Hecaté. 'You wish to join the fight, not baby-sit me.'

'No, it's just ...'

'I am not offended,' she assured him. 'It is only natural.'

'I just wish I could do something for you,' he said. 'I hate to see you like this.'

'You do not even know me.'

'I know, but ... You're just so... you – I,' he floundered.

'I like you too,' she said.

Stiles went red again. 'Someone like you shouldn't be chained up,' he said. 'It's wrong.' He grasped the chains in frustration.

* * *

They were barrelling along a corridor, still in silent communication, when suddenly Peirce stopped. 'What?' said Denny, impatiently.

'I can go no further,' said Peirce. 'I am – compromised. You can no longer trust me, at least not for much longer. The influence of the "Master" is taking control of my mind, I can feel it.' He looked at Tamar. 'I want you to succeed,' he said.

'You must leave me behind.'

'Suits me,' said Denny, shoving him into a nearby cell and slamming the door.

'Thanks for the warning,' said Tamar.

'I feel the power emanating from that direction,' said Peirce.

'How do we know you're telling the truth?' pointed out Denny.

Peirce grinned through the bars in the door. 'You don't,' he said.

'We'll just have to risk it,' said Tamar.

Denny brought his face close to Peirce' and stared into his eyes. 'I believe him,' he said, eventually. 'Let's go, we'll let you out later – if we survive.'

'You will,' said Peirce, almost winking at Denny. 'I have this feeling.

'*You,* I'm not so sure about,' he added under his breath, meaning Tamar who was already off and running, and he grinned, evilly. Then he frowned and shook his head as if to clear it. 'Wait!' he called. 'Wait!' But they had gone.

As they rounded the corner, it appeared that Denny had caught up with and overtaken Tamar. He halted and looked back at her. She nodded and stepped in front of him. 'Ladies first,' he said and smiled enigmatically.

'Very funny,' said Tamar frowning.

They burst into the chamber; there was no point in being subtle. The "Master" turned in his chair and smiled sardonically. 'Took you long enough,' he said.

'Askphrit,' said Tamar. There was no surprise in her voice; she sounded as if she were following a badly written script. She waited for the next line.

'Tamar my dear, how delightful to see you again.'

'You've gone too far this time. ' There was no passion in her voice.

Askphrit laughed. 'You have no idea how far I've gone,' he said. He looked at Denny, who nodded. 'Sorry babe,' he said and thrust the Athame under her ribs. 'Actually, I'm not, really,' he added.

She fell to the floor. 'Why?' she gasped.

'I want your power,' he said. He held up the Athame. 'Thanks for this,' he said to Askphrit. 'I guess it was you who gave it to me?'

Askphrit inclined his head, and threw a cage around Tamar. 'She may have lost her power,' he said, 'but you can't be too careful with this one, she has some tricks up her sleeve.'

At this point Stiles burst into the room.

'Jack, don't,' cried Tamar. 'Run for it, Denny's gone dark side on us.'

'What a shock,' said Stiles, as if it was anything but. 'I guess you didn't ...'

Denny casually manifested chains around Stiles and flung him telekinetically into a corner with a gag in his mouth. 'Shut up!' he hissed.

Stiles frowned, trying to understand.

Two burly vampires appeared, holding a struggling Cindy and Eugene.

'Ah,' said Askphrit. 'The gang's all here.'

~ Chapter Thirty One ~

TAMAR WAS STARING at Denny with despair in her eyes. 'What have I done?' she said.

'Ah,' said Askphrit in satisfaction. 'So you *do* understand? You always were a clever girl.'

'Yes, I understand. *I* did this with that foolish wish I made before I set you free.'

'Just to recap,' said Askphrit, 'for those of you just joining us.' Here he nodded to Stiles, Cindy and Eugene. This woman is the reason that you are all in this mess. You don't understand? Well then let me explain. I was a Djinn, and she wished me free, but before that, she made another wish, that this boy,' he indicated Denny, 'would have powers of his own.'

'I thought, I could avoid the consequences,' she sobbed. 'I assumed that you wouldn't be able to interfere and cock it up for him, not after I made you human. My arrogance did this. Denny always said that I didn't know everything.' She looked at Denny. 'I'm so sorry,' she said.

'Hey, don't be sorry for me babe,' said Denny. 'I never felt better.'

'Say that again when you're enduring the fires of hell. A red hot poker up the jacksy puts a different perspective on things, just ask Edward II.'

Denny lit a cigarette with his finger and leaned back, he was still wearing his unnerving grin.

Tamar looked away from him, as if she could not bear it.

'You were not entirely wrong,' said Askphrit to Tamar. 'But my non interference was dependent on my *not* regaining my powers. Which, as you can see, I have'

'You must have opened every bottle in the world,' she retorted.

'Ah ha, ha, no. I considered finding a Djinn, but the possibility was remote, especially with you out there, freeing Djinn all over the place. And as a mortal, I had limited time.'

'So, how *did* you do it, come on, I know you're dying to tell us.'

'Ah, that's a long story.'

* * *

'Done,' said Askphrit, and for your second wish?'

Tamar smiled. 'I wish that you were free.'

'What?' Askphrit shrieked, as he felt himself becoming mortal, he was furious. 'Why did you do that?'

'We *were* going to leave you in the bottle, but I can't do it. I can't sentence you to an eternity in captivity, even though that's what you did to me. Denny doesn't understand, but I do. At least this way, you can't do any more damage.'

'*Compassion?*' screamed Askphrit. 'That's the reason you're giving me? That you feel sorry for me? You bitch, you absolute ...' Words failed him, as he gasped and spluttered in his fury.

'Being human's not so bad,' she said. 'You'll get used to it, now shut up, don't make me hurt you.'

Askphrit glared at her. 'Can I go now?'

'You can do anything you want now,' she told him. 'Free will.'

Askphrit stalked off. 'Free will,' he muttered. 'Anything I want! Yeah, until I *die*. No way sister, this isn't over.'

*

Askphrit sat huddled in an alley, sipping out of a paper bag, it was raining. He had been mortal now for almost forty years, *forty years!* He was an old man now, and his bitterness against Tamar had escalated into a kind of madness, he would have his revenge on her, if it killed him. But time was running out, soon his mortal life would run its course, and then it would be too late, his hatred of her was the only thing that had kept him alive this long, the belief that he would find a way to make her pay.

He knew that in order to do this, he would have to regain his power, and to this end, he had been using his contacts, the ones he had made while masquerading as the sorceress, Kelon. He had a definite plan in mind, but it was dependent on finding a certain sorcerer. The parallels with Tamar earlier quest were not lost on him.

Because of his obsession he had not led a normal life, thus his current status as a bum. Homeless and friendless, he had experienced only the worst aspects of being a human; he had even spent time in prison. This only increased his bitterness toward she who had done this to him. But it was nearly over, he believed he had finally found his man, as long as he could cling to life long enough to see it through, he was going to make Tamar Black sorry.

A figure loomed out the gloom. 'This way,' it said, and led him to a large black limousine. Askphrit felt the excitement rise in him; it was finally happening. He felt his heart leaping. 'Be careful,' he admonished himself; he did not want to keel over from a heart attack now, not when he was so close.

'Askphrit old man,' the sorcerer greeted him. 'Sit down old man, you look done in, what can I do for you?'

'George,' acknowledged Askphrit. 'By God, you're a hard man to find, if I didn't know better, I'd say you'd been avoiding me; however, I am feeling a bit ... I'll get straight to the point if I may?'

George inclined his head.

'I need to go back,' said Askphrit, 'to change what happened to me. If I don't I'll die pretty soon, I know you can do it. Will you help me?'

'Hmm,' said George. 'You know that time travel is a tricky

business, you are not supposed to do it in order to deliberately change the past; it's tricky enough just going back to observe, you could make an awful mess, I don't know if I should ...'

'Oh cut it out George,' said Askphrit. 'You don't fool me with all this social conscience drivel, how much is it going to cost me?'

George considered. 'How far back do you need to go?' he asked.

Askphrit grinned, now it was just a question of the bargaining.

*

Askphrit's hands were shaking as he picked up the bottle and pulled out the cork, BANG!!!

He faced himself. It was the weirdest experience he had ever had. His other self thought so too. But it had to be this way, this was the only Djinn he was sure he could find (he just had to remember where he had been) and the only Djinn who would give him what he wanted – without consequences.

He explained the situation, in a highly edited form, to himself. 'In a few months,' he said. 'You are due to meet a young woman named Tamar. If you do, I am your future.'

His other self agreed that it was not a pleasant prospect.

'I propose a deal,' said Askphrit. 'You give me back my powers – without consequence, and we will both be free.'

As you can imagine, his other self agreed to this with alacrity.

As the wish was granted, the universe split into two distinct realities, in an unprecedented way. Rifts had occurred before, but nothing on this scale. Askphrit watched his other self vanish into the other one, to meet his future with Tamar, he would have no memory of this exchange; after all, it never happened in that other reality. 'By Allah, what a fool I was, I never did understand all that metaphysical stuff.'

Now, with his power returned, he could put his plan into action, after all, he now had all the time in the world.

* * *

'That's not possible surely,' said Tamar. 'Even the Djinn can't time travel, let alone a sorcerer.'

'They can if they have access to the mainframe,' said Askphrit.

Tamar gasped. '*No!*'

'Yes, old George had the codes,' said Askphrit, chuckling at her astounded face.

'I don't know how he got them; it must have cost him pretty dear. I watched him input them, he accessed the archives for me, and opened the file, and all I had to do was "enter". This was his house.'

'You killed him?'

'When I came back. I had the codes already, after all. What did I need him for? And this place was perfect, had the computer set up and everything.' He pressed a remote control, and a vast computer screen was revealed from behind the panelling.

'And all this time ...?'

'I've been in the other reality, moving through time at will, setting things up nicely, until it was time to return to this reality to find you (after all in the *other* reality you lived and died thousands of years ago.)

'Revenge is all very well, and it was my main objective, but what do you do afterwards? There's nothing like a little world domination to keep you busy, and the best part is, it's all your fault. You'll have to live with that.

'You see it occurred to me that I could use your heroic tendencies against you to further my plan. I already had control of the vampires, posing as Ran-Kur; I took over, oh about 200 years ago. In the other reality, they were flourishing under my protection, although in this one they had become timid and very few. So I went back again, about 7000 years (you know, before reality split) and wrote my little prophecy, I knew you couldn't resist that. And the vampires, well, I had them right where I wanted them. The only problem there was the *real* Ran-Kur, but well, you dealt with him for me.'

'Denny's dreams?' said Tamar.

'Yes, I did that; I knew you'd fall for it. Such a good little puppet he's been. You kept him on the side of good, fighting the evil inside, just long enough, although it can't have been easy, for him or you, but I knew I could rely on you. And now, because all the belief is still there, I now *am* Ran-Kur.'

'You used us to make yourself a *god?*'

Askphrit was enjoying himself immensely. 'Oh yes, ironic don't you think?'

'But, *why*? A Djinn has far more power than a god.'

'Yes, but a Djinn doesn't have the sway over the hearts and minds of his followers. Now that's *real* power.'

'You're insane.'

'Possibly, possibly,' said Askphrit mildly, 'wait until *you've* been a powerless mortal for forty years and we'll see how *your* sanity holds up.'

'You're not going to kill me then?'

'*Kill* you? What do you think I am, some kind of barbarian?'

'The thought had crossed my mind.'

'No, no, I want my revenge to last a long time, it's much more elegant this way, and far more satisfying.' He glanced at Denny, who was lounging against a pillar, looking bored. 'I want you to live with the knowledge that your arrogance destroyed the soul of the one and only person you ever cared about in your whole miserable, worthless life.'

Tamar blanched.

'Of course, I needed him evil anyway; he was the only one who could get near enough to you to take away your power, the only one you trust. And if you hadn't made that wish, I never would have been able to do it. In fact, it was your wish that gave me the whole idea. Now that's irony, I love it.' He laughed maniacally.

Denny yawned and took a long drag on his cigarette. 'I think maybe you've splashed on a little too much "Obsession for Dorks",' he commented, dryly, and started cleaning out his fingernails, in a bored fashion. He seemed supremely unaffected by Tamar's obvious distress

Askphrit ignored him; he was enjoying this. Far from being unaffected by Tamar's suffering, he was positively relishing it. He rubbed it in some more.

'It was fun,' he said, 'watching you run around like a

headless chicken, doing exactly what I wanted you to.

And you,' he turned to Denny. 'You came through like a trouper. When you killed those men – *wonderful*!' he clapped his hands in ecstasy, 'and this fool, didn't cotton on even then.'

Tamar gave a low moan.

Askphrit brought his face close to hers and mocked her through the bars. 'What was that? Something you want to say?'

'You'll never get away with it,' she said dully.

'Is that the best you can do?' said Askphrit, 'how unoriginal. My dear girl, I *have* got away with it. I have you trapped, your lover has betrayed you, the world is under my domination, you have made me a god, in fact, and it's all your own fault. Face it, I've won.'

~ Chapter Thirty Two ~

'GUESS AGAIN,' said Denny, stepping up and, without warning, thrusting the Athame into Askphrit's gut. Askphrit screamed in disbelief and fury as he felt the powers he had struggled so hard to regain ebbing out of him *again* and flowing into the Athame. Denny was wearing his, by now, trademark evil grin.

He threw a cage over Askphrit. 'Can't be too careful,' he quipped, 'never know what kind of tricks you have up your sleeve.'

'Why?' said Askphrit. Much as Tamar had done. 'It will not benefit you. You already have a Djinn's powers from *her*.'

Denny's body shimmered and an illusion dropped, revealing Tamar, she grinned,

'Fooled ya,' she said. Askphrit gaped.

Tamar snapped her fingers and the cage around what was now revealed to be Denny vanished. He stood up and stretched.

He looked at her, sardonically. 'Babe?' he said. '*Babe?* When did I *ever* call you babe? For God's sake!'

'Sorry,' she said. 'I thought it made me sound more – evil,

or something.'

'You cunning, cunning witch,' said Askphrit. 'Just how much did you know?'

'Well, we knew how you were having us watched for one thing,' she told him. 'It was Denny who worked it out. Clever really – the moths, they were vampires, weren't they? Pity *they* weren't as clever as you. *Talking* to a man so well versed in his folklore was a big mistake.'

Askphrit groaned. 'Idiots!'

'And I *knew* that the Athame was turning him evil – oh yes, I *did* work it out – and since he found it here, it wasn't such a great leap to work out that it was at least a possibility that you *meant* him to have it. So when I took it away from him to have it blessed, to remove the evil from it, I took precautions, to make sure you didn't find out what I'd done. I had an idea it might be useful to keep you in the dark. Of course, I didn't know who you really were at the time. I only knew about the "vampire" that Denny met while he was here. That was ... oh what was it – two months ago? Not long after he killed those men, actually.

'Jack knew.' she indicated Stiles. 'In fact, it was something he said that put me on to it. Do you want to know what it was? It's kind of silly really. You were right, all the other things he did, even killing those men, I had another explanation for it – I didn't *want* to see – but when Jack mentioned to me that Denny's guitar playing was pretty good, I *knew* something was wrong.

Denny, the Denny *I* know, would never use his powers for petty vanity like that. His guitar playing usually stinks you see? No offence,' she said to Denny.

Denny shrugged. 'It's true,' he said. 'My parents thought music lessons were for ponces.'

'That's how I knew that he wasn't Denny anymore, anyway.' resumed Tamar. 'He had been taken away from me, and the demon who was wearing his face was killing people. I must have been blind not to see it.'

She brought her face close to Askphrit's. 'If it's any comfort to you, when I realised what I'd done to him, I felt every bit as bad as you could have ever meant me to. I knew then, that it was my fault, that my wish had done it to him.'

Denny nodded as he remembered her distress and self-recrimination. 'It's true,' he said. 'Everything you heard tonight, she had already said on that night, I remembered it; I'll never forget it.' He glanced at Tamar repentantly. 'She'll never let me. I also remember that, at the time, I didn't care either. But I suppose that wasn't really me, was it?'

'Actually I was a bit worried when Jack came running in,' said Tamar. 'I thought he might give the game away, that's why I gagged him ... oh God.' She stopped. 'I forgot to let him go.'

She released him. 'Sorry,' she said.

Stiles shrugged. 'That's okay,' he said. He did not *sound* as if he were being sarcastic.

Cindy and Eugene were listening curiously (their vampire captors had fled as soon as they had seen their "Master" put in a cage.)

'Two months?' said Askphrit, disbelievingly. 'It was *after* that when you murdered that old witch.'

'That was actually an act of compassion,' said Denny. 'She had been a prisoner in that cave for thousands of years; it was the only way to release her, from what had become a torment. Also, it was time for the labyrinth to be closed forever. The power to kill gods is too dangerous. The witch knew that, she was worried about it. That was why she asked me to stay behind.'

'Well, you turned your landlord to stone,' argued Askphrit.

Denny shrugged. 'I'm only human,' he said.

Stiles laughed. 'The point is, he didn't *kill* him,' he said.

'I just wanted to,' said Denny. 'What? I hate that guy,' he added when Stiles frowned at him censoriously.

'Anyway,' Tamar continued, determined to tell her story, 'when we got here, and found Hecaté, that's when we *really* began to put it together. She had no idea who we were. When we thought we had met her, she was actually here. It had to be *you*, therefore, who had come. And why? To lure us here of course! What else could it be? And to trick us into killing Ran-

Kur, yes we worked that out too, we already knew that you would have taken his place, Peirce had told us that you were posing as him. Poor blighter, he wasn't very bright was he, he had no idea you were taking his name in vain, did he?

'And why did you want Denny evil? Because *you* didn't have the power to get past *me*. We didn't know it was *you*, of course, but what we *did* realise, was that whoever the "Master" was, he, that is you, wanted Denny evil, so that *he* would put me out of the way for you. Like you said, who else could do it? So we decided to give you what you expected.'

'*I* figured that part out,' said Denny. 'Being evil, gives you an insight into how a warped mind works, I *knew* what you expected me to do, I had even thought about doing it, while I was under the influence of the demon who made the Athame, and I knew that you would know that.'

Tamar resumed. 'Since, whoever you were, you wanted *me* out of the way, it seemed reasonable to assume that I would be able to handle you, otherwise *you* would have just taken me on by yourself.'

'When did you …' began Stiles. He gestured expressively to indicate the complicated plan they had apparently come up with in a matter of minutes. 'I mean there was no *time.*'

'Oh, it's amazing how much you can say in only a few seconds with telepathy,' said Tamar.

And Stiles remembered them gazing at each other, almost vacantly, inside Hecaté's cell. They had been formulating a *whole plan?*

'Why did you turn into each other?' wondered Stiles.

'Because we wanted him to spill his guts,' said Tamar. 'And we knew he wouldn't do that until he thought he'd won, he had to believe he'd got me. Believe me villains aren't as stupid as they seem in Bond Movies. But of course, *really*, I had to be free to deal with him, if it became necessary. I thought we played each other pretty well.'

'Very convincing,' said Stiles. 'You certainly had me fooled, 'specially since you had no time to rehearse.'

'It's easy when you live with someone – you know all about them.'

'It's *easy* when you're telepathic,' corrected Denny. 'Don't pretend you weren't feeding me lines.'

Tamar shrugged.

'Not just the lines either,' muttered Denny. 'I *felt* it; just what *you* had felt.'

Stiles heard this and raised his eyebrows; now that was some guilt trip, he thought. He wondered if Tamar had done it on purpose. Of *course* she had!

'You cunning, cunning witch,' said Askphrit again, who had been listening to all this in horror.

'I *said* you wouldn't get away with it,' she said.

'Oh, bite me,' snapped Askphrit petulantly.

'But,' said Stiles, 'you really *did* stab him with the Athame, I *saw* you!'

'Oh this?' Tamar held it up. 'It's a fake. I manifested it.' she held up the real one. 'Spot the difference,' she said. '*This* is the real one. The one I used on *him*.' She held it out to Denny. 'I suppose this is yours.' She looked at it thoughtfully. 'What a pity *you* weren't the one who stabbed him,' she said to Denny.

'But what can it matter?'

'If you had, then *you* would have taken the power he had.'

'So what?' then he got the point. 'Oh, I see, then I would have had a Djinn's powers too, and we could …'

'And then we could … as you say.'

'Denny took the Athame. A strange look came over his face. 'Unless the power resides in the Athame itself,' he mused. 'Like the demon's power it came with.' This, he felt, was a good point.

He was sure he could feel the power flowing through him. There was only one way to find out for sure, however.

He grabbed Tamar round the waist and held her fast. 'So far so good,' he said. He kissed her hard, as desperately as if she were his first drop of water after a month in a desert and Tamar realised how much he had longed to do this. He had hidden it well. Now, suddenly, he was like a man possessed. As if he had been waiting his whole life for this.

The others turned away, embarrassed in the face of such a

passionate display.

Finally he broke away. 'I don't even feel faint,' he said triumphantly.

'Well *I* do,' said Tamar. She was weak at the knees – finally!

'Well that seems pretty conclusive,' said Denny. He was glowing.

Really he looked almost handsome, thought Cindy.

Stiles, who had not really followed this, got back to the matter at hand. He shook his head. 'But you *did* stab him,' he said, meaning Denny. 'When he looked like you,' he added.

Tamar pulled herself together. She passed the "fake" Athame through her hand as if it were made of nothing more substantial than smoke. 'Misdirection,' she said. 'The hand is quicker than the eye.'

'Like one of those fake knives they use in plays, with a retractable blade?' said Stiles catching on.

'Wait a minute,' said Cindy, suddenly rounding on Askphrit. 'It was *you* who sent us on that rotten quest.'

Stiles rolled his eyes. 'What page are you on?' he said. 'We did that bit.

'Oh, oh right, carry on.'

'I think that's it,' said Denny. 'We just have to decide what to do with him.' He gestured to Askphrit.

'You'd better kill me this time,' said Askphrit. 'Otherwise ...' He made a threatening gesture.

He was largely ignored.

Cindy spoke again to Denny this time. 'You seem different now,' she said. 'If you were never really evil, at least, not since I met you, why did you seem so – so sinister and intimidating?'

'Scared you did I?' he asked, grinning. 'I *had* to act that way, we were being watched, remember?'

'It was damn convincing.' Cindy shuddered.

'I was working from memory, not so long before I *was* like that. But I'm a nice guy really – honest!' he grinned at her, and this time he did not look sinister – he looked almost goofy. Cindy smiled back.

'Well, it's going to take me weeks to sort all this out,' said

Stiles. 'Thank God I don't have to write a report about it. That's one good thing about vampire hunting, no paperwork. I still don't really know what the hell happened here.'

'Something good,' said Hecaté, appearing out of the shadows.

Stiles choked.

'Here,' said Askphrit, 'how the hell did *you* get out?'

'*I* released her,' said Stiles, 'although I'm not really sure how.'

Tamar smiled. 'I think I might have an idea,' she said. 'Destiny.'

'Explain,' said Denny.

'What Askphrit didn't take into account when he wrote his "little prophecy" was that now he's become a god, the prophecy will become true.'

'It is true,' said Hecaté. 'This is a divine power, to create prophecies. Any prophecy that is made by a god is bound to come to be.'

'There you see,' said Tamar. 'You turned Jack from an ordinary man into something special; he has a great destiny now.'

'Not to mention the end of vampire-kind,' said Denny. 'Betcha didn't see that one coming, Ha! Even if you'd won today, I think the scheme for world domination might have fallen apart.'

'Not if I'd killed him,' said Askphrit.

'But you couldn't have,' said Tamar. 'That's not part of the prophecy. But I bet Hecaté is. After all, this child's going to have to be pretty special. Hero-like, even. Half-god perhaps?'

Stiles and Hecaté were studiously avoiding each other's eyes.

Denny nudged Stiles and winked. 'Go on,' he said. 'You know you want to.'

'*Denny*,' said Tamar sharply.

'What?'

'Shut up!'

Hecaté suddenly slipped her arm through Stiles'. 'Well,' she said. 'You cannot fight destiny.'

'My, haven't we all changed,' said Tamar grinning at Denny. She and Denny were still entwined; she was hanging on to him as if her life depended on it. Cindy thought she would never let him go again. She, at least, understood what had happened for them, if nobody else did.

Suddenly, a dishevelled Peirce came careering into the room.

~ Chapter Thirty Three ~

THE ATMOSPHERE IN the room changed immediately. The effect that Peirce had on people could be described thus. If he were human, he would be the guy that, if your plane had crashed in the Andes, there were plenty of food supplies and the rescue helicopters had been sighted, you would *still* eat him.

'I came to, to warn you,' he gasped, 'he's ...' He stopped as he spotted Askphrit in the cage. 'Oh!' he said. 'I guess everything's ... I – I thought ... oh well.'

He shifted uncomfortably, like a kid who has just walked in on his parents in bed. They were all staring at him coldly.

'Well, I'll just ...' He started to slide backwards out of the room. Denny barred his way; he said nothing, just looked menacing.

'Or I could stay – why don't I stay?' He sat down on a chair in the corner of the room, he kept stealing glances at the cage, he seemed more than usually twitchy, even in Denny's presence, who he was clearly still terrified of.

'You know,' said Denny. 'This might be quite a nice house,' he strode over to the window, 'if it weren't so dingy in here.'

He pulled the curtains open, sunlight flooded the room. Everyone gasped. Peirce yelped and shuffled his chair backward into a corner.

'The sun's out!' said Cindy.

'Yes,' said Hecaté. 'The darkness has broken.'

They all turned to stare at her. She inclined her head. 'Least I could do,' she said. 'Soon the light will spread. Now that the monster is in chains.'

'I love the way she talks,' said Stiles. 'Don't you love the way she talks?'

'Very – goddess like,' agreed Denny. He was looking at her in fascination; Tamar trod on his foot.

'Ahem,' he said. 'Why don't we go through the house and round up all the vampires who are still here?'

'Good idea,' said Cindy, nudging Eugene, who was also staring at Hecaté.

'What about *him*?' asked Stiles, meaning Askphrit.

'He's not going anywhere,' said Tamar. 'That cage is unbreakable even by magic.'

'I can watch him,' piped up Peirce.

'Oh no you don't,' said Denny, hauling him to his feet. 'You can come with me.' He grinned wolfishly. Peirce gave him a bitter look.

'Okay,' said Stiles. 'So, there's,' he counted, 'one, two, three, four, five, six of us and him,' he pointed at Peirce. 'So shall we split up into three groups of two?'

'Okay,' said Denny. I'll go with Cindy, you go with Tamar and Hecaté can go with Eugene, no couples together, we don't need distractions, okay?'

There was a murmuring of assent. There was a deliberate distribution of power in this arrangement that everyone approved of. Cindy, for example, would be safer with Denny, than with Stiles or Eugene, who were not as powerful. But no one felt inclined to mention it.

'Okay,' he distributed weapons. 'Lock and load.'

'Star-Trek,' explained Tamar, when this statement engendered some surprised looks. 'Insurrection.'

'Ah,' said Stiles. 'Not the best of the series.' Tamar rolled her eyes, 'Men!'

'Peirce comes with us,' said Denny. Cindy's face fell, but she said nothing. 'After all, she thought,' Peirce is scared to death of him, 'it'll be all right.'

* * *

The house was large and gloomy, and there were plenty of vampires to be found in various dusty corners, most of which were easily dealt with by wrenching open the curtains suddenly, while saying, 'gosh, isn't it stuffy in here.' Resulting in Peirce dashing for cover, behind various items of furniture, as if the Jehovah's Witnesses were at the door.

Cindy was particularly useful at luring them out for this; she seemed to have been designed by nature to be the perfect vampire bait. The east wing was almost clear.

Tamar, in the south wing, was, unfortunately, too well known to them for this to be an effective ruse, however, battering them to a pulp seemed to be working quite well for her, and Stiles was an efficient partner in this activity.

Hecaté was flooding the west wing with indoor sunlight, and Eugene was clearing out the darker corners as a dragon the size of a rocking horse.

Down in the dungeons, though, it was a different story. No windows down here, and it was not long before Denny found himself in a concerted battle with at least seven cornered vampires. Cindy was surprisingly useful; she pitched right in there and brought down at least two of them on her own. Between them and the distracting cheers of the prisoners, Cindy and Denny were a bit too preoccupied to realise that Peirce had slipped away unnoticed.

When they had cleared the house and led the prisoners blinking into the sunlight, it was Stiles, of course, who suddenly said, 'where's Peirce?'

Tamar looked at Denny, reproachfully. 'You lost him?'

They all looked around; he was nowhere to be seen. 'The chamber?' said Cindy.

Denny swore. 'Askphrit!'

Without exchanging another word, they all ran, leaving the bewildered prisoners, standing in the garden.

* * *

Askphrit was standing by the computer, grinning, Peirce was lying on the floor beside him, he was unconscious.

'You're too late,' jeered Askphrit. He pressed "enter" just as Denny reached him, and vanished. 'This isn't over, sister,' he said, as he de-materialised.

They were speechless. Tamar did not even have the heart to say 'damn!'

They kicked Peirce until he came round.

'How did he get him out of the cage?' asked Stiles. 'I thought you said it was unbreakable, even by magic.'

'Well, it wasn't!' snapped Tamar. 'There's no such thing, if there were *he* would have used it on me. I lied so that he wouldn't try to escape.'

Peirce claimed to have no memory of what had happened. 'He had control of me,' he whimpered, plaintively.

'Where's he gone?' Denny demanded to know.

'I don't know – ow, ow, owww, aaagh, all right, all right, he went into the past. That's all I know, I swear.'

Denny twisted his arm further up his back. 'Where?'

'Doesn't matter, anyway,' said Tamar. 'He can go anywhere he wants from wherever he is; he's not going to stay in one place, or time, is he?'

Denny let him go. 'There's nothing we can do then?'

'I didn't say that.'

~Chapter Thirty Four ~

A GLOOM HAD descended on the house. Cindy had left with Eugene and Stiles with Hecaté. They had felt awkward and out of place and had made their excuses. There was nothing more they could do anyway. They had promised to keep in touch, and maybe they would. Tamar had dealt with the prisoners. A memory modification, more for the trauma than anything else, after she and Denny had transported them to various hospitals; the official story would be a train wreck.

They had decided to put a kicking and screaming Peirce in the chapel that they had found attached to the house. 'I'm surprised they didn't tear it down,' Denny had said, but Tamar explained that that would probably have entailed going inside at some point. And besides, the very stones it was built of were blessed by years of worship. The vampires would have avoided it.

The gargoyles over the door had howled in protest, as it is their duty to warn against evil trying to enter. But they had not howled as loudly as Peirce had.

'Serves you right,' said Tamar. 'Now shut up, or we'll tie you to the crucifix.'

And now it was just Tamar and Denny again.

'I suppose we should go home,' said Denny.

'I suppose.'

There was a silence.

'It *is* a nice house,' said Tamar.

'Yes.'

'I suppose it'll just stand empty now. With Askphrit in the past somewhere, I don't suppose it really belongs to *anyone* now.'

'No, I suppose not.'

'And that computer, all set up, it'd be a shame to have it just sitting there, it'd be very useful to us now, it may even have the codes to the archives on it somewhere. Save us looking for them.'

'Yes.'

'And we will need those, if we're to go after him.'

'Uh huh.'

Tamar wandered over to the window. 'There's a nice big garden,' she said and grinned at him.

He grinned back. 'Yes,' he said.

They surveyed their new home; they had a lot of work to do. They went into the garden; both of them had a longing for the sunshine.

'One thing I've been wondering,' said Denny, as they made a start.

What's that?'

'What *was* Hercules' real name?'

'Trevor.'

'You don't really expect me to believe that, do you? You're such a liar. Do you know what I think? I think you just make things up half the time, because you can't stand to admit that you don't know everything. '

Tamar turned to him and grinned mischievously. 'Bite me',' she said.

THE END?

Epilogue

THE TALL, thin man faced his cohorts around the table. (You had to call them his cohorts. They certainly could not be called his friends – or anybody's friends.) 'Well!' he said. 'What a complete and utter cock up.'

There was muttering around the table.

'It turns out that we have been made fools of by this – this Askphrit character, and not for the first time. We have played his game. We sent out our champion on a fool's errand, and if she hadn't …' He took a deep breath. 'Well, a great calamity was narrowly averted.'

'He has escaped,' pointed out a voice from the shadows.

'She will go after him,' said the thin man. 'And we must help her.'

'We are not supposed to interfere,' pointed out another.

'We have *already* interfered,' said the thin man emphatically. 'If we had not, this would not have happened. Now we have a dangerous lunatic loose in the past, who knows what kind of damage he will do?

'No, we have no choice. She *must* stop him, and we must help her. Tamar Black is our only hope.'

'There is the prophecy, he himself wrote it, might that not...?'

'We cannot wait. For a child to be born, grow up and destroy all vampire-kind, thus destroying he whom is now their god. No, we cannot wait. Imagine how much damage he will do in that time! She has the power to kill him *now*, and she alone. She *must* do it.'

'It must be her own decision,' came another voice, squeaky and high pitched.

The thin man glared 'I *know* that, Lucien, you pedantic prat.' he snapped. 'And it *will* be; do you really think she will just let him *go*? Ha! Not her! Besides, soon she will have no choice.'

About the Author

Nicola Rhodes often can't remember where she lives so she lives inside her own head most of the time, where even if you do get lost, it's still okay.

She has met many interesting people inside her own head and eventually decided to introduce the rest of the world to them, in the hopes that they would stop bothering her and let her sleep.

She has been doing this for ten years now but they still won't leave her alone.

She wrote this book for fun and does not care if you take away a moral lesson from it or not.

You have her full permission to read whatever you wish into this work of fiction. As she says herself:

"Just because I wrote this book, doesn't mean I know anything about it."

www.ingramcontent.com/pod-product-compliance
Lightning Source LLC
Chambersburg PA
CBHW050420260626
47156CB00003B/1093